# EARTH, WIND AND FIRE

An American Indian Nation's legacy
of glory, defeat and resurrection!

Manuscript Written by

## Sam Bass

Trafford
PUBLISHING

Order this book online at www.trafford.com
or email orders@trafford.com

Most Trafford titles are also available at major online book retailers.

Note for Librarians: A cataloguing record for this book is available from Library and Archives Canada at www.collectionscanada.ca/amicus/index-e.html

Printed in Victoria, BC, Canada.

ISBN: 978-1-4120-6069-1

Jeff Gold-Sam Bass                        Registered
13900 Panay Way, M307                      WGAw
Marina Del Rey, CA. 90292                  Copyright
Jeff Gold 310/827-9165
Sam Bass 501/952-9729

*We at Trafford believe that it is the responsibility of us all, as both individuals and corporations, to make choices that are environmentally and socially sound. You, in turn, are supporting this responsible conduct each time you purchase a Trafford book, or make use of our publishing services. To find out how you are helping, please visit www.trafford.com/responsiblepublishing.html*

*Our mission is to efficiently provide the world's finest, most comprehensive book publishing service, enabling every author to experience success. To find out how to publish your book, your way, and have it available worldwide, visit us online at www.trafford.com/*

 www.trafford.com

**North America & international**
toll-free: 1 888 232 4444 (USA & Canada)
phone: 250 383 6864 ♦ fax: 250 383 6804 ♦ email: info@trafford.com

This book is dedicated to Jessie Cordelia Stowers Beard, my mother. Jillian Hancock Bass, my wonderful wife and Grandmother Dirteater, a full blood Cherokee and my dear friend. These ladies are and were the metal in all strong and caring women and an example to us all.

## CHAPTER ONE

## CHEROKEE NATION, STATE OF OKLAHOMA, RURAL SUBURB OF THE TOWN HULBERT, UNITED STATES OF AMERICA

## 1953

## ARE YOU THE SALT OF THE EARTH?

A small stocky-built blonde boy runs from an old wood house letting the wooden screen door slam behind him. He clutches a full, brown paper bag in his little hand. This is a daily routine for him during the summer. The boy's pretty dark-haired mother hangs wet clothes on a line that runs beside the house.

The youngster cuts his blue eyes toward his mother as he rushes up the well traveled trail through a flock of Rock Island Red hens as he steadily moves towards a steep wooded hill in the distance. The birds squawk and complain as they reform their flock after the little boy passes them. His mother yells out after him, "Samuel, where are you going?"

He yells back, "To Grandma Dirteater's house."

She nods and goes about her work as she speaks. "You're just five not twenty-five, be careful."

The little boy smiles and waves as he goes. Out from under the front porch of his house runs "Poochy," his blue and tan colored part beagle and hound dog. He joins Sam on the trail. In a minute they come to an old well that has a black oak post standing over it, fashioned to form a squared arch. The structure holds a large rusty metal pulley in the center with a rope threaded through it connected to a torpedo looking cylinder.

Samuel and Poochy's eyes scan the set-up. He places his brown bag on a rock and grabs the smallest galvanized bucket sitting in a row of three pails close to the well head. He positions the bucket immediately next to the well and drops the cylinder down the shaft toward the hidden fresh water below. Poochy looks down the deep hole, barking and listening to his own echo. The rope attached to the metal cylinder spins away as it drops down the open hole until the boy hears a splash. Sam wait's a few seconds for the torpedo to fill with fresh water and begins his struggle to pull it up from the depths. Hand over hand he pulls, his face red with the struggle until finally the water comes to the top. He manages to pull a trigger on the torpedo to release the water and fills his little bucket while Poochy licks at the splashing droplets.

The child looks toward rolling hills in the distance. He singles out the steepest mound next to the gravel road near the well. The boy wipes sweat from his tanned forehead. He grabs his precious brown bag and water bucket then immediately cuts across the trail before him with a quick determination walking toward the steep mound. He struggles with the full bucket spilling water occasionally on his jeans and white tee-shirt and filling his cowboy boots. Poochy pants and trots behind Sam in full support.

Samuel finally makes it to the foot of the hill and enters the thick green forest. He still struggles to carry his bag and bucket, but moves steadily on. In a few minutes he is deep into the dark forest and cool surroundings. The young boy can see movement in the near distance. Poochy's ears perk up and he scans the area. Sam moves on, he then sees a six-feet-long black snake, which is a little bigger than a shovel handle, on the trail. It does not move for a moment then flicks his tongue tasting the air. The big snake's head rises higher as he scrutinizes the area. Sam and Poochy stop thinking what to do next. The snake slowly begins to move toward them. Sam suddenly runs as best he can through the woods lugging his now half full bucket and brown bag. Poochy takes the fight to the big black snake with little success, because the snake has a fix on Sam and continues to move toward him, striking at Poochy occasionally to ward him off.

Sam looks back as he runs and sees the snake go flying through the air from the end a stick that has scooped him up. Poochy gives chase as the large snake disappears in the leaves. The youngster stops and looks back to see Ms. Dirteater, known to him as Grandma Dirteater. She stands leaning on her long oak staff smiling. Her slim ninety-two year old full blood Cherokee frame is strong and healthy. Her smile reveals exceptionally good teeth and a real happiness to see the boy. Grandma speaks to Sam in a perfect English accent. "Oh-si-yo (hello),

Well little so-qui-li (horse) where have you been?"

Sam smiles looking in the direction of the snake and Poochy. "I had to get your water."

She says, "Don't worry about that old snake. He is an ornery Coach Whip snake, and they are just too pushy for their own good, besides Poochy would have finally done him in had he stayed around, and we would have had dinner."

Sam grins and moves next to Grandma. "Yeah tasty, I brought you something."

She pats his back and pulls him toward the trail. "Let's go to my house and take a look."

She takes the water bucket, and they walk together with Poochy in tow. A few minutes up the trail, and they arrive at her small log cabin. It is picturesque; a one room log cabin with no modern appliances or utilities. The little house stands in a clearing not much bigger than the cabin. The moss covered wood-shingled roof looks like an oil painting.

Grandma and Sam move to a red oak log lying next to a burning campfire. Sam sits on the log and Grandma puts the bucket on a wooden table near the end of the log. She places more firewood on the embers and folds the coals in on top of the new wood. Grandma

7

then turns to a large, well oiled metal frying pan that sits on a hot rock next to the fire and stirs the very slow cooking meat inside. Grandma takes a piece of meat from the pan with a fork and wipes the grease from it on a nearby sack cloth. She blows on the meat to cool it then tosses it to Poochy. Poochy grabs the meat and lops to the corner of the house and lies down in his usual spot, wallowed out from many months of use to enjoy his treat.

Grandma smiles at Poochy and sits next to Sam hugging him. "How's my little man. I missed you so much. It's lonely around here without you and Poochy."

Sam is shy but happy about his relationship with the grandmother. "I have something for you Grandma."

She says, "Really. Should I guess what it is first or should you just give it to me and I'll be spoiled and open it."

He smiles. "You'll love it, guess."

Grandma smiles. "Yes, ah, it's a pound of gold."

Sam grins. "No it's something you really wanted."

He hands her the paper bag. Her aging brown hands take the bag and then she brushes the boy's hair back from his eyes with her fingers.

Grandmother Dirteater opens it and looks inside. "Oh how nice, twenty-two bullets."

Sam is beaming. "Yes and they are twenty-two shorts just like the ones you like, so they don't tear up the meat when you hunt."

She hugs him. "So they are and four boxes. It must be my birthday." Grandmother Dirteater stands and goes to the cabin speaking as she talks. "Well let's try them out."

Grandma retrieves a twenty-two single-shot rifle that sits just inside her cabin door and goes back to Sam.

Sam is excited about shooting the gun but not about shooting lunch. "Grandma, let's practice shooting."

She opens a box of shells and puts one in the chamber and closes the bolt on the shell. Grandma looks toward Samuel. "Stay put now."

She pulls the bolt's cocking mechanism back and aims at a wild daisy at the edge of the clearing. Grandma fires. The daisy flies from the stem.

Sam is amazed. "Ga. How do you do that? Can I try?"

Poochy looks up but is undisturbed by the familiar sound. She smiles, puts the rifle back in the house and returning to Sam she says, "Sorry little man, I will teach you, but not this day. You have to be at least seven before I will teach you."

Sam is sad but he knows her and respects her wisdom. "All right, but I could do it now. Hey, my dad told me you know a lot of good stories."

She smiles and pats him on the head. "I know only true stories and they are all about people, I don't know any fairy tales."

Sam says, "Mom and dad say I am part Choctaw. Do you know any stories them?"

She Gets a tin cup from the wood table and pours strong coffee from a pot that sits it near the fire to keep it warm. "Yes, I know them, tell your mother to bring me some coffee next time she goes to town. I'll give the money before you go."

Sam is in thought. "My mom says you are the salt of the earth and I'm not to take any money from you, just tell me what you need. What about the Choctaws."

Grandmother Dirteater says, "Your mother is the salt of the earth. I am just old."

Samuel pushes a little more. "Not what my mom said. She says you are special. "Please, tell me about the Choctaw."

She smiles. "Well I know a little about them. They were friends to my people, the Cherokee. I know they were fierce warriors, the fiercest of them all. If you had a Choctaw on your side you would not lose when in battle. The most important thing about the Choctaw people is they were always honorable, and when you are all of that there is little more to be said."

Grandma is curious while in her afterthought. "Salt of the earth, huh?"

Sam is proud. "Yes, what is a salt of the earth?"

She smiles. "Something special and salty, like me." They both grin together."

Sam is hooked to the story-telling and wants more. "What about your people, were they the same?"

Grandma loves this part of her life and begins to tell the story. Poochy comes over and puts his head on her lap while Samuel scoots closer. "Yes, little Samuel, they were the same, good and honest, but at the same time in many ways they were very different from your people. I remember a story told by my great aunt when I was very little. It happened right in her own village. I think it was around seventeen-ninety-eight, and the Blue coated army of the United States was everywhere. The army said they were in our country to make peace, but the strange part of this was if they had not been in our country there would be no fighting. Oh, I'm sorry I got off on that, back to the story. My Aunt Susan Deerinwater's village was in a valley next to a river somewhere in Georgia where a lot of people traveled by raft and canoe. Nearly every day people traded goods there, including Indian people from other friendly tribes and white's that lived in the area. Many merchant/traders also came to the village, especially the Scottish and French, and a few British. Not only did they travel on the river, but they traveled through the hills on horses and mules with pack animals. Then one day, the soldiers came and our time of prosperity changed to tragedy like a storm of fire and wind."

# CHAPTER TWO

## CHEROKEE NATION, GEORGIA REGION, UNITED STATES OF AMERICA 1798

### KILL ME FOR THE SAKE OF KILLING.

Grandmother Dirteater continued to spin her tale. "Yes I remember the story about the hateful Indian agent that gave our family the harsh name that I carry now. He did it just being mean and arrogant." She is in thought, "Oh, back to my people's story. I remember Aunt Susan always told her own story with a quiet sadness. It was hard for her to tell the story. This was the time of the soldier, she always said."

It is becoming morning, thick white spring time rain clouds laced with threads of black roll in over the lush green valley above her village. Two hundred blue-coated United States cavalry troops quietly hide, erectly mounted on restless cavalry horses just behind the wooded rim of the steep valley wall. Their animals fidget and snort under the sounds of the pre-dawn forest. A young and very ambitious Captain Daniel Sevier lies on the ground looking through a brass telescope at the Cherokee Indian village below. It's still too dark for the captain to see much through his telescope. The village is made up of well built dug-outs covered by log and bark roofs and a few log homes. The village resembles a frontier town more than the typical Ancient Indian community. A few people are up and getting ready for the day while others are already trading goods with the people arriving to do business.

Through the scanning telescope the captain can see a sleepy

Susan Deerinwater cooking a piece of deer meat on a spit over her out door fire in front of the family dugout. Her son John comes from the corner of the house and tears a piece of hot meat from the spit tossing it from hand to hand to cool it off. Susan looks at her son with loving eyes. "John you need to wait for the meat to finish cooking, you'll get a stomach ache. We'll eat soon enough."

He smiles and hugs his mother. "All right, I'm going to go play stickball. Call me when it's ready."

She smiles and pats him on the butt as he passes on his way to the sport field. This band of Cherokee loves to play their game of stickball against other bands and tribes in the area, so they practice almost every day. This is the national sport of the Cherokee and other neighboring Indian nations. The game is played very much like the game of Lacrosse. There is a question as to who played the game first, the Indian nations or the Europeans. It is clear this Cherokee band is extremely secure in their centuries old homesite.

Inside Susan's dug out, her daughter, Rebecca Springwater and Rebecca's husband, Dennis are staying with Susan while they build a new home of their own. Susan's daughter lies awake next to her sleeping husband while her happy baby, King is resting on her other side. The baby is almost ten months old and is big for his age. Her husband says the baby will be a great hunter and probably a war chief one day. Rebecca respects her husband, but she is not sure this is what she wants for her child. She is sixteen and has already seen war and its ugliness. Her mind is etched with the bloody wounds, men killing men and running for her life. She says a little prayer that her baby will never know these things.

Rebecca doesn't know why she is awake this early. She usually sleeps much later. Rebecca tries to relax and she snuggles further under the blankets, but sleep will not come. Something is wrong. She can feel it. There is a thunderstorm headed towards them; she can hear it approaching. Whatever it is that's wrong, it's not the storm. Rebecca can hear the thunder roll down the valley, almost as if it were the hooves of thundering horse.

Above the village the captain stands and mounts his seasoned war-horse. He has a better view of the whole village from atop his horse and he uses it to scan for the signal from his scouts. His intense dark eyes scan the early-morning forested valley floor. Soon he sees a bright spark near the front of the village in the early morning forest. It is followed by one from the rear and then one from each side of the village. These are the signals he has been waiting for. They mean his scouts are in place, using their fire starting flints to throw off bright sparks, signaling they are ready. His scouts wait to kill only Cherokee sentries watching over their unsuspecting village. The captain waits a moment and relaxes while watching the future battleground.

Other soldiers have also seen the signals. They all know the attack on the village will be soon. The captain can feel the tension in the troops as he waits to give the command to start the attack. He takes a moment to compose himself and run through his mental check list one last time. He is satisfied; they are prepared to be the best they can be.

The captain turns to his sergeant. "Sergeant Prince, ready the men."

Sergeant Prince quietly relays the order down the skirmish line of the troops. He turns back to the captain. "The men are ready, sir," he reports.

Captain Sevier wait's a moment longer, feeling the tension grow around him, when he feels the moment is right, he gives the command loud and clear: "CHARGE." On his command the ready troops come crashing down the side of the valley wall to the forest floor hell for leather. Branches from the trees break away and fall, while flying green leaves plummet to the ground and dust boils from the dry forest floor. The troops break out of the forest and into the valley itself just as Sevier's scouts have methodically finished killing with surprise and knives any Cherokee sentry that stood guard around the village. The scouts complete their mission by guiding the invading troops straight into the heart of the Cherokee community.

The commanding officer pushes them hard as he yells orders over the rage of battle, guiding the cavalry charge against the village. Just before the real thunderstorm hits, the cavalry attacks with total surprise smashing into the village like a thunderstorm from hell. It is then that a blistering rain descends blinding the soldiers and their prey. Captain Sevier's troops are well trained, even with the driving rain and the confusion of battle it changes nothing, every living thing remains under attack. The troops are methodical and merciless, destroying and slaughtering the village and its inhabitants. They view the Indian people as less than human. The Indians are considered savages and are, "The Enemy" and thus must be destroyed.

Captain Sevier commands the attack, yelling orders and directing his troops as best he can in the rain-swept battle. The captain has them strike one area and then another as the slaughter engulfs the entire village. The mounted soldier's blast through the rain soaked streets and shoot every villager they see. The quickness of the attack and the large size of the village gives the Cherokee men little time to make any coordinated defense. The ones that do are cut down before they can get into position. The rage of battle immediately sprawls across the entire Indian town and Susan Deerinwater and her family are caught up in it. A soldier slashes at her with his saber. She ducks and runs toward her son who is advancing toward her. The boy dodges cavalry horses and homicidal soldiers to reach his frightened mother. He grabs her and runs for the forest under the cover of the receding rain. Another soldier attacks, and John is able to pull him from his horse into a large smoldering campfire. While the soldier is busy getting the hot coals off of himself, John and Susan are able to get to the forest and watch the massacre from the cover of the undergrowth.

The mounted soldier's are still attacking the people in the hard rain, shooting every villager they can; including woman and child. The rear guard troops follow through, hacking away at the stragglers with glistening sabers. The troops orders are clear: kill every Indian and Indian sympathizer you see. A few more brave warriors arrive from a hunt and are able to rally a small but fierce force and fight back, but they are quickly dispatched by overwhelming numbers of soldiers with rifles. The government needs this land for new settlers on the way to this virgin frontier, and this attack is labeled retaliation for attacks on the army. A convenient and regular method of grabbing land without a treaty.

Nothing, not even the live-stock, is to remain alive in this village an example must be set for the other villages. The white European traders are killed just as savagely as the Indian people they traded with. These traders are considered friends of the red man because of their commerce and their acceptance of the Indian and the Indian way of life. Some of these traders have taken Indian wives. This act is especially repugnant to the young captain Sevier who sees these marriages as totally immoral. He feels these White men that lie with Indian women and have half-breed children are in his view, no better than the savages he is ordered to kill. Thus, Captain Sevier's orders to kill every living thing in the village includes the traders. As the battle progresses it becomes more and more apparent it is a slaughter and less a battle.

Rebecca's husband, Dennis and their baby, King were killed along with her in their bed at the beginning of the battle. A soldier shot her husband in the chest as he rose up to protect his wife and child. Another trooper shot Rebecca and her baby before they could turn to look. Fortunately her mother and brother lived to get away under the cover of blowing rain.

The battle is spent and the rain lessens. The battle- hardened troops complete the mission in that, they shoot all remaining livestock. The price of war in this time is bitter and no quarter is given even to the children. The cavalry troops' commander signals for his men to regroup and assemble. The surviving, weary soldiers rally their winded war-horses into a skirmish line with sabers ready. As they linger, a final view of their gory action against the peaceful village confronts them, women and small children lie dead throughout the encampment, and home fires smolder inside the rain soaked homes.

15

EARTH, WIND AND FIRE

The carnage is total and complete. Five soldiers bury six of their number that were killed in the line of duty. The Cherokee and traders bodies will lie where they have fallen, to rot or to be eaten by wild animals and vermin.

By the time the U. S. Cavalry is ready to leave, the village is completely destroyed either by fires inside the homes or soldiers tearing them down. All of the villagers, about four hundred men, women, and children, are dead as are the few White traders that were there that unlucky day. The sight of pigs and chickens bodies mixed in with the Villagers is a horrifying sight of destruction.

The mud mixed with the river of blood still clings to the men and horses legs. The smell of death is in the air, and it can't be washed off. It can't be slept away; it will be in the memories of these men for life.

When the realization of the slaughter comes to the commanding captain and his seasoned campaign veterans, they find no victory in the death and destruction, and an uneasy quiet falls with a simple tone of bereavement. Sergeant David Prince is mounted next to the captain. The sergeant looks across the rain soaked village watching the soldiers complete the burials. They mount up and join the formation with Prince and Sevier. Wolves cautiously circle the camp, looking and waiting. Prince turns to the captain. "I suppose we should say a few words over our dead."

Sevier looks at Sergeant Prince, bows his head and prays. "Heavenly father take these men into your kingdom, amen."

Prince takes notice of the short prayer that does not include him or the other soldiers, but says nothing. "I guess that's what it comes down to, you either survive or you're something's food."

The captain nods and gazes around the area. He orders Sergeant Prince to form the men into a column of twos and make ready to move out. The sergeant relays the order. The men fall in and make ready to move out in columns. The soldiers stand ready. Daniel Sevier speaks in an uncharacteristic quiet tone to Prince. "The army has no place in this land grab. I did have a realization today. We shouldn't be

16

here, but we're in it now, and I'll have to make the best of it. It does seem Washington could bring in negotiators and settle the problems with the Indians and make a way to live together."

Prince lightens the conversation. "Well we know that's not going to happen. Their brain works only when talking about money and this land is money."

The strictly military Captain Sevier grins while his eyes still search for any possible trouble. "Move'em out Sergeant Prince we're headed up-river."

Sergeant Prince ask, "Why did we attack this village captain?"

Sevier answers, "It was ordered because someone said a few warriors from the village attacked white settlers and an army troop." Prince nods. He and Sevier move out, and the troops follow.

While the soldiers go out of sight. Susan and Dennis come out of hiding and go from person to person seeing who they can help.

In two hours the veteran troops are getting near another village up-river. This village is small compared to the town they had left. Scouts ride on the flanks and front of the cavalry column. They begin to report by yelling out. "Movement in the brush to the front." "Got activity on the right flank."

In a brief moment all seven scouts have reported some kind of activity. Sevier's and Prince's eyes search the area. Sevier snaps. "Rifles ready, eyes sharp."

Everyone in the company watches for anything moving. At once, a hundred Cherokee braves in full war-paint attack from all sides. The braves vermilion faces with black paint make their eyes look especially fearsome. They fire American made rifles, their own traditional blow guns loaded with long, large needle-like darts and flint headed arrows at the troops. Fifty unaware soldiers fall to the ground wounded or dead before they can fight or take cover. Sevier draws his saber and goes to work on his enemy, as does Prince.

Sevier pauses to command: "Second platoon, skirt them, out flank them on the left."

The platoon sergeant takes notice and yells orders to his thirty men to follow. They move into the forest and manage to get in behind and to the side of the enemy force. The soldiers fight hard doing large amounts of damage to their ferocious enemy. Cherokee warriors fall from the sabers and bullets of the platoon. Suddenly Pushmataha, the chief of all Choctaw and friend to the Cherokee people, moves in on the platoon with fifty men and makes short work of the detachment using arrows and tomahawks to kill every man. Pushmataha and his seasoned unit now begin to work on killing the rest of Sevier's men. Sevier can see his numbers have dwindled and Pushmataha's hardened warriors are rapidly evening the odds.

Sevier yells to Prince as they fight for their lives. "Recall the troops to rally on me. We are moving into the woods."

The sergeant yells out to every man as he moves around the killing field and finally the troops begin to break off the fight and follow Sevier as he retreats into the forest. Finally, the captain and his men are blasting through the dark woods at full speed on their exhausted mounts with the Cherokee, dead on their heels. Pushmataha is curiously no longer needed.

Sevier rounds a corner of an out cropping of tall gray rocks and finds a small detachment of thirty soldiers directly in front of him positioned to defend. Sevier's men pass through the front ranks of the ready soldiers. The positioned soldiers begin to fire on the Cherokee warriors. A few Cherokee men fall from their horses and the remaining Cherokee break off. They quickly return toward their village under fire from the soldiers.

Sevier rides toward the Master Sergeant in charge of this saving force. He talks as he goes. "Sergeant Prince make the men ready to defend."

Prince nods and begins to position the men for a possible fight. The captain moves on to meet the sergeant in charge. "Thanks sergeant for saving our ass."

The sergeant smiles. "Thanks for making so much noise we heard you coming." They smile at one another; Sevier dismounts and shakes the Master Sergeant's hand.

Sevier is concerned about the wounded and dead. "I hate we can't go back and bury our dead. God bless'em they'll just have to take their blessing where they lie."

Sevier mounts and turns to Prince. "We've had enough; better get our wounded taken care of at Gillespie's. I think it's probably over for now."

Prince acknowledges and moves to form the men to move out. The captain turns to the sergeant. "You better come with us."

The sergeant replies, "We will be along. This is our regular patrol. My troops will follow as your rear guard." Sevier nods and returns to ride with Prince in front of his troops.

The captain looks at the disheartened troops and speaks to console them. "We are going to Gillespie's station for re-supply and a little heal-up time. Keep your eyes open, this is the heart of Indian Territory as we just discovered. Move out."

Sergeant Prince signals the tired and weary troops. They form a column of twos and fall in behind the Sevier and Prince.

The sergeant glances up on the wooded ridge above them in the exact spot they had rode from. A bold looking painted warrior sits on a magnificent bay stallion with beads woven in the horses flowing black mane. The stocky middle-aged warrior just stares. His steady image is like a subtle warning beacon. This warrior is obviously a leader, according to the bright colorful turban he wears and the weapons he posses, all a sign of wealth and power in his nation. A beautiful well made tomahawk, slim and deadly looking hangs from his belt. A thick leather quiver full of long and well feathered arrows, made for maximum range are across his back along with a long slim hickory bow. A highly polished single shot, ornately carved French pistol is secured in his belt. Abruptly fifty more warriors ride up on the ridge on either side of him, each armed equally as well.

Sergeant Prince looks at his commanding officer. "Sir, up on the ridge, dead ahead, that's Pushmataha, The chief of all the Choctaw tribes. That fierce son-of-a-bitch has never been defeated by anyone.

He's the one that attacked our flank back there. We should try and ease out of here before he tries to kill us again."

The fatigued troops are also staring up at their next fight. Sevier looks at Sergeant Prince. "What the hell difference does it make to him? The people we fight are Cherokee."

The sergeant is becoming agitated with his stubborn captain. "Sir, the Choctaw are friends of the Cherokee. The Choctaw gave them their name. I have been around these parts for a while, and I know Pushmataha, he is not one to negotiate, and the old devil is not afraid of retaliation by the army. He will kill us just for being in Indian Territory. Let's move on before he gets the advantage and attacks again."

The captain nods and gives a hand signal for his troops to move out. "O'Reiley, Camron, Burns, and Kelly form a rear guard, look sharp. Franklin, O'Shea, and King guard the front of the column, you know the drill. Yell out if you see anything." They begin to move cautiously through the well-traveled woods.

---

# CHAPTER THREE

## WASHINGTON, D.C., UNITED STATES OF AMERICA

**1866**

### LET THE PEOPLE KNOW MY STORY.

Cal Chase, a well dressed, athletic, and handsome young man stops writing to look at his work. He is a recently hired news reporter for the popular *Washington Chronicle* newspaper. Cal lays his pen down from this adventurous frontier tale that is his passion. He looks at the page before him. It is a chronicle of the assault on a Cherokee Nation Indian village in Georgia that he plans to finish for a front page headline as soon as he interviews one last person. Cal gets up from his very old and well-used oak desk. He puts on his coat and walks to the door of his small office. A fellow reporter and new friend notices him leaving. "Where you going Cal, got a headline you want to share?"

Cal strolls out smiling. "I've got business with an Indian Chief." He starts down the long hall.

The middle-aged reporter grins. "You're a funny man. Hey Cal, I'm seeing the Queen of England, later. Want to have tea with us?"

Cal smiles and speaks as he walks. "This road to genius is blocked only by you." He continues down the hall.

Cal steps from the ornate office building doorway framed in carved hardwood and onto the busy sidewalk. He says to himself.

"What a great day."

Red and silver sunbeams pierce the unusually-overcast gray summer sky. The morning sunlight spreads across the busy city. The light of this day dawns on a new political era for the United States of America. An era that sets the stage for bitter reflection and badly needed reconstruction for post-Civil War America. Cal moves across the bustling avenue still talking about the end of the Civil War and the South's surrender, a year after the surrender. He passes colorful people from many different countries, recognized by both language and dress. His thick blonde hair appears almost golden as the bright sunlight flows across his broad shoulders.

Cal quickly continues toward the front of the prominent Brown's Indian Queen Hotel, a local landmark. The Indian Queen is a stately hotel that provides a pleasing scene of something a little more than reality. A portrait of fine architecture that is so well done it is more like a picture than a real building. Its grounds are green and lush and inside is more picturesque reality. Suddenly, an ebony horse drawn convertible carriage ornamented in brass, rushes from the hotel crossway near Cal. It is filled with the rich of the day and their trappings of wealth. The coach's highly polished finish reflects rippling images of pedestrians as it moves down the hectic street.

Cal is impressed by the sight of this stately transportation. He thinks to himself. "As I look at these powerful black horses drawing this blatant political transport that is probably paid for with political favors that only the rich can deliver the lone animals worthy to pull it are Thoroughbred horses. Only they could look so regal in such an environment. This most beautiful breed of horse that is raised for racing is now hitched to a coach as ornamentation for the politically powerful. I knew I had seen the consummate Washington scene."

Cal steps to the side as the universal Washington conveyance speeds past. He crosses the street and onto the hotel steps.

Cal sees his buddy, the doorman, Constantine. Constantine is the best source of local gossip in Washington. He is a robust doorman with an ear for gossip. He towers over his friend Cal by at least a foot, but his personality is always on the level with Cal and his other friends. Constantine's British green uniform is tailored with a military cut, setting the theme for the elegant four-star hotel.

Cal smiles at his pal and ask. "Morning, Con, is he here?"

Constantine blurts out his reply with a grin and a new joke for his captive audience. "Yeah, hey Cal, did ya hear about the guy that went to the doctor? His head has a fat green frog growing out of it. The Doctor looks at him and the frog with a medical curiosity. Then the frog speaks to the surprised doctor. "Hey Doc, can you get this growth off my ass." Constantine laughs out loud at his own joke.

Cal smiles and chuckles a little. He tries to be a little more reserved than his friend. "Yes, I know how that frog feels some days." Cal says.

Constantine joins him in their small laugh. Just then an older Cherokee Indian man dressed in a dark suit and tie, sporting long black graying hair and wearing a very colorful yellow and black turban rides past on a strong gray-dapple horse saddled with fine leather. He brushes Cal slightly, giving him a start; they look at the proud Indian man in the city. Thunder rolls in the distance behind dark clouds hovering outside the city. A peculiar day for Cal. First the thunder on a sunny day and now an Indian man in the city brushing past him. Could this be a sign of something about the Indians or just coincidence? Cal is not usually superstitious, but today he feel something unexplainable for him in the air.

Cal and the ever grinning Constantine look back at each other and shrug their shoulders. "Almost forgot, Cal. He arrived a few minutes ago."

Cal is appreciative. "Thanks, Con."

Constantine opens the mahogany door to the hotel for Cal, and Cal moves inside. He sees a beautiful carved dark mahogany-trimmed lobby and a number of attractive well-dressed people, including high-ranking soldiers and politicians from all walks of life scattered throughout the well appointed entrance hall. These high level patrons appear to be enjoying the trappings of affluence.

Cal stops at the well appointed registration desk and drafts a short note. A high-browed, aging hotel clerk addresses Cal from behind his polished cherry-wood counter. "May I help you, Sir?"

Cal folds the note and pulls a shiny gold coin from his pocket. "Yes, announce to Principal Chief John Ross of the Cherokee Nation, Cal Chase of the *Washington Chronicle* would like very much to see him."

Cal hands the note and the coin to the well-starched clerk. The clerk smiles and smoothly puts the gold piece in his vest pocket then looks towards an employee dressed in a gray uniform, cut similar to the one Constantine wears. He rings his desk-bell and the bellman quickly answers his page.

The clerk creases the note again and gives it to the

waiting bellman with a silver dime from a tray on his desk. "Take this to the Principal Chief Ross Suite and wait for an answer, please."

The bellman takes the note and quickly departs. The clerk glances at Cal. "Please have a seat in the lobby. We will call you when we get an answer."

Cal stares at the clerk a moment longer than necessary, letting him know he had seen him cheat the bellman on his tip. Cal moves to the lobby and waits.

A harsh looking American Indian Warrior walks past Cal. The warrior is dressed in a union army uniform with general's stars on his soldiers. The general's classic uniform is topped off by his long black hair and a short gray feather as decoration. He nods and Cal acknowledges with the same. A major sitting nearby stands and speaks to the general. "General good to see you."

They sit and talk with other military officers. Cal thinks to himself. "This is an odd place for a chief of an Indian nation and an Indian army general. A sight that is not that uncommon in the time. These men are powerful symbols of nature and the outdoors, not at all like the lavish hotel they reside in now."

Cal knows why John Ross stays here. He is a wealthy man in

his own right and does not need support from anyone, but these men are soldiers on lower than average pay. They must be supported by someone to live here or be independently wealthy. Cal knows it is likely they are supported by someone requiring favors for their backing. A tried method of survival in Washington.

Cal smiles again and glances at the grinning formal counter man. He walks to a nearby floral sofa and sits on the cloth flower garden. Cal casually glances around the busy Rococo lobby. Throughout the lobby, men sport fashionable dark wool suits and the ladies wear expensive silk dresses styled for summer while highly decorated military officers carry on their business with civilians. All of this is the attire of a political city with its people vying for high position, easy money, power, or the vanity of fame. All of this is telling him that Washington is a capital of negotiation for high stakes by people with a lot to lose and any stories about these people and their activities will be hard to come by. He can only hope Chief John Ross is a different man than these.

The privileged few continue to stroll in and out, while other fortunate ones sit in red leather, wing-backed chairs sipping their first-rate coffee or whiskey. The elegant chairs are just wide enough to fit their well-fed behinds with a little room left over for them to rise without taking the chair with them. In other parts of the hotel, advocates and politicians consult across ornate inlaid cherry-wood tables and enjoy the aroma of the best South American and French coffees. All of this sets a final picture for Cal of overwhelming wealth and high opportunity for all who come here. Cal's messenger has at last returned. "Mr. Ross said he will see you, but just for a few minutes. He isn't feeling well."

Cal stands and gives an amiable acknowledgment and a generous tip to make up for the dime. He hurries up the dark staircase. The wall adjoining the flight of stairs is a montage of brilliant blue and green male peacocks strutting across the scenery of India further marking the wealth of this city like many of the patrons of the hotel.

Cal reaches the top of the stairs and walks down a long plush hallway whose walls are decorated with rows of British fox hunt paintings in gold leaf frames. He moves on past the paintings towards the Chief Ross Suite. Cal pauses at Chief Ross's door, which is secured by two husky Cherokee Nation guards. They ask for Cal to identify himself. Cal quickly complies. One guard goes inside while the other stays with Cal and looks him over. In a moment, the sturdy seventy-six-year old Chief Ross comes to the front door and the guards go back to their silent posts. Chief Ross's salt and pepper silky hair and smooth face give the illusion of a much younger man.

This man of history impresses Cal. "No," he thought. "This great man is history: Principal Chief of the Cherokee Nation, a one-eighth Cherokee Indian and seven-eighths Caucasian. His father was Scottish, a man at peace with the Indian nations with whom he earned his living as a merchant trader in their territories and his beloved mother, a part Cherokee woman who continued to live the traditional Cherokee life of tribal unity and living off of what nature has to offer. She made one exception to help her husband at his trading post sitting on Cherokee land deep in the nation."

Cal Chase continues to think, "John Ross has risen to the high position of chief in his own nation and, in Washington D. C., as an honored diplomat in the worst of times in America when Indian people are totally rejected as a part of American society, and any one with Indian blood is considered inferior. John Ross is the elected National Leader of his Sovereign Nation, the Cherokee homeland. He was elected again and again for most of his adult life. It is ironic that the Cherokee people elected their officials long before most modern governments functioned on this continent. The same governments that now call the Indian nations uncivilized."

Chief Ross wears a conservative dark wool suit as everyone else in Washington does, a starched white shirt, and topped off with a black tie. He is an eloquent man, more diplomat than Indian Chief. "Hello, Mr. Chase. Welcome, please come in."

Cal gladly enters the boldly decorated suite that is more like a British Hunt Club than a common hotel room. He sees an elderly man with his back to them looking out the window. Chief Ross turns to his elderly friend and introduces him to Cal. Cal recognizes him from the street; he had let his horse brush Cal as he passed. "Talmidge, this is Mr. Cal Chase, of the Washington Chronicle. Mr. Chase, Talmidge Watts."

Talmidge slowly turns from the window and extends his aging hand. "Nice to meet you, Mr. Chase."

Cal smiles and shakes hands with the tall and stalwart gray-haired, Talmidge. "We've met, nice to know you, sir. Are you with the Cherokee Nation?"

Talmidge smiles. "Well yes, I am Cherokee. I suppose that makes me with the Nation."

Cal replies. "I'm sorry, are you an official of the Cherokee Nation?"

Talmidge is a mischievous character. "You mean like a politician. You could say I'm an insider or you might even say I lobby the chief for dinner and favors frequently. So, yes, I'm an official politician."

John smiles and moves to a nearby Queen Anne table topped by a brilliant green Tiffany Lamp and a crystal vase filled with crimson red roses, John's favorite flower. They remind him of Quatie his late wife and her beauty. "He is modest Mr. Chase. Talmidge is Chief Counsel to the Principle Chief of the Cherokee Nation. Coming to the point is not his strong suit."

John then sits in a brown leather chair and looks at Cal with his ever-quick smile, then turns to Talmidge. "Will you stay for dinner?"

Talmidge turns slightly toward the door. "No, John. I'll be going. Nice to have met you, Mr. Chase."

"Mr. Chase, Talmidge is an Indian, you know, doesn't talk much. It's not you." John smiles.

Cal doesn't know what to say. Talmidge retorts. "I can see I'm not the butt of this joke. I'm the whole ass."

EARTH, WIND AND FIRE

Mr. Watts moves to the door, opens it and speaks as he walks out. "I'll see you for breakfast, around six. Be ready."

John acknowledges with a nod and a smile. "I'll be ready."

John turns back to Cal. "Talmidge has been my friend for over fifty years. I know him better than he knows himself."

Cal smiles with his gracious demeanor. "Did the two of you grow up together?"

John smiles with pride. "Yes, he has protected me and supported me like no other. You could say we are best friends."

Cal agrees, "A friend like that is rare, very rare."

John is kind and gets back to business as quickly as he strayed. "How may I help you, Mr. Chase?"

Cal gets comfortable and grabs a fist full of confidence. He looks into John's warm eyes and speaks as eloquently and sincerely as he can. "Well, Mr. Ross, I have deep regard for the Cherokee people and their plight. My mother was part Cherokee."

John remains kind and supportive of the young, eager reporter. "Your mother told you about her people?"

Cal says, "Yes some, my mother Mary Deerinwater past on stories from my grandmother Susan Deerinwater. Did you know them?"

John smiles. "Yes I did know your grandmother, Susan. She was a bold Cherokee woman and a good friend. I always thought a lot of her."

Cal smiles proudly. "My father, Jonathan Chase, told me more. He was from here in Washington. Father was in a battle with the Cherokee when he was a young cavalry soldier and was so impressed by that event he never forgot them and their ways. Because of his experience father eventually went back to the territories, met my mother and here I am. But the best stories came from my grandfather when he was captured by the Cherokee and released."

John chuckles. "I'm glad they let him go, or I wouldn't have met you. Your family certainly has a rich history with the Cherokee."

Cal musters more sincerity, trying to show John he is truthful about writing a quality story about the Cherokee Nation. "Yes sir, But I'm here because you lived it your whole life, and my mother and grandmother spoke of you often. They were supporter of yours."

John's eyes glint with a bit more interest. "I told you we could only take a few minutes. However, I feel a little better now. Let me tell you a grand story about the glory of a nation, your mother and grandmother's nation. A story about glory, defeat and resurrection."

He begins his tale with Sir Alexander and King George of England.

# CHAPTER FOUR

## CHEROKEE NATION

### 1730

### A GENTLEMAN CALLS.

John's voice gets stronger and more proud as he begins to reel off a tale of a grand legend that he has not before told in such detail. He begins with great care. "Long before you and I were born things were very good for the Cherokee Nation. They were a formidable force in their homeland, now known as the state of Georgia and all surrounding regions from Georgia to North Carolina. The Cherokee, for that moment in history, were comfortable in the position they held."

An English explorer, Sir Alexander Cuming, a handsome and likeable dark-haired English gentleman was dispatched by the English monarch, King George himself to parlay with the leaders of the Cherokee Nation in the United States of America, specifically, over a region now known as the state of Georgia, but then it was a beautiful forest. Sir Cuming was to come to a compromise of trade and military support for the British soldiers and other British citizens exploring in the region. The king also wanted protection for British government official should trouble arise with the French troops and explorers already in the region. Alexander rode casually through the old growth Cherokee forest, day dreaming and whistling a tune expecting a welcoming reception because the Cherokee had always been friendly to the British. He hoped to meet an interpreter along the way knowing they were plentiful in the region. Suddenly three rebel Cherokee warriors rush him from the undergrowth. To their surprise Cuming quickly turns his horse towards them. Cuming is no novice, but now he has to prove it.

Cuming charges, running one down under the horses sharp hooves and then knocks a second one to the side with the full force of his horse's body. A third fires his ancient pistol and misses. Cuming turns his horse with pistol drawn, ready to shoot. Six Cherokee warriors and a husky powerful chief are quickly on the scene surrounding Cuming and the warriors. Attakullaculla, the chief, yells out in perfect English. "Stop!"

Cuming pauses and draws his aim on the chief as his horse moves under him. Attakullaculla is calm. He looks at his waiting warriors, all aiming their rifles at Cuming. Three of Attakullaculla's men take the ailing young warriors in hand. The chief speaks harshly to them. "You disgrace your people. You are thieves and robbers. Go, take the good-for-nothings and put them under the whip, fifty lashes"

Attakullaculla's warriors take the three injured men away. The remaining Cherokee warriors hold steady aim on Cuming to protect their chief. Sir Cuming continues to stare down the barrel of his pistol at Attakullaculla.

Attakullaculla smiles and continues to speak a high quality English. "What do we do now, Englishman?"

Cuming appears relieved. He uncocks his pistol and puts it away. "I am looking for the Principle Chief of the Cherokee Nation."

The warriors stand steady. Attakullaculla nods. "What is your business?"

Sir Cuming is still brave and forward in his bold manner. "Do you know him?" Attakullaculla nods again with a yes. "By the way how did you know I am British?"

Attakullaculla smiles. "Your clothes. Only the British wear such fancy clothes in the woods."

Cuming smiles slightly and continues. "Will you take me to

31

Attakullaculla?"

Attakullaculla nods and says. "Is this something he would not kill you for? I say again, what is your business?"

Cuming realizes he should be concerned and more sincere. "He will thank me for coming. Please, if you know this man, take me to him. I have a message of great importance."

Attakullaculla sees his urgency and recognizes him as friendly, but remains cautious. Cuming is in luck. Attakullaculla likes the British. "Come, follow us. I will take you." The warriors and Attakullaculla get their horses. They mount up and ride away with Cuming in tow. Both sides understand there is an uneasy peace in the Cherokee Nation. All sides rush to gain allies to survive. In these times numbers mean power.

The British badly need an alliance in this new land with the Cherokee Nation, because the Cherokee are the most powerful tribe in the eastern half of the continent. If the English are able to control this region they can improve trade and also assure the safety of their soldiers and settlers. Unknown to anyone in the Cherokee nation, the British secretly want to control the entire continent and over a period of time make it a part of the empire. King George has personally asked Sir Alexander Cuming to seek an alliance with chief Attakullaculla and the Cherokee Nation. The King's first step is to keep his country's foothold in the new world by joining with the Cherokee.

Finally Attakullaculla and his party arrive at New Echota, the mother town of all towns and villages of the Cherokee Nation. It is a sunny and serene day, a good day for talking. Sir Cuming looking very British boldly rides into the village with Chief Attakullaculla. Cuming and the Cherokee party pass two sentries, standing ready to attack if he makes the wrong move. The streets are lined with well-kept log homes and dugouts. Cherokee children gleefully play stickball. In the background, Cherokee women prepare the evening meal.

Everyone in the village looks up and takes notice as they ride past. Cuming pauses as Attakullaculla steps down from his horse. Thirty warriors form around their chief. Five times that many warriors watch from locations around New Echota, their home. The chief speaks to Cuming, still amused at his audacity. "Step down, it is very brave for a white man to ride alone on our land and into our village. Why do you do this?"

Cuming is bold out of necessity. "I have come as a messenger to offer peaceful term for an alliance with the Cherokee Nation. Do I need an armed escort for such business?"

Attakullaculla chuckles and nods. "Not if you are British."

Cuming relaxes a little seeing the humor in Attakullaculla and ask out of necessity as he dismounts. "Am I going to see the chief?"

Attakullaculla says, "I am chief of all Cherokee. My name is Attakullaculla.

Cuming is relieved. "Thank God, I am Sir Alexander Cuming, Representative of King George the Second of England. I have urgent business with you and your people."

Attakullaculla is interested in his new friend's name. "Cuming, where is Going?" He smiles.

Cuming is more serious. "Your command of the English language is very good, but Cuming is my name, C-U-M-I-N-G." He stops and smiles. "I see it was a joke." Cuming smiles. "Good, very good. Just like not telling me you are the chief."

Attakullaculla smiles with a more somber tone. "I still say it is very brave for a white man to ride into our village and not come to the point."

Cuming tries to conceal a distressed smile and attempts to speak confidently to the chief. "Not brave, Sir, by order of King George."

The chief is more interested. "What is a King and who is George of England?"

Cuming smiles. "He is a chief, like you are a chief." Everybody in the village laughs out loud.

Cuming does not understand. "What's funny? He is like ah, Chief George of England."

Attakullaculla laughs. "I am chief of all chiefs."

Cuming is a little nervous with all of the unusual looking people around him and the unknown of whither they may burn him at the stake or something worse. Duty calls, however, so he proceeds on. "How did you come to speak English so well?"

Attakullaculla answers casually. "English traders taught me when I was young."

Cuming presses on to get to the point. "Good, very good. As I said, I am, Sir Alexander Cuming, Ambassador of King George, the Second, of Great Britain, chief of all chiefs in his nation. I would like to speak with you about an alliance between our nations. An alliance where both of our nations will profit with trade and both will enjoy the safety of numbers."

Attakullaculla looks at Cuming sternly. "This is your business with the Cherokee, Sir? Sir is a strange name for a white man. For any man."

Cuming smiles. He is eased a little by the chief's good demeanor. "Yes, that is my business."

Attakullaculla is friendlier now and smiles with a gentle gaze. "Good."

Cuming wants to make friends quickly. "Sir, you speak excellent English. I am sorry I can't do as well in your language."

The chief speaks like a teacher. "You are, Sir. I am Attakullaculla."

Cuming tries very hard to show he is friendly and not speaking down to the chief. "Walter is my name. Sir is just an expression of respect."

Attakullaculla responds with an order. "We will call you, Sir. I will be called Attakullaculla."

Cumming cuts it short in order not to cause any trouble. "Sorry, well, please call me Sir. I like it. I will not insult you with worthless gifts, may we sit and talk?"

The chief gestures for his people to prepare a place. "We will council."

Three Indian women and two small girls spread colorful crimson red and black woven blankets over a log that is cut flat on top making a seat that lies near a campfire. Other women put more wood on the massive campfire.

Cuming says, "Thank you, Chief Attakullaculla."

The chief turns and walks to the comfortable blankets. A young boy takes their horses away. Cuming walks to the warm campfire.

The chief sits on the log at his favorite place. "Sit, Sir, and welcome."

Cuming's smile is a little ill at ease. He is concerned that Attakullaculla will not get to the point of this meeting. He is thinking the chief may be stalling for some reason yet to be revealed. Cuming sits as he talks. "Yes, Sir, thank you."

Attakullaculla glances at Cuming and answers sternly. "You are Sir. I am Attakullaculla; State your business from George."

Cuming squirms to sit properly on the hard log then starts his statement like the diplomat he is. "I met with Choctaw Tribesmen and the Creek." The chief nods in understanding, "And they say the Cherokee is the most formidable and most powerful of all the Indian Nations."

The chief nods again and corrects his pronunciation. "Chillaki." Cuming smiles anxiously. "That's what I said, Cherokee."

The chief nods with a smile. Cuming continues. "The Choctaw also said your tribe controls most of the land in this region and I thought since you own most of the land north to south on this part of the continent, we should talk about a treaty between you and my King. A treaty that would benefit both Cherokee and British. With this agreement our nations would be able to keep the peace and prosper without the losses and waste of war, not to mention the profitable trade between us. We only ask that you don't trade with or defend the French."

The chief is amused. "You talk with many words when just a few would do. What is continent?"

35

Cuming tries to explain. "Well, ah, it's a piece of land bigger that yours that goes from sea to sea."

The Chiefs nods and cuts a large piece of meat from a deer flank roasting over the campfire. He gives it to Cuming and cuts one for himself. "Eat."

Three camp dogs gather around for scraps. Cuming takes a bite. A dog turns his waging tail to Cuming's leg distracting him. The tail beats hard against the side of his leg. Cuming dodges the tail and another dog grabs his large slice of meat. Attakullaculla laughs. "Sir, you make friends fast."

Cuming grins and throws out his chest in jest. "I am a friendly old boy most times."

Attakullaculla shows obvious pride. He loves the big dog. "The fast one, the one that took your meat, is my dog, Horse."

Cumming is amused. "Dog is named Horse? I guess that's as good as any name, Horse is a dog? " Cuming grins. "Horse smell like dog."

Attakullaculla has grown to like Sir Cuming and tries to make him feel more welcome with a friendly joke. "You know what you call dog with big balls that drags them through campfire?"

Cuming is grinning. "No, what?"

The chief laughs at his own joke. "Sparky." They laugh together.

Attakullaculla became a little more serious. "About your business, Sir, I will speak for all of my people; I believe we should meet with your King before we talk of any agreements."

Cuming answers with sincerity. "He lives a long way from here and time is very short."

The chief is interested in the uncommon speech and eloquent language of his new friend. "What does it mean, long way?"

Cuming thinks out loud. "Well, ah, a lot of sunup's and sundown's."

The chief holds up his fingers on both hands. "More than my fingers in sunup's and sundown's?"

Cuming looks around and sees a toddler and his mother sitting nearby. Cuming points to the happy little boy. "That boy, half the time he has lived to get to my king."

Attakullaculla is agreeable. "I will take Council of our nations Minor Chiefs, and we will decide together. This is our law."

Cuming's face forms a satisfied look. "Capital, just tell me how long? As I said, time is critical."

The chief and Sir Cuming look at each other. The chief smiles and gives him a firm answer. "I will tell you our answer in five Suns. You stay and be with us until we decide."

Cuming cheerfully agrees and quickly gets on to more pressing business. "Chief, the border problems you have with the other tribes and the White Settlers? Will you keep your Minor Chiefs from attacking our settlers and soldiers until we can finalize this matter?"

Attakullaculla agrees, "Yes, I will stop the chiefs until we decide. Now, we eat."

Cuming smiles in agreement and says. "Wonderful, please do this as soon as possible."

The chief smiles and nods. The women serve more food and drink with the Cherokee utensils made of wood and clay. Attakullaculla cuts meat from a roasting deer flank for Cuming and the nearby children.

In five fleeting days, Attakullaculla has his anticipated answer along with several ambassadors from the villages to participate in the, "liaison." Everyone is happy and jubilant about the trip to London. The entire village celebrates the decision.

Cuming sits next to a campfire burning in front of the Cherokee Council House. Attakullaculla walks to the campfire and sits with him. "We have agreed to become friends with you and your people when we meet with King George, the Second."

The serious Cuming looks at him with urgency on his face. "Is there another way without meeting the King? Time is important."

Attakullaculla shakes his head, no. Cuming hesitates. "Time is so important. The balance of power rests on this liaison. If we don't hurry, this will soon change and neither of our Nations will survive here."

The chief is sincere. "I understand the French are moving fast to make agreements with the other tribes and that our nations combined are stronger than one alone against these enemies but, Walter Alexander, the Council of chiefs has spoken. We will meet with George before we agree to join with you."

Cuming nods in submission.

## CHAPTER FIVE

## NEW ORLEANS SHIPYARD, PIER THREE TO LONDON

### 1730

### IS THIS THE PEACE WE SEEK?

Ambassador Cuming has quickly arranged a departure for New Orleans harbor where the group has managed to catch a British Warship bound for London. Attakullaculla is a happy, fun loving man, smiling as he rides horseback with six Minor Village Chiefs and Cuming. The Chiefs are dressed in deer skin pants with colorful cotton shirts and traditional Cherokee colored turbans wrapped around their heads like a multihued bandage. Some of the turbans are red, others are yellow and purple. Each chief has their own colored robe draped over their shoulder to protect them from the cold on the voyage.

Cuming rides along in his British traveling clothes which are, of course, very tailored. Attakullaculla has brought two armed Cherokee warriors and Cuming has arranged for four British cavalry soldiers to ride with them. They ride and talk as they go. The Minor Chief named War Eagle munches on parched corn and berries as they move down the well-worn trail. He speaks with his mouth partially full and grinning. "Did you hear about Attakullaculla?" He then farts like a trumpet.

Cuming is amused and joins in the banter. "Sounds like an

explosive story."

Attakullaculla grins. "Sounds like hot air to me." They all laugh.

War Eagle chimes in. "Did you hear a dog bark?" He laughs out loud.

Cuming pipes in. "Confucius say, man who farts in church, sits in his own pew."

Attakullaculla smiles trying to be silent, but he can't resist. "I will give War Eagle new white man name, Bugle-ass." The group laughs again.

A warrior guard carries on. "We can't take War Eagle anywhere. He always gives away our location."

Another Minor Chief, Whitekiller adds his part to War Eagle's story. "Did you hear about man standing behind War Eagle in battle? He got burned from the powerful force of War Eagle.

Cuming supports the story. "He's a new secret weapon? Last night in camp I thought I heard a trumpet. I guess it was just War Eagle testing his capabilities."

They all chuckle. Attakullaculla has another story. "Did you hear about the Choctaw and his friend white man, riding their horses to town? White man begins to gallop his horse. Indian speeds his horse beside him and yells out. "Why do you go so fast?" White man replies. "Faster you go cooler it gets." The white man grins like an opossum and pushes his horse to go faster. He finally leaves Indian in the dust. After a while Indian and his horse slow down and ride into town. He sees white man standing beside his poor dead horse, lying on the ground. Indian stops and looks at the horse then at white man. White man is sad. "I don't know what happened?" Indian stares at the horse and back at white man. "Um, must have frozen to death."

They all laugh again. War Eagle laughs with them. He turns his attention to Cuming. "Sir, do you know about the little people?"

Cuming appears puzzled.

War Eagle continues. "Little people hide in the forest and create mischief. They have dogs with two left legs."

Cuming is interested he ask, "How little?"

War Eagle holds his hands in a position to show about two feet tall.

Cuming is more curious. "Have you seen them?"

The Minor Chief smiles. "All Cherokee know them. They are our trouble. They are the people that make bad happen. The smaller they are the worse they are. The little people are mostly mean. If you catch one, you will rule the little tyrants."

Attakulaculla adds his part. "Catch one and you'll think you've got a Bobcat by the tail. They are little, but mighty. Fierce devils."

Whitekiller grins. "It is said they will steal your children."

War Eagle adds more. "I hear the little people are cannibals and like fat men best."

Whitekiller laughs a little. "You don't have anything to worry about War Eagle. "They will not eat you. The little people can die of food poisoning and they know it."

War Eagle has more. "The little people have more lives than a cat; they make sounds like a frog and croak every night."

Attakullaculla laughs. "War Eagle is probably why his village has never experienced the little people. They're afraid of Bugle Ass and his explosive greetings."

Attakullaculla looks back at his Minor Chief and asks, "War Eagle, do you know the story of Sun and Moon?"

War Eagle is a jolly man, but groans a little at the idea of another story. "No, tell us the story of Sun and Moon."

Attakullaculla who loves to tell stories, smiles as he speaks. "At one time, Sun burned down on the children of the Earth harshly. She was so hot she burned them and sometimes killed them. She burned most of the day with only a little at night. They decided to defend themselves. But Sun was smart, so they knew they must be smarter."

"Finally a mighty chief sent the boldest blacksnake and rattlesnake to kill Sun. At that time Sun came up in the west. The snake brothers waited for her at the edge of Earth. When Sun came up, Blacksnake was blinded as he tried to strike and Sun killed him. Rattlesnake rattled and ran away striking out wildly. He accidentally killed Sun's daughter that was nearby. Sun was angry and sad about her little daughter's death and sadly went away from this revolting deed. The people began to suffer while Sun was gone. They froze and were miserable. The people's toes turned black from frost bite and the worst one's long noses froze and fell off from getting into other people's business. Now their noses have grown back. The old long noses are all sizes and the worst ones are called nosey by their people. The mightiest chief of all went to Sun and said he was sorry about her dear little daughter and begged Sun to come back and love her people again. She said no, but her cousin, named Moon, could take her place. Moon always wanted to join with people, but Moon did not have the bright smile like Sun. Moon finally did come to join the people and gave them moonlight, but only for part of the day, because Moon was cautious and remembered the deeds of the people before. Sun was begged again by the mighty chief to come back and was offered many things, but she would not."

"After many years of sadness and staying away, Sun missed her people and came back, but only for a short time each day and she came up in the east to avoid any more ugly surprises from bad men. The story of Sun and Moon has two lessons. Sun suffered a serious loss for being mean to her people. The people suffered more for meeting her meanness with their own. It is written: You must do justice to all to get justice from all."

War Eagle really likes the story. He adds to it. "Sun remains good now, but is still sad about her baby daughter. She has decided to go away early every day to remind us of our bad deed and hers, hoping it would never happen again. This story is like me. Burn like the Sun. Strike like a snake."

Attakullaculla is amused and replies, "An old and blind Snake."

War Eagle grins. "You know how Attakullaculla got his childhood name? They called him two dogs then."

Cumming is interested. "No how did he get his childhood

name?"

War Eagle's grin is much bigger now. "When Atta was very young he went to his wise mother as he was curious about this odd name given him by his father, and ask how he came by this unusual name. His mother told him Indian people name their children after the first thing the father sees when the child is born. She said, like your sister, she was born and father looked across the forest and saw a running deer, so he named her Running Deer." War Eagle turns to Cuming in a very serious demeanor and speaks with sincerity. "His mother is kind and looks him in the eye and says, 'why do you ask two dogs humping'." War Eagle breaks out laughing as does Cumming and the rest.

They arrive at the busy New Orleans docks and dismount near a very regal British warship sporting all of its colors. Attakullaculla looks up and up at the ship's mast with the British flag flying high. Cuming speaks to Attakullaculla. "Chief Attakullaculla, bring your people along. We will board now."

Attakullaculla looks at Cuming and then at the armed warrior guards and soldiers riding with them. "Take the animals back." The two warriors acknowledge and mount up taking the chief's horses by the reins. The soldiers stand fast. The warriors ride out.

Attakullaculla looks at his Council Chiefs. "Come, we have an adventure."

They walk to the ship's gangplank. The chiefs all board slowly, while looking and talking. Cuming is in a hurry. He knows his miscalculation of time to get from the village to the ship made them a little late and the ship's captain will be irritated, but he necessarily remains the diplomat.

Cuming turns to the chiefs as the last one comes on board. "Wait here, I'll tell the captain we've arrived and get your quarters ready." Attakullaculla acknowledges as Cuming walks away.

The colorful Chiefs watch four sailors using ropes and pulleys to load cargo onto the huge ship. One of the four sailors closest to the Chiefs speaks in a thick British accent to Attakullaculla. "Well gentlemen, what do ya think of our old war-horse?" Attakullaculla looks at him with a question on his face. The sailor smiles and continues the explanation. "Our ship."

Attakullaculla looks at the sailor with his charming demeanor. "First time I have seen floating house, but I like it, it is a fierce looking house."

The sailors laugh. One of the sailors explains. "It is built for long voyages."

Attakullaculla acknowledges by smiling he says, "Good, we are going on one."

Cuming returns and the sailor goes back to his work. "Follow me, gentlemen. I have your quarters ready." The Chiefs smile apprehensively and follow as Cuming turns and walks toward the cabin hatch.

In the background of the cabins sailors are beginning to set small sails to move from port and clear the harbor were they will finally set full sail. A gang of sailors heave off the port docks and the huge ship slowly floats away from the pier toward the open bay. The small sails at the fore front of the ship begin to completely open as a slight wind is caught. The ship cracks and pops as it works the kinks out moving toward the open sea.

The chiefs enter their small, crowded, and scantly furnished cabins. They look out the port holes elbow to elbow for a last look at their home that is becoming far way and going out of sight.

Outside the Chief's cabin the main sail drops and catches a good wind. The sailing is smooth as they get underway. The ship moves almost silently out to the high seas and gracefully cuts through the rising waves all through the clear day.

Attakullaculla watches the dark ocean roll against the afternoon sky. As he looks to the port side, Attakullaculla sees a Sperm Whale break the surface. The site pleasantly surprises the middle-aged chief. He turns to War Eagle who is standing with him. "Now, that's a fish."

War Eagle nods. "If you catch him, it would be a fight to decide who eats who."

Attakullaculla smiles and answers. "Everything is so big out here. We float in our canoes and catch fish the size of our hands. These people float in full size houses and can't catch fish. Who is better?"

War Eagle is amused. "These people don't think ahead. They just make war."

Attakullaculla is thinking out loud. "They do. We just don't know what it all means yet."

Three more playful family members join the giant whale. The site is spectacular for Attakullaculla and War Eagle. The two men continue watching until the gigantic Mammals swim out of sight.

Two months have passed, and they are still at sea. The warship goes about its patrolling duties slowing the trip down a little, but still traveling steadily toward Great Britain and the meeting with King George. Everyone is anxious to see land and feel it under their feet. The sun begins to set and fortunately the waters are calm. The remaining Minor Chiefs join Attakullaculla and War Eagle at their favorite spot on the deck of the ship as does Cuming. They all enjoy the scenery since they have finally gotten their sea legs under them, and no one has gotten sick from the constant rocking of the ship. They have become sea worthy whether they liked it or not.

Alexander Cuming speaks to Attakullaculla while looking across the calm seas. "Chief Attakullaculla, you're going to love England. It is beautiful and full of wonders from new inventions of science to fine architecture."

Attakullaculla has a question on his mind knowing from experience that everything is not always as it is told. "What is England? Is it a land of woods and game or blighted by a city with too many people? Like the settlers camps where we live."

Alexander patiently explains. "My land, where my King lives, where I live, is like your nation. Some of it is beautiful with green woods and bountiful game while other regions are blighted by cities that are too big and over-populated. This is the way of modern man. He has become too lazy to hunt and live from the land as nature provides. So he relies on making things for others. These things he makes are sold for money to buy food and shelter."

Attakullaculla is still curious. "Money, we have dealt with money it seems to create a greed for more. The more important question for me is George? I mean, is he like you or is he greedy like the people you speak of?"

Cuming answers as a teacher would. "He is the leader of our people in our nation, as you are the leader of your people in your nation. You will meet him very soon and decide for yourself. I am sure the two of you will become great friends."

Attakullaculla acknowledges. "I look forward to meet George."

Cuming responds in kind. "And I am sure he looks forward to meeting you."

Attakullaculla smiles. "You are a good man, Sir Alexander Cuming, and a loyal friend to George; he should be proud."

Cuming pats Attakullaculla on the back. "Let us get some rest, we have a long day tomorrow."

Attakullaculla smiles and watches as Cuming leaves for his quarters. He turns back and looks across the sea for some time after Cuming has gone.

It is becoming dark now. A bright moon looms overhead casting a pale light across the calm seas. Several colossal humpback whales swim near the ship singing to each other. Attakullaculla is impressed by these animals and continues to watch their moonlit images. A large male comes near the ship and the chief can see his eye, it looks almost human. Attakullaculla speaks to him. "Hello big one, we will not hurt your family." The whale swims on blowing water high from his head. The wise chief smiles to himself and moves from the rail to his quarters.

Late the next morning the British Warship slowly sails into the English Channel and on toward Britain. It is not too long until the ship cruises the crowed London Harbor. The sleek ship moves into a large British Navy slip near the Harbor Master's office. They begin docking procedures. Two sailors throw ropes over the side to waiting dockhands. The deck hands tie the ship off while four sailors aboard ship lower the gangplank. Attakullaculla and his chiefs are on the deck of the ship watching the harbor's heavy activity with great anticipation.

There are many ship's captains, local traders and traders from around the world, walking from place to place, negotiating cargo deals. A large number of freight wagons drawn by giant draft horses bring cargo to the loading docks. In another area of the commercial pier, three English Navy men supervise the unloading of cargo from a large freight wagon.

Attakullaculla looks up to see a sizable white-faced clock with black hands surrounded by a gold colored round frame, hung on the outside of the Harbor Master's building. A sign rest under it: "London, England."

People on the well-worn dock gawk and chatter while some point at the colorfully dressed Cherokee Chiefs. A sailor aboard the warship stops as he walks past the chiefs. Their attention is still taken by the huge clock. The sailor takes notice. "Say mate, ya never seen a harbor clock that big before?"

Attakullaculla looks at the rustic sailor. "What is harbor?"

The sailor smiles and answers. "It's ah, this place we are in, where the ships dock. Like back in New Orleans. Ya know docks with water around them."

All the Chiefs look as if they understand. Attakullaculla starts his quizzing process again. "What is clock?"

The sailor is condescending. "Well, what you're starin' at of course. You tell time by it."

Attakullaculla nods his head yes and smiles like a fox. "What is time?"

The sailor tries to figure a way to answer. "Well, it's

what happens from, well how long it takes to do something, you know time?" Attakullaculla nods yes. The other chiefs look on with a straight face nodding.

The sailor looks at the clock. "Blimey mate, you fellows really haven't been anywhere, have ya?"

The Chiefs look at him harshly. Attakullaculla retorts. "You know what Buffalo is?"

The sailor is surprised. "No, can't say as I do? I suppose it's an American wild animal or somethin'."

Attakullaculla smiles a mischievous smile. "You are not the sharpest knife in the house are you?" The seaman appears a little angry. All of the chief's eyes get wide and wild looking waiting for the sailors next reaction. Attakullaculla continues. "You really haven't been anywhere have you?"

The sailor smiles. "Well, I guess the jokes on me!" He laughs and the chiefs laugh artificially with him.

Sir Cuming walks up to the group curious as to what has transpired. The sailor speaks to Cuming. "Hello governor, just visiting with the natives."

The Chiefs and Attakullaculla glare at the sailor just too playfully intimidate him for his earlier remarks. "Well I got work to do, good day gents. I enjoyed our visit." The sailor leaves.

Cuming apologizes for the seaman. "Please don't think anything of him gentlemen. He was only making conversation and probably not a very good one."

The grinning Cherokee chiefs listen in silent private amusement as Attakullaculla speaks to Sir Cuming. "What is a clock?"

Cuming appears rushed. The captain of the ship is hastening everyone off so he can get the ship organized and leave himself. "It is, well, time, something we are very short of."

Attakullaculla nods. "Is this is an important thing that you have little of, like gold?"

Cuming is pressed for time. "I thought we had discussed this before. No matter, I'll explain everything at your training session to meet King George, but yes in many ways it is more precious than gold. Particularly if you are an important man like yourself. We really must go. The captain is battening down the ship and wants everybody off as soon as possible."

The Principal Chief is amused at Cuming's hurried explanation. "Do we have time?"

Sir Cuming smiles. "No, time ran out. Let us be off. The carriage awaits." Cuming turns and walks off the ship and the Chiefs follow surveying the area, taking in every sight. They walk down the long brick street toward an awaiting Royal Carriage drawn by four black powerful horses. People along the craggy streets stare at Cuming and the Chiefs as they pass them by.

Three ladies stop in the middle of their conversation to watch this strange parade of colorful natives go by. The crowd begins to whisper behind their hands. "I've never seen anyone like that. I heard they were to be in the city. Are they savages? Look at the big one. He must be chief. I wonder what's under those feathers!"

The Cherokee Chiefs stare at the ladies with their huge feathered hats and long puffed dresses. They like what they see.

One young Cherokee Chief cannot seem to help his curiosity. He leaves the group and walks to a nearby young and pretty lady to look at her beautiful peacock-feathered hat. Her hat's plumes hit the curious young chief in the face as she turns to talk to the middle-aged woman next to her.

Cumming and the Council of Chiefs turn and watch the young man. Cuming starts to go to him. Attakullaculla puts his hand out and gently stops Cuming and continues to watch his young chief. Cuming stops and waits patiently.

The charismatic young chief looks closer and admires the Peacock plumes by touching them. He taps the woman on the shoulder. The rest of the Minor Chief's group is still patiently waiting. The crowd holds their breath watching for his next move. The woman turns around reluctantly and faces this fierce warrior chief. "Yes?" She asks. "What do you want?"

The young chief points gently to the hat in total admiration. He speaks in broken English he has learned from Attakullaculla. "Plumes are beautiful."

The woman touches her hat. "Why thank you, sir." The Cherokee pulls a raven feather from the braids in his shiny black hair and hands it to the woman. The woman is puzzled by the young chief's action and is aware she is being watched by everyone. The woman looks at the feathers, still curious. She ask, "What, do I do, with this?"

The young chief smiles with sincerity. "I will show you." He takes the feather and places it in a special place on the side of her large hat. The young chief then takes a peacock feather and puts it in his braided silken hair. "The feather of the raven will bring you good luck. Keep it in your beautiful yellow hair."

The pretty woman touches the feather. "I will, what a lovely gesture, I hope my feather brings you as much good luck."

The young chief is proud and smiles. The woman warms to him. He turns and walks to the diplomatic group with a grin on his face. Cuming smiles at the goodwill the chief has displayed to the English people. As he walks the Peacock feather moves in time with his stride from a dangling braid in his black mane. The woman continues to watch the young man with a kindly expression. The powerful young chief turns to the restless horses hitched to the carriage where the footman waits with the coach door open. He walks to the animals side and begins to stroke their necks and heads. They calm down and relax, warming to his touch. He looks at the people surrounding him. "They are tired." He says to the interested crowd.

The crimson group along with the youthful chief walk on a few feet more to the Coach. Cuming urges everyone into the coach. They enter the large Crested Royal Carriage leisurely. The young chief is the last one in. Cuming gets in and the footman shuts the door. The young man looks back at the woman and smiles. She is impressed by his proper manner.

The horses jump nervously and fidget rocking the carriage while the driver awkwardly tries to control them. The young chief gets out and walks in front of the sweating horses. Cuming takes a deep breath knowing he must not offend these people and waits patiently. The chief begins to stroke their necks and heads again as he speaks softly to the proud animals. They immediately calm down again.

The young man notices everyone is still watching. He smiles and speaks out as he turns to get in the carriage again. "They want to go home and rest. No more waiting."

He walks past the driver of the royal carriage. "Take these horses home, feed and rest them when we get to the George house. I will come and see to be sure that it is done. If you do not I will come for you." The chief waits for an answer.

The driver stares for a moment then says, "Good, good, I will do it soon as we get to the castle, right-o."

The young chief smiles and gets in the coach with the delegation and rides away.

## CHAPTER SIX

## BUCKINGHAM PALACE, LONDON ENGLAND

## 1731

## A STRANGE WAY TO LIVE.

The stately official carriage of King George's Court winds its way around the London streets until it reaches a long cobblestone avenue leading to the palace entrance.

The ebony coach rolls through the courtyard of the grand Palace with the Cherokee Chiefs and Sir Cuming riding comfortably inside. The chief look out interested in the castle.

Attakullaculla turns to the others. "This must be the castle."

Cuming smiles. "Yes, this is the castle, where George lives."

They all nod unceremoniously.

The royal conveyance stops in front of the ancient residence. A servant wearing a black tailored uniform opens the carriage door and the well groomed footman puts a wooden step below the door. The dignified chiefs wait for Cuming to exit. Cuming gets out and then helps his guest to exit. The chiefs blend well with the royal environment. The Cherokee traditional and colorful apparel is well suited to the fanciful wardrobes of England. A servant opens the massive carved oak doors trimmed with brass that covers the front entry. Sir Cuming moves everyone inside while still being courteous. "Come, gentlemen, follow me."

The young chief looks at the waiting driver of the coach. The driver tips his hat. "We're going now governor, food for everybody including me and the footman."

The chief smile and strolls inside with the group. He glimpses the outside of the gigantic royal estate as he enters the palace. The large doors swing shut behind them.

Attakullaculla looks at War Eagle. "George must be very rich. I wonder if he as good as he is rich?"

Cuming smiles while he walks between the two chiefs. "Very rich indeed."

The foyer and the room beyond are ornamented with polished oak and marble trim. Huge briar oak furniture and colorful royal blue trappings set the style. Cuming opens a large door off the palace hall secured by two ceremoniously uniformed palace guards that stand on either side of the door.

Cuming says, "This way, gentlemen."

They enter the large beautiful room. The chiefs are awed for a moment by the opulence of the decor. In a brief time King George enters. The King puts up his hand casually, to motion them to relax. Cuming bows, the Council Chiefs do not see the need.

The King is respectful to the chiefs. "Gentlemen, be seated." The chiefs nod and begin to seat themselves.

The King is casual to his friend Sir Cuming. "Alexander, who are these dignitaries?"

Cuming turns toward the Principal Chief. "Your majesty this is Chief Attakullaculla, Principle Chief of the Cherokee Indian Nation." The chief stands very proud, looking at King George. "Their nation is located near the Colonies, and these other gentlemen are his village chiefs and trusted counsel."

King George puts on a very big smile. "I'm glad you came gentlemen and Principal Chief Attakullaculla. Please be seated and relax. I apologize for rushing ahead, but we do need to get right to our business, I have many pressing engagements today."

The King sits in his chair decorated to look like a small throne that sits at the head of a lengthy oak table. His guest sit with him in elegant chairs on either side of the table. "The problem I have in your land, your nation, is that I need an alliance to protect my countrymen and someone to trade goods with. For that I will protect your villages and people from trespassers with my armies and give you favorable trade agreements. Our nation will buy and trade things from you as well as sell you goods you may need."

Attakullaculla looks interested and almost royal himself with his regal manner. "We will discuss this matter in Council and speak tomorrow."

The King smiles in agreement. "Splendid, before you go, I have gifts for you; then you may rest and, gentlemen, thank you for coming, we are grateful."

King George motions for four people in the wings of his meeting room to bring the gifts. The people enter with splendid English tailored clothes. They stop beside the King and await his instruction. "Gentlemen, I have garments for you while you tour London."

The King nods for his people to fit the Cherokee. They begin to fit and measure each of them. The Chiefs observe with guarded caution as the tailors measure. The tailors pull on the arms and legs of the chiefs and call out numbers. A nearby scribe writes every thing down.

The next day after a lot of quick sewing by many tailors, Cuming and the Chiefs are dressed to the style of the day. They exit the Palace and into the front courtyard. They pass a striking and well cared for rose garden and continue toward a covered Royal Coach where coachmen and footmen wait. Sir Cuming is enjoying himself and wants the Chiefs to enjoy themselves too. "Gentlemen, we are going to tour the city and visit many important places."

The Chiefs smile and acknowledge the plan. Cuming directs the coachman as he gets closer to the carriage. "Take us to the Belvedere Hotel please."

The Footman opens the door and puts the step down for all to enter. The coachman nods as Cuming enters last and the footman takes the step away then closes the door. As the coach's door clicks shut the coachman drives away. After a short trip the carriage stops in front of the elegant and international Belvedere Hotel. Crowds of inquisitive Londoners gather when they see the Royal Coach. London Bobbies hold the people back, until they discover it's not the King or Queen and the crowd walks away uninterested.

Cuming exit's the carriage and waits while the footman holds the door open for the others. For a moment no one comes out. Cuming smiles patiently as finally Attakullaculla sticks his head out of the carriage doorway and looks around. He continues to look around at the few remaining people gathered around the carriage. Attakullaculla slowly steps out smiling and strolls to the hotel doorway. He then looks back at the other chiefs.

They are still in the coach. Attakullaculla shrugs his shoulders as the doorman open the door. He walks inside the hotel. His dress and his manner give no clue that he is a stranger to this place.

Cuming continues to smile and patiently wait for the other chiefs. Slowly and reluctantly they emerge from the carriage uncomfortably clad in their new clothes. Cuming escorts them inside as a few onlookers gawk at their long hair and Indian adornments.

They pass through the eloquent hotel lobby while Cuming points the way to a large ballroom. As they enter the ballroom, the elegance of the room entrances them. It is decorated with golden colored drapes, white table clothes and crystal chandeliers that throw the gas light around the room like a hundred small suns. The Chiefs are duly impressed. They now see a long, narrow, elegantly decorated platform sitting in the center of the room. Cuming guides them to an area on the platform that appears to be set up like a museum display. "Come with me, gentlemen, his Majesty wants the Royal and wealthy of Great Britain to see you."

Cuming asks them to change to their wilderness clothes behind a nearby dressing curtain. They just look at him. Attakullaculla speaks with the power of a chief. "What is this display of men?"

Cuming is apologetic. "It is completely all right, Chief. You and

55

your Minor Chiefs will stand on the platform and be observed by our citizens, it is our custom. They have never seen men like you before, you do understand?"

Attakullaculla is rigid in his statement. "No, I do not!"

Sir Cuming tries not to offend his friend. He speaks in his best diplomatic inflection. "It is our way. I am sorry Principal Chief Attakullaculla. I will ask no other favors of you."

Attakullaculla is disgusted. "We will do this, but a single time as a friend to you and England, but especially for you. If you ask your friends to embarrass themselves again, you will be displayed tied to a stake."

Cuming is relieved, but guilty about what he has been forced to ask. "Good show, Chief, never again. I do value your friendship."

Cuming hurriedly gets the men behind the curtain and they dress in their own clothes. As they come out Sir Cuming positions the Chiefs while Attakullaculla signals them with his stern eyes to comply. In a few minutes British citizens file into the large room looking at the proud chiefs. A great number of people gather around the Cherokee Woodland Royalty. The Chiefs look at the British people with the same curiosity and finally settle into their role in this demeaning display. A loud little boy with red hair pulls away from his mother trying to get closer to Attakullaculla. "Mother", He ask, "Is he a savage?"

The mother looks down at her small son with a frown. "Charles, please be quite."

Attakullaculla has a kindly smile for the young boy then suddenly opens his eyes very wide and makes a false motion toward him. The boy and his mother screech from the site. The boy hides behind his mother's full dress looking out from behind her hips. Attakullaculla and the crowd laugh. The mother is relieved it's a joke. Three hours pass and the chiefs are getting tired. Whitekiller kneels, just down the platform from Attakullaculla, talking to a middle-aged woman.

He is totally engrossed in telling his embellished story. "Yes, on that cold day I killed four black bears that attacked me and I had only these powerful hands to protect me."

Chief Whitekiller shows the engrossed woman his thick strong hands. She looks at them almost as if they are artifacts and says, "My God, the wilderness in America is truly a scary place to live!"

The Chief confidently smiles and remains enchanting in his story telling. "And on the way home, I was so hungry I chased a deer down only by running longer than he could. When he finally gave out I captured him. He was completely tired and defeated but I was strong. I cooked him and ate and ate until there was no more."

The woman is completely engrossed in the story. "Then what?"

War Eagle turns from his position on the platform next to Whitekiller and speaks to her. "And then he died, a fat man of exhaustion."

The woman is surprised and then laughs. "Oh, what a story teller!" She smiles and walks away.

The two Minor Chiefs turn to each other. Whitekiller is not very happy about War Eagle interrupting his story and lets War Eagle know about it. "You hurt my story, bugle ass!"

War Eagle smiles and is mischievous. He reasons with Whitekiller. "Me hurting your story is better than your being hurt by Attakullaculla. If he hears you lying your lying will get you lashes."

Attakullaculla looks down the platform curiously at the two men. Cuming returns to the ballroom. There are a few people left still talking with the Chiefs. They filter out while Cuming waits. He moves closer to the platform. "Well gentlemen, a good days work, thank you. Shall we go to the dining room?"

The chiefs are a little puzzled, until Cuming clears it up. "Let's eat!"

The Cherokee immediately get off the platform. Cuming walks while talking. "His majesty has a very special meal prepared for you." The Chiefs casually look at each other and follow.

Cuming escorts them through the entry hall, to a large table with beautifully decorated plates of food. "This way gentlemen and thank you again for allowing our people to observe you. We are having lunch here at the Belvedere. One of the best eating establishments in London"

Sir Cuming sits to his left of Attakullaculla, who takes the head of the table. Cuming nods to a nearby waiter for everyone to be attended. The headwaiter turns and motions for three more waiters to begin serving the food.

War Eagle watches the waiters serve the flamboyant foods. A lanky very British waiter steps beside him. The Chief looks up curiously at the courteous waiter as the waiter takes a large white cloth napkin and shakes it loose. The waiter starts to place it in the chief's lap. Instantly War Eagle jerks back. The professional waiter is startled and also frightened of this fierce wilderness man. The waiter stands unsure of what to do. War Eagle sees he has frightened the waiter and kindly takes the napkin from him. He looks at his own lap and back at the waiter. He decides to offer a bit of sage advice. "I am man." He points to Whitekiller. "He is woman."

The waiter smiles nervously in acknowledgment and serves the others. War Eagle comments to Whitekiller. "Strange custom for men." Whitekiller takes his napkin from the waiter and nods. Cuming quietly burps.

Attakullaculla looks at him. "We do not do such things out loud, where we eat."

Cuming is embarrassed. "I am sorry, gentlemen. Please excuse me."

Attakullaculla nods. Cuming begins to eat more slowly. All of the Chiefs glance at each other and then at Sir Cuming. They continue this process for a few seconds. Attakullaculla copies Cuming's style of eating. The other Chiefs mimic him. Soon they are all in cadence and following Cuming exactly.

Sir Cuming looks around the chic table. He smiles and acknowledges by raising a fork while he eats. The Chiefs all raise a fork with their pinky fingers protruding out. They have a great laugh from their newfound skill.

Over the next several days Cuming and the Chiefs toured London from museums to pubs. Their names were on the lips of every person, but in just a few more days they were hardly noticed.

The Chiefs and Sir Cuming had great fun. They laughed and talked while walking the streets of London on their way to the next event. Curiosity seekers wanted to know more. They stopped them or sometimes just watch from afar as the Chiefs passed by.

As they walked down a dark street two men with knives step before them and demand money. Attakullaculla cuts his eyes to his youngest chief as a signal to stop the men. The young man pulls out a hunting knife and positions to fight. The muggers look at each other and run away.

Cuming smiles broadly. "Well now that's a good bit of police work."

The young chief smiles and puts his knife away. The Royal group continues on to a Shakespearean play. The Chiefs are in awe of the play and compare it to some of their own ceremonial interpretations of the world. The Cherokee and Cuming have finally gotten a full taste of the nightlife in London and are ready to go back to their rooms. Within an hour they are back at the Palace and take a detour through the Royal Stables to look at the fine thoroughbred horses and then on to the rose garden full of red roses. They have come full circle, and soon they will have to leave England.

The next morning the Royal group is back in King George's meeting room to finalize the British/Cherokee treaty between their nations. The Cherokee leaders sit around the same beautiful large oak table where they had first met George. They casually talk while three male secretaries lay parchment paper in front of each of them. King George strides into the room and begins to talk to everyone. Sir Cuming stands and bows. The male secretaries bow. The Council of Chiefs take notice but do not rise.

King George smiles and says, "Please everyone, keep your seats."

He sits down. Cuming reseats himself. The male secretaries

continue their work.

The King is friendly. "Gentlemen, I hope you have enjoyed your time in our country. Well, let's get this over so you will be on time for your departure."

Attakullaculla speaks in his direct manner. "We agreed to be friends for all time. What more is needed?"

The King smiles. He takes a parchment in his hand. "This gentlemen, is an article of our agreement, a contract. It states: We will be friends. England will buy goods from you and protect you from intruders and you will do the same for us. I give you my part of the bargain in exchange for loyalty to England. You will trade only with us and protect England's interest in our absence. For that we will send rifles and goods as a simple gesture of good will. Just as we have spoken before."

Attakullaculla is pleased. "Then we do agree?"

The King manufactures an amiable smile for his guest. "Yes, all we need to do is to put our marks on the paper to seal our good faith."

Three male secretaries show the Chiefs where and how to make their marks. The Minor Cherokee Chiefs surprise everyone by eloquently signing their names in English. The documents are witnessed and sealed by the King's proficient Secretaries. Attakullaculla smiles and signs. He looks up at the King and Cuming while rolling the pen between his fingers. "Missionaries, they said we would need to know this one day."

The pledge is completed. The King makes a rare exception by letting the Chiefs shake his hand. Cuming bows to the king and shakes the Chiefs hands. They all walk from the desk to the front door of the meeting hall.

The King expresses his gratitude to the Cherokee. "Thank you, gentlemen, for coming to my country. I hope we are friends for the life of our sovereignties. I know you will fare well."

Servants open the front doors of the Palace. Attakullaculla turns and speaks to the King. "Friends."

The fresh and rested carriage horses are just outside the front doors of the Palace with the footman waiting. The chiefs quickly enter the conveyance for their trip back to the docks and the long voyage home.

Alexander Cuming reluctantly say's his good byes before the footman shuts the carriage door. "I'll miss all of you, but you must get back and forge our unseasoned alliance before the French become more powerful. The driver of the carriage will take you directly to your ship, it is named the Challenger." The Chiefs nod to agree and the carriage rolls through the massive palace gates.

Attakullaculla talks to the others inside the carriage. "This thing, time, must be very important. Everybody keeps saying that they are short of it."

As the Council of Chiefs arrives at the docks, they see their ship, the Challenger, being loaded with supplies. The chiefs nonchalantly exit their carriage and walk toward the mammoth ship. War Eagle stops and looks around at the people and the busy docks. "These people are truly strange. But I like them, sometimes."

Whitekiller speaks mostly to himself as he walks. "I think they are related to the little people." He smiles and walks on.

War Eagle grins and follows. Within minutes of the arrival of the Council they unceremoniously board the giant British Warship. The ship heaves to and eases from the harbor slip. It slowly begins to move under light sail and full colors toward open sea. The chiefs emotions are high, they want to go home and see their families. Finally the main sail drops and they are moving out to sea. The Council of Chiefs thoughts of home and family are still on their minds and nothing else seems very important.

Attakullaculla and Whitekiller relax against the portside bulkhead watching silhouettes of accompanying British Warships riding high on the rolling ocean horizon. Attakullaculla thinks out loud: "I hope our new friendship with these people and their King is more formidable than the insincere friendships our people have made with others like them."

Whitekiller is solemn. "Friendship with the white man is an ever changing thing, as the wind. Cherokee friendship is like the stone, but to them we are not very important, especially when we both need something. They always come first. I hope our people never learn these ways."

Attakullaculla stares into the distance. "I think the closer our peoples become, the more we will mature as one. I'm still not sure this is the wise way for our people, but our course is set by fate not by us."

War Eagle walks from his cabin next to Attakullaculla. "What are you doing Whitekiller, looking for some fish to poach for favor with the chief?"

Whitekiller is ready for his friend. "I need not take what is mine, but you, I think, a lot of face paint would improve your looks and our scenery."

War Eagle is amused. "Does this mean you are insulting me old friend? Should I listen for more of these childlike remarks from minor sources?"

Attakullaculla loves his Cherokee Brothers. "I have known both of you since we were boys. I do not remember a silent moment between you."

Whitekiller pats Attakullaculla on the back. "Brother Attakullaculla, you are our best friend."

War Eagle speaks up. "Yes, we love you Brother Atta for your money and your women."

The sun sets as they laugh together and walk to their small cabins.

Over the next couple of months, sailing is smooth and uneventful. The British Warship and its passengers arrive at the New Orleans port intact, just after dawn. The ship's crew docks with ease and the gangplank is put down. The ship is tied off. The bright eyed chiefs walk from the ship to a lone waiting warrior holding their horses for them. They mount up and ride away. All very unceremonious for such a large slate of events and international transactions. This is way of the

Cherokee; everything is taken in the stride of the day.

# CHAPTER SEVEN

## CHEROKEE NATION, INDIAN TERRITORY

### 1775-1781

### TAKE MY LIFE BUT NOT THE HOLY LAND.

Cal has sat for an hour already and is glued to every word. Chief Ross continues to spin his golden fable. He describes his Tribe's fate as if he could see it while he speaks. "It was the new agreement of commerce with the British that caused our people to get closer and closer to the White Man. The British treaty was terminated after the war of independence between them and the colonies. The colonies were angry about the war and we were left to suffer the consequences for being friends of the British. Every time we get close to the White man there is usually a tragedy to be suffered, particularly by us."

John remembers the day Attakullaculla rode into the mother village, months after the British agreement, only to find most of their people sick with small pox. Many families wrap their dead for burial and others try in vain to help the sick and dying.

John Ross speaks from his heart about the sad events. "Our people became ill with the disease of Small Pox, over one-half of them died within a very short time. Thousands were unceremoniously buried or burned as quickly as possible to avoid spreading the disease to other tribes and villages. It has been said the local English allowed small pox carriers to handle the food and rum sent by the King, hoping to spread the disease in retaliation for a regional dispute with our people after the agreement with King George. But this did not stop our tribe from progressing, nor do I think the British did it."

The elderly John stares at a crystal vase of red roses. "I love roses, they are beautiful and strong. Crimson red is my favorite color." He is in deep thought as he speaks. "Mr. Chase, if you tell our story, I don't know that it will do any good. Many people are now against us. We have come so far and lost so much. We don't have the ability to fight anymore. Most of our people have been lost through murder and disease."

"The Cherokee Nation's dilemma began long before I was born. Our people were always fun-loving and happy, until, as a great old chief once said, "I think we would have more friends if we didn't have so much land.' Our land was what everyone wanted, and we had to fight to survive."

The old diplomat continues his passionate tail of the Cherokee people. He and Cal flow back into the distant past, to a dark autumn in a Tennessee forest. "Later in the history of our nation another meeting takes place very much like the meeting and agreement with the British. Unknown to our people their way of life relied completely on the events of this day."

A huge campfire licks the sky six-foot high stoked with large logs in the center of a small well-guarded clearing deep in the remote woods of what is now known as the state of Tennessee in a country that will become the United States of America.

A group of white English traders gather around the warm autumn fire hoping to negotiate a deal with the principal Cherokee Chief of this Counsel for land. The rustic traders sit with five Ani-Yun-Wiha warriors and three traditionally decorated counsel chiefs. The chiefs wear colorful turbans and leather clothes suitable wardrobes for wilderness royalty. This Indian group under the guidance of their Principle Chief is close to carving out the land deal hoped for by the traders. They are for no known reason selling their homelands.

John's sage voice floats over the evolving clandestine scene. He paints a realistic portrait of lush green forest and plentiful game, helping Cal with the visualization. "In the early seventeen hundreds, a Council of Indian Chiefs of the Ani-Yun-Wiha tribe met with English Traders. Ani-Yun-Wiha roughly translated meaning "Real People." They were also known to their friends, the Choctaw as "Chillaki" meaning, cave dwellers and finally for all time as Cherokee, a derivative of Chillaki. This meeting with British traders in the remote forest is for convenience and discretion."

"How I wished I had lived in the beginning, maybe I could have helped change our poor destiny in some way, but you know our people were very wise. I doubt there was much that could be changed. Time is always the enemy, and we had so little of it left as free people."

The Cherokee Territorial Chiefs sit around the new Council fire. They strut all of their pomp and circumstance of Indian majesty. "It was truly a time of greatness, and the hour of our decline. I don't think I would have had the strength and vision to resist those times of promised wealth, either. Wars fought with money are stronger and more fierce than wars fought with bullets."

"The Council finally agreed to sell another portion of Cherokee land. This poorly planned and short-sighted sale was the beginning of the White Man's massive intrusion onto Cherokee lands and the splintering of the once great and unified Cherokee Nation. I'm afraid that breach still exists in our tribe today."

The Council is well underway. The leaders eat roasted venison while they speak of mutual interest. The high burning fire lights the dark sky and sets the perameters of the negotiation field.

Dragging Canoe is a lofty and muscular Minor War Chief of the Cherokee Nation dressed in full leather and armed with bow, arrow and large hunting knife. He waits in the shadows with a favored warrior. The warrior whispers to Dragging Canoe. "They are so white."

The warrior is curious. "I wonder why? Were they born early and never matured?"

The chief agrees that is the case. "Some of them have eyes of blue and green, like water. I am sorry for them. How do they survive?"

The chief shakes his head. He surveys this covert meeting. His long black hair and dark skin partially camouflage him in the darkness. Dragging Canoe's dark leather pants and shirt are ornamented in his traditional bright colored war chief raiment of bright metals and high colored red turban, a standard for him. The powerful chief waits intensely for the right moment.

Abruptly the fierce chief steps from the darkness with thirty battle hardened warriors solidly behind him. He scans the shorter less proportioned Principal Chief of the Nation, Black Fox. Black Fox is angry about the unexpected abrupt intrusion.

Dragging Canoe turns his gaze to each white man around the blazing and crackling fire. He then focuses on his Principal Chief. The young war chief manages a peaceful tone as he articulates in eloquent English. "You cannot sell our homelands. They are sacred."

The cold gaze of the hostile war chief makes the white men anxious. They stay close to their weapons. Principal Chief Black Fox is not intimidated. He turns to Dragging Canoe and answers firmly while his angry black eyes send a clear message of mandate. "Dragging Canoe, you do not decide at this counsel-fire. I, Black Fox, I am Chief of this Counsel. I will decide this destiny."

Dragging Canoe looks deep into the eyes of his powerful chief. The courageous young chief pauses, he then scans the entire group like a skilled politician. He directs his message to the Cherokee Chiefs and warriors with Black Fox. They all sit in the background. "Our people no longer carry sacred tribal names but take the names of White men and speak their complicated language. The White hunter takes our game until there is no more. Our Women marry them and raise half-breed children that have no identity in either Nation. The worst of it is, now, you give them our sacred homelands."

Black Fox stares at Dragging Canoe's glistening eyes. Everyone is frozen in place; any wrong move could provoke an irreversible incident. Back Fox softens his stance slightly and speaks. "We have agreed to sell our lands. We must make our word good. It is only a small portion."

Dragging Canoe glares at him, humbling himself again to make a final plea for his people's ancient ancestry. "This small portion is the great hills and streams of our forefathers. We must not barter our souls."

The Principle Chief smiles and relaxes. He feels there is a weakness in Dragging Canoe. "Do not be concerned. We have much land."

Dragging Canoe is angry. He directs his gaze at Black Fox with a raging fire in his eyes. This bold warrior-chief is not concerned with the amount of land or money, but the hallowed tradition of his people.

A sudden cool wind blow Dragging Canoe's long black hair back over his shoulders. The immense campfire lights his strong and angry face. He is no longer humble, but demanding. He speaks from his claimed authority for his people. "Our people are of earth, of wind and of fire. These things are our spirit. They will be forever. I speak of this so you may know, I can never allow our ancestors home to be taken from us."

Black Fox is fatherly now, hoping to cool down his fierce warrior-chief. Black Fox does not want an embarrassing incident in the middle of his personal pact with the anxious traders. "You are too suspicious my young chief. Leave this to the old heads."

Dragging Canoe is adamant. He refuses to listen to any explanation. Dragging Canoe turns away from his chief and speaks directly to the Minor Chiefs and warriors. "Their agreements mean nothing. Our people number more than the seeds of the mountain flowers. We have the warriors to resist peacefully or at war. Let us do it now before more come and we are finally destroyed."

The chief is calm, but annoyed by Dragging Canoe's persistence. "Do not speak of war at this council. These men are friend to us."

Dragging Canoe's manner changes again from firm pleading to cold demanding. "I will never stand by and watch my people wither away under the White Man's silent aggression."

Black Fox lashes out in contempt. "I warn you, Dragging

Canoe!"

Dragging Canoe ignores the Principal Chief and interrupts. He speaks directly to the entire group in a final compromise. "Soon the lands that our people have so long occupied will be demanded and taken by the White Man. Then the remnants of Ani-Yun-Wiha that was once so great and formidable will seek refuge in a distant wilderness. Remember these words. This is a cowardly destiny without our formidable opposition."

Black Fox is harsh with Dragging Canoe. "You speak with no authority. I am Chief, here. I decide!"

The leader of the White Traders stands and walks beside the Black Fox. He hopes to resolve this conflict and save his own life at the same time. The Trader speaks directly to Dragging Canoe. "We mean you and your people no harm. Our lot is simply to trade goods in this new land."

Dragging Canoe glares bitterly at the dominant trader. His ready warriors stand firmly behind him. All of the White Men grip their rifles. The Minor Council Chiefs and warriors stand ready with their chief. Black Fox gives Dragging Canoe a final warning. "You have gone too far, Dragging Canoe. Your time is over."

Dragging Canoe is passionate. His words ring out in harsh reality. "I will not tolerate the stealing of our lands by these White Vultures and their Wolf Pack of settlers. I warn you! Dragging Canoe will destroy all Whites on the lands of the Ani-Yun-Wiha. This is my promise."

Dragging Canoe takes a last cold look at the tense traders as if to imprint their nervous faces on his sharp mind. Abruptly, he and his men yelp a deliberate war-cry and leave in a fury. The Principal Chief turns to the white traders in an effort to make them feel secure in his care and save the land transaction, He speaks with authority. "Our trade will stand." The merchants smile in agreement and relief.

The leader of this powerful trading company reassures Black-Fox of his intentions. "You are an honorable man chief. I will have the trading post and goods turned over to your people and the money will be ready tomorrow, but you must control Dragging Canoe."

The Principal Chief nods in confident agreement. "Agreed."

The white trader pats Black Fox on the back and continues to play the politician. "Chief you just made one of the largest land sales ever achieved, you must be proud." They smile and shake hands.

Old Chief Ross turns to Cal. "A simple merchant sealed the fate of the Cherokee that day. I often wondered what the motives of each of the parties were. I do know the greed of that Principal Chief and the merchant set the Cherokee people on a tormented course."

John Ross is proud of his beloved Cherokee Nation. He relates their affluent history with a heartfelt drama. A Nation that governed and owned land from the western parts of what are now the Carolinas, parts of Kentucky, all of Tennessee, through parts of Georgia and Alabama. A national treasure everybody wanted.

The Cherokee homeland is filled with large forested mountains and glistening mountain streams flowing through the foothills. Deep in the lush valleys, busy Cherokee Villages bustle with teeming commerce beside beautiful rushing shallow rivers.

The villages are alive with colorful and happy people. Adult Cherokee women go about their work gathering water, making bread with flour made from acorns and smoking meat over low burning campfires. More mature children monitor the small children playing stickball. Throughout the Cherokee Nation's history their communities identified themselves as regions and towns. The regions and towns are named for their historic location or a great Cherokee forefather. This land system consists of upper, middle and lower Cherokee towns. Unmarked, but mutually agreed on, Cherokee borders separate their neighboring tribes. These disputed boundaries cause conflicts at times, but rarely a fight to the death.

In the beginning the Cherokee people had always been the largest and most powerful tribe in the region. With this distinction came the job of peacekeeping for all in the area, a huge task and unpopular duty. Almost immediately after the land deal with the council, white settlers and traders began to homestead the land. New settlers encroached on the Cherokee territory lands not owned by the British land company. This unorganized sale of property created many bitter confrontations between Cherokee and settler, death and destruction rained on both sides.

The presence of new citizens in Indian Territory gave their White Government a reason and the authority to push for westward expansion.

This is the very situation that created angry warriors like Dragging Canoe and his battle hardened followers. This fierce group had made their threats good. They had attacked any white settler they saw.

Dragging Canoe continued his attacks on the encroaching White population all of his life. The passionate chief knew if he did not hurry, the White man would outnumber all of the tribes in Indian Territory and there would be no formidable resistance. Dragging Canoe's vigilance was relentless. He knew time was his enemy and he wasted none of it. The War Chief and his thirty-one Cherokee warriors were determined to fight the white population, to eliminate the growing numbers of Whites settlers.

The warring Cherokee wore battle markings of vermilion face paint, with one eye circled in white, the other eye circled in black. This band of intolerant warriors was on the warpath with more fury than ever before. It seems the harder they fought, the more settlers came to fight. Dragging Canoe's men were always battle ready. They were armed with red and black war clubs for close in fighting and poison dart blowguns for distance. A few of the warriors had managed to confiscate badly needed pistols and rifles.

The battle group readies themselves and their weapons for an attack. They watch two settlers chopping wood next to their wilderness log cabin sitting on Cherokee land. The settlers have been warned to move. They have chosen to ignore the warning. A well-hidden Cherokee warrior suddenly springs from the tree line and hits the nearest settler with his sturdy war club, killing him instantly. The remaining Cherokee attack while the other settler runs for his rifle.

Before he can reach it, three warriors hit him with war clubs and crush his skull. The second settler falls to the ground dead.

Ten warriors have rushed inside the settler's log home. They drag two women and three children from the house screaming and kicking. The warriors hold them while Dragging Canoe looks them over. A pretty and petite light-haired woman is terrified. She shakes and cries as she begs, Dragging Canoe. "Please don't kill us!"

Dragging Canoe continues to look them over appearing proud and forbidding. The second woman with light skin and dark hair has already resigned herself to the evident fate they face. She screams out in defiance. "They're savages; they'll kill us, because we're White."

Dragging Canoe moves closer taking a closer look at the dark-haired woman. He then glances at his warriors and back at the light-haired woman while giving his warriors instructions. "Let this one go, you warn the other Whites to get off of Ani-Yun-Wiha land or die. Take the small children with you."

He turns and looks at the dark-haired woman and continues to instruct his warriors. "Take this one to our village and put her with the women. She can decide if we or the white man are savages." The warriors let the light-haired woman and the children go. She and the children scurry to the cabin.

The dark-haired woman screams out for help. "Help me, somebody, please help!"

Dragging Canoe softly puts his hand over the woman's mouth. He looks directly into her somber blue eyes with a piercing glare. She is kindly warned. "If your tongue wag's again, I will take it for a pouch."

Her eyes widen from fright; she is silent. Dragging Canoe takes his hand away and smiles. He motions for the warriors to get their horses. Two days later after leaving the white woman at the settlement, Dragging Canoe and his men are mounted on their war-horses surveying a trading post that has encroached across the border into the Cherokee Nation without authorization from the Principle Chief. The covert warriors are secluded high on a timbered ridge just inside the tree line. They prepare for and anticipate the attack. The trading post looks more like a frontier fort, it is built with logs to fortify the perimeter. All of the frontier posts have become fortified to defend against attacks from numerous parties.

The well-built outpost is bustling with people, Indian and White, inside and out. Dragging Canoe's eyes measure the fortress for the attack. He gets comfortable sitting on the ground while he waits for the right moment as his horse grazes in his background. A seasoned warrior rides from behind Dragging Canoe to his side. He speaks as a loyal friend. "Mighty chief Dragging Canoe, should we attack the whites again, so soon after the border trouble with the other tribes. We fight on too many fronts. The men are weary of daily battle and need a long rest to be at their best."

Dragging Canoe watches the settlement and appears firm in his answer. "Our people still trade with the Whites and act like their dogs. We will fight!"

The warrior earnestly attempts to give his leader a compromise. "Let us stop these attacks for a time. We can go to the Charlestown settlers. They will pay us with money and guns to fight our old enemy, the Tuscarora tribe. We need those weapons."

Dragging Canoe stands and turns to him abruptly and gives a cold order to an old friend. "We will fight this intruder first, then Charlestown."

Dragging Canoe mounts his grazing horse, yells a war-cry and motions for the warriors to attack in force. They all yell a bloody whoop and charge with full force toward the unaware outpost, just a few hundred yards away.

Before the settlers and trading post owners realize it, the Cherokee are on top of them. They blast through the people on the outside of the post. Dragging Canoe sets the pace of destruction. He swings his battle club like a knight with a mace.

A robust settler jumps from a supply wagon outside the fortress and knocks Dragging Canoe from his horse. The two regain their footing and fight hand to hand. The settler pulls out a huge hunting knife. He slashes at Dragging Canoe. The chief dodges and picks up a tomahawk to defend himself. The two combatants clash again. The settler swings his big knife across Dragging Canoe's chest. The blade opens up a long gash. Blood flows down his body. At the same moment the powerful chief slams his tomahawk into the skull of the daring settler. The man drops to the ground dead.

The chief grabs his war-horse and remounts as if nothing had happened and continues the attack, disregarding his bleeding wound. Dragging Canoe's warriors are still in the skirmish killing friendly Indians, settlers, and traders with swift blows from their battle clubs. In seconds the Cherokee are moving inside the fortress destroying everything in their path. The only defense from the marauding warriors was to close the front gates, but the people are too late; Dragging Canoe crashes through the fortress with a crushing blow to anyone in his path. In minutes the job is complete and the seasoned combatants ride away as quickly as they come, leaving behind a brutal warning about trespassing.

A fleeting week later, Dragging Canoe and his men stop their horses in a clearing to be sure their raiding party is out of rifle range of the well-established frontier fort known as Charlestown. The War Chief still favors the wound he received at the last battle and is moving slower. Dragging Canoe looks around and motions for one of his most trusted Cherokee to come to his side. A fierce warrior rides beside Dragging Canoe and stops his war-horse. Dragging Canoe takes the warrior's brilliant red and black battle club and ties a white cloth around the tip of it. Dragging Canoe gives the warrior instruction on contacting the white men inside the frontier fort. "Hold the white high. It means we will talk. Sometimes they honor it and other times they don't, so be very careful of these whites. If they talk, tell them we will fight the Tuscarora, in exchange for guns and money."

The warrior rides toward the fortress. As he rides, three Cherokee burst from the tree line and stop him. They talk for a few seconds then the four of them turn and ride at full speed back to Dragging Canoe. The Cherokee stop in front of the War Chief. The leader speaks to him. "The formidable Dragging Canoe. It is good to see the mightiest warrior."

Your respect is accepted, Dark Moon. Why do you watch the Charlestown Fortress?"

Dark Moon is respectful. "We do not watch the Whites. We left The Charlestown war with the Tuscarora tribe because they did not pay us what we agreed on, and we found the war was to take Indian prisoners for selling into a life of work. They are called slaves. I only warn you, it is not wise to speak with these White men, you could become a slave."

Dragging Canoe thinks out loud. "No one may be a master of men. Men must be led. You are right. We do not wish to talk with these men."

The warrior completes Dragging Canoes statement. "We fight for honor."

Dragging Canoe is determined. "We came for guns! Let us take them."

Dark Moon warns. "They have many Guns and many warriors. Let us go to my village and rest."

Dragging Canoe looks toward the fortress. "If they have guns, we will take them!"

Dark Moon is concerned. "Let us not fight. We will give you guns from our taking. Let us go to our village, the village of the Chickamauga band. We will rest and become more fierce while the other tribes fight and weaken themselves."

Dragging Canoe looks back at his tired warriors. "You speak well, Dark Moon. We will go to the village of the Chickamagua band, with your guns, we may return at our pleasure."

The warrior relaxes and makes conversation as they ride. "The White man's gun is not good for our land. Since it came, our game has vanished. The Whites are like hungry winter wolves hunting the last deer."

Dragging Canoe smiles like a mountain lion with his teeth sunk deep in his prey. "We should teach them the Cherokee way."

The warrior is curious. "The Cherokee way?"

Dragging Canoe smiles again. "Yes, the way off of our land!"


They chuckle and ride through the forest toward the distant mountains and into the sunset.

Even after a long rest for Dragging Canoe and his tested warriors, he is still enraged. The war-party continues to make many attacks on the white settlers, traders, and their trading posts. Dragging Canoe continues to lead as a minor war chief of the Chickamauga band of the Cherokee Nation. After years of fighting throughout the Cherokee Nation, this band has become the only hostile Cherokee group left. After losing warriors in almost every battle Dragging Canoe is desperate for fighters, he begins to take on any fighting men that can shoot or wield a knife, no questions asked. His band includes hostile Creek warriors, Shawnee's, British Army deserters and British Tories. This Chickamauga band chief would do almost anything to keep his war alive. The other bands of Cherokee, governed by the Minor Chiefs are not allowed to help. They are obeying the ruling Council and Principal Chief that governs them all.

Many bloody battles rage throughout the Cherokee Territory. The Chickamauga Band keeps the fires fueled with their continued rampages. In retaliation, White Settlers attack Cherokee Villages, thinking they are the Chickamauga band. Straightaway the normally peaceful Cherokee warriors would retaliate. Peace and war were on a roller coaster for every faction in the region, and now the other chiefs are fighting back again. Time is vital. More and more, white settlers and soldiers pour into Indian Territory, their numbers grow beyond the numbers of the Indian Nations. The balance has changed.

The People now begin to see Dragging Canoes prediction coming true. Most Cherokee feel they must eliminate the White population any way they can, before their numbers grow beyond the point of no return. The Cherokee Council is finally pushed into a decision to come back as a tribe. The will of the people has spoken. The final torch of war is lit. The traditional war-pole is struck across the nation. When all of the chiefs strike the war pole, war is declared on behalf of the entire tribe and the War Chiefs take over the council until peace comes again. The first major skirmish was when a collection of volunteer white soldiers attack a Cherokee village. They shoot all of the warriors and put their long sabers to use that day on the warrior's families.

Cherokee homes burn, lighting the way for the soldiers exit. Up and down the Hiawasee River all Cherokee villages are attacked and burned. At the high point of the conflict, daily battles rage throughout the Cherokee Nation. Every band of the tribe is at war. Finally, every Indian Nation in the region is back in the fight. During the battles the white settlers continue to encroach on Cherokee land. It was red man against white man and red man against red man. The unity of the Cherokee Nation was maintained in loose-knit, small roving bands of war-parties led by independent war chiefs.

Dragging Canoe's band has shrunk from six hundred to fifty. He is badly scared from many battles. The brave chief sits at a campfire with his rugged warriors. Dragging Canoe reflects. "After so many battles the whites still come like locust."

A warrior chimes in. "They are like ants from an ant hill."

A young warrior speaks up. "I thought they would have all been killed by now, and the British would have come back to help us."

The warrior speaks again. "I miss the old ways."

Dragging Canoe contemplates. "Talking about the old ways, there is a story told by our friends, the Choctaw. In a dry season there is little food for Deer, so he had become thin and weak. One day old deer meets possum. "Possum, how fat you are. How do you get so fat, when I cannot find enough to eat anywhere?"

Possum answers with a smile. "I live on persimmons. They are good and big this year and I have all I want to eat everyday."

Deer looks at him with curiosity. "How could I get the persimmons?"

Possum grins a little possum grin. "The persimmons grow high on the tree, so I walk from the tree, back and back then turn and run as hard as I can. I strike the fruit tree with my head so hard, the fruit falls from it. Then I eat all of the ripe fruit I want."

Deer is impressed by his new friend's skills. He turns and finds a persimmon tree. He looks at Possum. "It is easy for me. Watch I will get all of the persimmons." Deer goes to the top of a hill. He charges and runs head long into the tree. Deer is killed; all of the bones in his body are broken.

Possum sees what has happened to Deer lying there so sad. Possum starts to laugh, harder and harder, so hard it stretches his mouth. That's why it is still stretched today like a silly grin and that is why people say grinning like a possum. Possum cooked deer and ate him. That is how deer became food to eat. So, if you don't want a stupid grin or to be somebody's food get smart."

Dragging Canoe explains. "Like us, the strength of deer did not help him. Like deer, our people were tricked, by the best trickster of them all, white man. We need to get smart."

All of the warriors chuckle and mumble their own stories to each other. Dragging Canoe stares into the blue and yellow campfire.

# CHAPTER EIGHT

## CHEROKEE NATION

### 1781-1798

### AN UNEASY PEACE.

John continues to tell his story. He says that the old ways have changed for the Cherokee. Dragging Canoe has not been heard from in a long time, and the war of Independence is over between the British and the American colonies. "The British left our nation, and we then saw a need for change, a new direction to keep us safe. We began to build seminaries and schools to teach our children many things. Knowledge is power."

John imagines the proverbial little red schoolhouse with many Indian children playing outside. A teacher walks onto the school porch and rings a large hand held brass school bell. John then proceeds with his people's story. "From the beginning of our association with the white man we began to teach the English language in our schools and encourage our people to learn reading, writing and arithmetic, adult or child. We feel that knowledge is armament and our best weapon against the aggressive white government.

John says, "In seventeen-hundred-eighty-two, a learned, but short sighted colleague of yours, Cal, from Pennsylvania by the name of Mr. Hugh Brackenridge wrote about our people."

John describes the bold block letters blazoned across the newspaper headline that whirls into his mental view: THE ANIMALS

CALLED INDIANS SHOULD BE EXTERMINATED.

John continues his story. "Our people continued in spite of the hate and ignorance. We ignored such things and persevered, making many treaties for peace and equal treatment, all broken to get more land."

John saw a parchment document signed by the Cherokee Council of Chiefs that holds the terms of the well known and historical Hopwell Treaty. John describes the details to Cal. "This treaty promised no more land to be taken, and our people would be treated as equals, for as long as the sun shall burn and statements like that.

In seventeen-hundred-eighty-eight, an aging chief and six Cherokee meet a group of ten settlers; suddenly, one of the settlers fired his rifle, killing the Principal Chief. It was said, the panicked settler had just made a mistake. This mistake set off many bloody battles that led to another full scale war on every border of the Cherokee Nation between Cherokee and white. The Hopewell Treaty was terminated not to be revived."

"The bitter border war was finally settled, but many people claimed property through fires and destruction and the grudge killings continued. Several years later the fighting still flared from time to time throughout the land, but it had eased a lot from the early days. On a fateful cold day in early March those hopes of a final lasting peace were dashed when several persons of the Kirk family were killed just a few miles south of Knoxville Tennessee by an unknown band of Indians, not Cherokee. They were, probably a mixed breed of renegades, others believed they were simple outlaws. No one ever really knew for sure. That same band of renegades attacked another settler's cabin and set it on fire, then shot down two men, a woman, and three children that ran from the blazing building. Their bloody bodies were left lying in front of the burning structure for all to see."

"A veteran colonel of the U. S. Army, named John Beard, was hell bent on retaliation for the murderous deeds of the renegades. This need for retaliation was fueled by the Kirk's relatives. Revenge was on their minds for the deeds the Cherokee did not commit. Beard was well prepared to attack the Cherokee; he had raised a large number of civilian troops and whipped them into an efficient military unit. He marched against every Cherokee town he could find."

John Ross' story comes to life with all the color and adventure of his real life legend. Around May of seventeen hundred and ninety-eight Colonel Beard sits at his post desk at the U. S. Army frontier fort he commands. It borders the Cherokee Territory to keep the peace and he is in charge of investigating the Kirk killings. There is a knock on the door.

"Enter!" Says Colonel Beard.

Sergeant Chapman, his first sergeant, enters and salutes. "Sir there's a man named Kirk outside who says his family was murdered by Indians."

Colonel Beard stands. "Damn, keep him away from that barracks of the Choctaw soldiers. Their just passing through, and I don't need more trouble. I hope the idiots in Washington know what they are doing making these Indians soldiers and officers."

Chapman chimes in. "The Choctaw General, Pushmataha, has beaten a white soldier down with the flat side of his saber. He'll be in later to make amends."

Beard is in thought. "Damn, more trouble, send the civilian in, sergeant. I'll deal with it later"

The sergeant turns to leave. "Yes sir."

A very angry, short and wiry man, by the name of Thorn Kirk enters the office. "Colonel this has gone on long enough! Those heathen Injuns attacked our place two nights ago and killed my pa and two brothers. If you won't do something, me and my kin will!"

Colonel Beard is angered both by the embellished report and Kirk's threat. "I'm sorry about your people, but you are in no position here to give orders or decide the course of action to be taken. Tell me what happened."

Kirk is not backing off. "They killed my kin! Do something, Colonel."

Beard thinks for a moment. "Sergeant." The sergeant enters. "Get a detail together and stand by."

The sergeant turns and leaves. "Yes sir."

Colonel Beard gives Kirk a consoling look. "Mr. Kirk, do you know who attacked your family?"

Kirk is angry. He spits out the words. "There is no mistake, they were murderin' Cherokee."

Beard continues his support knowing it is probably someone else. "Which way did they go when they left your place?"

Kirk can see progress with this strict officer and happily answers. "They went back north toward the Hiwassee River."

Beard wants to give Kirk advice without ordering him, hoping to keep peace in his area of responsibility. "You go home and take care of your family; I'll take care of this military business."

Kirk is still mistrusting and reluctant, but agrees. "All right, but I want to know what happens."

The colonel acknowledges with a nod. Kirk leaves the office and promptly, First Sergeant Chapman enters with General Pushmataha. "The detail is ready, sir. Provisions and ammunition for a week are on the pack animals and sir, this is General Pushmataha, he is here to resolve the troop beating issue."

Beard looks at Pushmataha. "Thank you sergeant, I'll be along. Now General, why did you beat my man?"

Pushmataha is a strong and powerful looking man, but he manages to humble himself to tell the story. "As you know our families travel with us. When we entered the post the soldier insulted my wife, and I wiped him with my saber for his ignorance"

Colonel Beard is rough. "General this behavior is not tolerated at this out post. You will need to control yourself."

Pushmataha is civil to Beard, but harshly direct. "Sir, I beat the soldier for his insulting ignorance to my wife and family. A man like you that knows better I would have killed, and let me remind you of your position and rank colonel."

The colonel stares at the general stars on Pushmataha's shoulders. "Sir, we need not settle this here. You are leaving for New Orleans tomorrow on your campaign, and I am leaving today. Please control yourself until your departure."

Pushmataha smiles and leaves. "You can be assured of it."

Colonel Beard glares at the door as it closes. "Sergeant Chapman!" The sergeant promptly enters.

Beard is firm. "Locate Captain Winslow and inform him what has happened. I'm leaving him in charge during my absence."

The sergeant complies. "Yes sir."

Sergeant Chapman leaves the office. Colonel Beard takes his saber and pistol belt from the wall hangar and puts them on. He looks through some papers and then checks his weapons to be sure they are ready for use. After a few minutes he exits his office. The colonel walks from the headquarters office and mounts his horse. He rides to the front of his awaiting troops. Beard turns and speaks to Sergeant Chapman mounted and waiting. "Move'em out sergeant." The colonel rides toward the post gate.

Chapman gives the command. "Column of twos, yoo!" The troops form ranks and follow Colonel Beard and the sergeant out the front gateway. After moving the troops hard all night, the colonel locates his target. He and Sergeant Chapman watch a Cherokee village from a thick forested timber line. Beard stares at the morning activities of the large village lying next to the Hiawassee river bank. Children play games, the women work preparing food, and just a few warriors are present. A familiar scene for these people.

Beard is restless. He speaks to his sergeant. "This entire village has been destroyed before; you would think they would learn to make peace. Instead they murder white people and expect to be left alone."

First Sergeant Chapman glances toward the village. "These Indians don't learn, sir. They are just ignorant savages."

Beard nods in agreement. "Get the troops ready, sergeant. Maybe this will satisfy Kirk and send the Cherokee a message: make peace or die."

Chapman is eager. "Yes sir!" The sergeant rides back to join the waiting troops in the background. The day is eerily quiet and clear making everyone a little nervous. Within a few moments, the mounted soldiers are poised for the assault. Beard draws his saber and motions forward. The troops start the attack at a canter and follow the colonel as he begins to speed forward, now at a full run. The troops blast out of the timberline yelling and screaming. A few soldiers are shot off their horses by Cherokee sentries' arrows hitting their mark. The sentries are quickly shot and the troop speeds on. They blast into the open space of the river bank and across the shallow river and into the innocent village.

The Cherokee are caught unprepared. The troops charge through the Cherokee town shooting and slashing anyone they encounter. A charging soldier rides down a fleeing woman and her child. He raises his saber and kills the woman with a single blow. The child runs into the forest. The raid continues until most Cherokee are dead and a handful captured. The soldiers also suffered a high death toll losing more than half of their number. An ugly reminder of what has happened is the scene of a few men and women lying dead in the shallow river, killed while trying to cross to the safety of the forest. The battle is over. Colonel Beard scans the area. He looks to Sergeant Chapman. "Burn it. Leave nothing."

The sergeant complies without compunction. "Yes Sir." He turns to his troops and yells out. "Burn it. Leave nothing that can be used. Barker, finish off the survivors."

Suddenly Pushmataha and his fifty soldier/warriors emerge from the forest and swiftly attack the other soldiers. They are fighting hand to hand, horse to horse, hatchet to sword. Pushmataha's Choctaw soldiers begin to get the best of the offending troops. Beard and his men retreat into the forest at full gallop. Pushmataha signals his warriors not to follow. They begin to help the surviving villagers that were to be shot.

Deep in the forest Colonel Beard reorganizes his troops and gives an order. "Sergeant dispatch a runner to general headquarters and report this bastard so they can terminate his ass, if we don't do it first."

Chapman nods and goes about his business. Beard turns to his troops. "Men, we were caught unaware, but now we have the advantage. No one knows where we are. We now have another objective. This troop is going to wipe out every nuisance village along the Little Tennessee and Hiawasee Rivers, so we can finally stop dealing with these wild savages. Maybe they'll see we will not tolerate any more attacks."

Beard forms his troops. They begin the campaign and leave many burning villages behind with Pushmataha close on their trail. After the attacks the troop rides hard for three more days toward their outpost. They manage to attack a final undefended village on the way back. The territory is ablaze with turmoil and war. Colonel Beard wanted to punctuate his threat by destroying Indian villages, but, instead of pushing the Indians into making peace, he has started a territorial uprising.

About two o'clock in the afternoon, Beard and his troops break out of the thick forest. They see the log fortress they call home, sitting dead ahead. The troops catch a short breath of relief. They thank their good luck that there was not an ambush.

Colonel Beard and his trail-worn troops ride into the fortress. The scars of battle show both in their wounds and the battered horses.

Captain Winslow waits on the steps of the out-Post headquarters. Colonel Beard stops his horse and dismounts, handing the reins to a corporal standing nearby.

Captain Winslow salutes the Colonel. "Looks like you had some tough times, Colonel. Do you think things will settle down now?"

Beard is tired and worn. "No, but we had better get them before they get any stronger. They may decide to unite all the tribes, then they will kill us all."

Captain Winslow says, "I sent word to the Chiefs, if they come in and talk about the Kirk family, we can work things out."

Colonel Beard is in an evil mood. "Maybe, but we stirred up a good bit of hell out there. If they come it'll be a miracle."

Winslow says, "I hope so, Colonel. We're paying a big price on both sides and now the Choctaw are beginning to help the Cherokee."

Beard snaps, "That son-of-a-bitch Pushmataha attacked us after he left this post. If there was ever any doubt he changed that."

The Colonel is ready to end the conversation. "I need to rest now, Captain. I'll go to headquarters tomorrow and report directly to the General, so we can resolve this disaster." Beard and Winslow turn and walk to the Post Headquarters Office.

A week passes with routine duties until the Kirk's have their inevitable encounter with the Cherokee. Kirk and two relatives are talking to an army private inside the fort stables. A guard stands watch high on the fort wall, inside his log overlook. "Friendly's comin' in. Chief Tassel, Abram and four riders."

Kirk and his relatives turn quickly toward the gate. The gate is opened and two friendly Cherokee Chiefs with four warriors ride in unarmed. Kirk and his relatives commence firing as the group clears the gate. All six Cherokee are caught totally by surprise; they fall to the ground dead. Captain Winslow and Sergeant Chapman walk down the steps in front of the headquarters office as the shooting starts. They coolly stop and watch the troop check the Indian bodies. "Well sergeant, that crazy Kirk just took care of the Indian problem. You better clean it up."

The Sergeant glances at the Captain with a look of authority. "Yes, Sir, looks like trouble to me." He goes about his business.

Colonel Beard comes from his office. "What the hell happened?"

The Captain is informal about the killing. "Kirk got his revenge."

Colonel Beard takes notice and sees he needs to do something to defend the fort since this disaster has happened. "Damn, Captain.

This has got to stop, here and now. We are caught seriously off guard and outnumbered in this territory. Prepare the fort to defend. There will be trouble."

Captain Winslow just wants to make the colonel happy. "Sir, Kirk did it. Let them take their revenge on him."

The Colonel is angry. "Are you completely stupid? I wiped out six villages, and we were just getting past all of that, trying to make peace, and Kirk kills their Chiefs. To them that means we are liars and can't be trusted. We have screwed this up. Especially if we don't arrest the Kirk's and punish them."

Sergeant Chapman looks out the open front gate. "Too late to worry about that now. They're here."

Warriors can be seen stirring in the trees three hundred yards from the fort.

Beard thinks out loud. "The only good thing about this is general headquarters has dispatched Pushmataha to New Orleans, not as good as hanging, but good for us right now.

Chapman stares at the Cherokee. "They must have suspected something would happen.

The Colonel is back to reality. "Chapman, assemble your men!"

Chapman turns to his men, yelling orders to assemble for battle. "Shut the gate. Assemble the artillery battery! Corporal, take charge of the cannons."

Captain Winslow immediately goes to his troops and readies for the attack. Beard is now on the catwalk of the well secured fortress wall ready for battlefield command. His green eyes search the ground before him. Then suddenly two hundred Cherokee warriors appear on horseback from behind the trees with an invisible reserve hidden behind them in the forest.

Beard scans the group looking for a weak point. "Firing positions!" Every soldier aims his rifle toward the war-party.

An anonymous chief rides from the battle-ready group with a white flag tied to his rifle with six warriors as security riding behind him. He holds the flag high and gallops to the center of the battleground. Beard takes note. "Sergeant Chapman, get four men for security and follow me." He hurries down the catwalk steps.

In moments Chapman is ready, waiting on horseback, with mounted security guards and a horse for the Colonel. "Open the gate."

Beard mounts his horse and leads his party outside. He and his men gallop toward the chief when out of the dark forest General Pushmataha appears with his soldier/warriors. Beard has a shocked look on his face. Suddenly two hundred Indian rifles raise and fire, killing Beard and all of his party.

Inside the fort, Captain Winslow and his men are stunned. "Fire! Fire your weapons!"

Soldiers on the fort wall fire their first volley of shots at the Indians. Four cannons fire. Both sets of weapons are out of range.

The Chief yells out in haste while bullets fall short in front of him. "This is the penalty for murderers and liars." He hastily exits.

Pushmataha's troops are ready for the fight. He orders the charge. His Indian troops charge, firing their weapons as they go. A volley of bullets rains down on the Chief and his warriors killing five of the Indian troops. The charge continues. Pushmataha's men slide their horses to a stop and dismount close to the fort wall so they will not be shot. The fort has not received badly needed cannons and lacks a solid defense without them.

Captain Winslow reacts. "Keep firing, damn it fire." He turns to the soldiers on the fort catwalk. "Shot those Indian soldiers next to the wall."

Rifle volleys from both sides now--gun-smoke is heavy in the air. Two hundred Cherokee warriors charge the small fort. They jump from their horses and cling next to the fort wall with the Choctaw soldiers. When the white soldiers lean over to shoot, a designated warrior at the wall will shoot the soldier before he can fire. Another designated group of Cherokee set twenty different fires on the fort walls using lamp oil and lard to stoke the flames.

The first wave of Choctaw retreat under a hail of gunfire as the fort begins to blaze high. As the second wave retreats a hundred flaming arrows are in the air flying towards the fortress. Then another volley of flaming arrows and another, until the entire fort is engulfed in flames. The Choctaw and Cherokee watch and wait inside the forest timberline.

The Fort gates open. Captain Winslow and his soldiers charge out trying to get away from the heat and defend themselves. They fire their weapons in a skirmish line being cut down as quickly as they join the line.

The Captain is finally shot and knocked down. He manages to stand and fight in spite of his mortal wounds. A Cherokee warrior rides past. He hits Captain Winslow from behind with his red and black battle club that kills Captain Winslow instantly. The Cherokee warriors regroup on the battlefield and watch as the fort burns to the ground. Pushmataha forms his men and begins to leave for New Orleans to fight the battle he is paid to fight.

An Osage Indian scout and a white private lie next to each other wounded. They see the Cherokee chief and a few of his men in the distance. The private looks at his comrade. "What are we going to do now?"

The scout grunts from his wound and grins. "What are you talking about White man?"

The private is not amused by his fellow combatants remark. "This no time for jokes," he says.

A battle weary Cherokee Chief sits astride his restless war-horse looking down at the wounded pair while Pushmataha and his soldiers ride away in the background. The young man and the scout are brave but have no doubt of their immediate fate, but the Cherokee Chief surprises them. "You will live young ones. Go to your people and tell them about this day. Let it end here. You, army scout, mend your ways, you are Indian, quit fighting your people."

They are stunned; the chief is letting them live. The private speaks up. "Yes sir, I will. I will tell all of my people about this."

Warriors help them get on their feet. The private supports the scout. They turn to walk away. The Chief wonders about the soldiers sincere attitude. "Soldier, what is your name?"

The young soldier turns back to the Chief. "Jonathan, Jonathan Chase. This is Samson."

The Chief says, "He is Homer Big Eagle, an Osage, not a man from the church people's book. I know him. Samson is his white name."

The Chief signals a waiting warrior to bring two cavalry horses they have captured. "You and Big Eagle are horse soldiers, Jonathan Chase. You ride proud, not walk ashamed. Go home, Big Eagle, your mother will be glad."

The young men nod and take the cavalry horses. They mount and ride away. The Chief and his warriors turn and ride in the shadows of the forest as quietly as they came.

In a different part of the Cherokee domain the ambitious Sevier still looks to make a name for himself and when he hears about Colonel Beard, he is more than ready to seek revenge. After an intense pursuit of the Cherokee for killing his friend, the Captain has arrived back in the heart of the Cherokee Territory in the future state of Georgia during the summer of 1780.

He leads four hundred and fifty troops to attack a Cherokee Village near Chattanooga, Tennessee under orders from his Territorial General Command. When the troops arrive, Sevier finds only a few utensils left behind in the deserted village.

This is a simple lesson for this captain and his commanding generals who have made a very common military mistake of coming back to trap the enemy when they still feel the wounds of the first trap. You can't burn the same villages, kill most of the people, and expect more to be there when you return for the next attack. Both *Indian and soldier have become lax in their battle plans. Every man is tired and sick of the fighting, wondering when it will all end.*

Sevier wants a fight and is mad because he missed this one. The

Cherokee are now aware of his movements and his bad attitude. They watch his activities as they lead him further into Cherokee Territory.

Captain Sevier begins to shout orders to his troops. "Set up camp here. Post sentries, and survey the area, high risk area."

He turns to the nearby loyal Sergeant Prince. "Sergeant, we're a long way from White's Fort were I plan to re-supply. The commanding officer there has put aside provisions for us, and we need to stay on the move so we won't run out before we get there."

Prince acknowledges the command with that over used declaration of subservience. "Yes, Sir."

Captain Sevier speaks with more authority. "Sergeant Prince, tomorrow morning I'm taking a detachment and will proceed ahead. The scouts say down river a few miles there's a small Cherokee village . I'll take the village and wait for you there. Take charge of the troops in my absence."

Sergeant Prince is ready. "Yes, Sir, any special orders, sir?"

Sevier is cruelly harsh. "Only one. Kill any Indian you see. The sooner they are all dead, the better off we'll be."

The sergeant looks out into the distance, expressionless. "Yes sir."

Captain Sevier spent the rest of the day getting ready for his scouting expedition and letting his troops rest. The uneasy morning came, and the troops reluctantly pulled out to encounter the elusive Cherokee. After a half day's ride through thick forest and mountainous terrain, they get closer to their target.

Sevier and three platoon captains ride in front of one hundred seasoned frontier troops through a heavily forested and narrow pass between two sandstone bluffs. They discuss their reluctance to go through the narrow pass, but it is the only way through the thick forest. Above them Cherokee warriors wait to fight. The Ridge and Stan Watie, two of the youngest and boldest warriors in the Cherokee tribe and brothers watch from behind a pile of shale and rocks. No one really knows why they have different names, but they are full brothers. The very young eight year old John Ross and his friend,

Talmidge Watts the same age, watch from behind a log nearby as the troops slowly advance into the pass. They are abruptly surprised by the ambush. Cherokee warriors rise from hiding to attack the unsuspecting soldiers. Arrows, poison blowgun darts and rifle fire rain down on the unsuspecting troops.

The soldiers shoot back. Some dismount to take cover. There is no place to turn or escape they are caught out in the open. More arrows, darts and gunfire fill the air. Soldiers fall from their horses wounded or dead. The able troops pick up their wounded and make a defended retreat. The sound of battle is suddenly silent.

They look to the rocks and trees above, and see nothing, then they see Cherokee warriors moving down the slope toward the wounded. Three Captains and ten troops lie dead in the opening between the bluffs with a few stranded soldiers standing ready to fight.

The retreating troops have stopped a safe distance away from the killing field. Sevier surveys the area while his soldiers regroup and regain their mounts. The troops are mute with fear and anticipation.

The Captain takes charge again. He looks at a group of seven troops. "You men come with me." Captain Sevier speeds forward with his men to save the stranded soldiers and wounded.

The Captain's alert eyes search the area as he moves swiftly forward. The seven cavalry troops ride close behind the Captain ready to defend against another attack and getting ready for what's ahead. The remaining troops stand as rearguard, ready for anything. They watch every step, scanning the area with a refined vigilance.

Sevier watches the waiting Cherokee in the draw near his men wondering why they don't attack. The soldiers stop beside the wounded and dismount, ready to defend, they watch and wait. The quiet is almost eerie, compared to what the soldier's senses had experienced minutes before.

Above them Stan Watie raises to shoot Sevier. A rock he stands on gives way and he begins to fall. Stan grabs at John Ross for support and they both fall down the wall of the narrow pass and directly in front of Sevier. Stan gets up and slashes at Sevier with his knife.

Sevier draws his saber and block's Stan blows. John Ross's eyes lock on a pistol Stan has dropped in the fall. He grabs it as Sevier cuts Stan's hand and causes him to drop his knife. John's small hands cocks the pistol and points it at the Captain. The fight has stopped, the Cherokee and soldiers are at a stand-off. Stan yells out, "Shoot him, John."

The youthful John just stares at the captain. Sevier does not move. Stan yells to John. "John, shoot him."

Suddenly a towering authoritative looking Cherokee Chief, John Watts, appears on the bluff just above them. All of the soldiers aim their rifles at the Chief. Over two hundred warriors appear on both sides of the bluffs above them ready to shoot any soldier that makes the wrong move.

John Watts' voice booms across the small canyon. "I am, Principal Chief John Watts of the Cherokee Nation. Tell your generals, if they continue trespassing they and their followers will be executed by order of the Cherokee Nation."

The soldiers are nervous. Chief Watts continues. "Take your wounded and leave. Let the fighting stop!"

The captain nods in agreement. John lowers his weapon and stares at Stan. Sevier motions for his men to pick up the wounded. He says, "All right, put'em on their horses."

The troops hastily gather the loose mounts and put the bodies of the three Captains and soldiers on their horses. They mount up under a constant vigil. The Captain stops his horse beside John. "What's your name?"

John just looks at him without a sign of reacting. The Captain speaks again. "I only want to thank the man that didn't take my life."

John looks at him. "I am Cherokee that is all you need to know."

Sevier is kind in his acknowledgement and rides away. Chief Watts watches them move out. He turns to a warrior next to him. "As

Dragging Canoe once said, white men come every day. If we don't stop them now, they will reign over us and will be the wardens of this land."

Stan Watie kicks dirt at the soldiers and glares at John as he rejoins his warriors. It was a hard trip back to the encampment for Sevier and there is a lot of talk among the soldiers about why they were there, "On these peoples land, anyway." The worn down and traumatized troops finally find the encampment of sergeant Prince in the late evening on their exhausted mounts.

Captain Sevier and his men ride into the camp like a parade of ambition gone wrong. The officers' and men's bodies lie across their cavalry saddles as a grim reminder of how military mistakes have harsh realities. Sevier dismounts and looks back at the bodies. He walks to the Corporal next to them as the parade moves past. "I'm sorry about your friends, Corporal Burns?"

Corporal Burns stops his tired horse. From his sunburned thick-skinned look, he's been in the territory for a good while, the rest of the drained troops stop behind him. The camp soldiers gather around to help with the incoming troops' horses. The Corporal can't hold back any longer. "We are tired of this senseless killing, sir. Chief Watts warned us. He said he would kill all of us if we continue to trespass."

The other camp troops have gathered and are listening to the Captain question the exhausted Corporal. "Are you afraid of that chief, Corporal?"

Corporal Burns pauses and looks directly at Captain Sevier. "Sir, those Indians fight for their home. We fight for pay."

Sevier speaks up. "I'm not afraid! I'll catch him and hang him."

The other troops talk among themselves. They are concerned. Suddenly the Corporal speaks up with a surprising statement for the Captain. "Our blood is not yours to spill, sir. We ain't goin' back in there. We'll go to the stockade, but not back there."

SAM BASS

All the troops join in, mumbling and talking among themselves. The Captain appears extremely angry and speaks as he walks back to his command tent. "Get some rest. We'll talk more tomorrow." He walks past Sergeant Prince. "See to it, Sergeant Prince." Before he can answer, the Captain is inside his tent.

The camp went through a restless night of tension from the possibility of being attacked and the troubles that will come with the ultimatum laid down to Captain Sevier by the Corporal. If the Captain orders them back in and they don't go, things could get bad fast. The penalties for disobeying orders in times of conflict are severe.

Dawn breaks and the troop's mill around, rolling bedrolls and making coffee. A few gossips about the night before. Sevier considers his options in the command post tent. Prince enters. "Good morning sir, what is the order of the day?"

The captain is distressed. "We'll regroup and return to White's Fort. There's fighting all over the territory. We need to keep the men in good shape."

Sergeant Price is of the same opinion. "We need them in good shape to survive the return trip. Considering all of the turmoil in the region."

The Captain agrees that discretion is best. "They're too confused and worried to make a proper battle. No use losing more lives for no reason. We'll return when conditions are more favorable."

Prince is a little confused by the Captain Sevier's new attitude, but relieved. Relieved, because he knows some of the men may have refused to go, if the Captain tried to stay and fight. "Yes sir. I'll prepare the troops to move out for Gillespie' Station posthaste."

Captain Sevier hears his sergeant and speaks almost to himself. "Good, I know we have lost valuable time here. We must succeed now, or they'll grow stronger and destroy us all."

The sergeant understands as he moves out of the tent. "I'll get the troops mounted, sir."

The captain approves with a nod while in deep thought. Throughout the territory full blood and mixed blood Cherokee

95

citizens observe the conflict from their own point of view. The battles rage on. Deep in the Cherokee Nation terra firma a trading post sets nestled in the forested foothills near the Hiwassee River.

Jack Fourkiller, a middle aged full-blood Cherokee man runs up the steps of the large Trading Post. He rushes inside ready to make conversation. Inside the Trading Post, the owners, Mr. and Mrs. Ross, a white man and a mixed blood Cherokee woman are dressed in typical store clerk attire. Their young son, John Ross, walks from the storage room carrying stock to be put up.

Jack Fourkiller checks his bright colored Cherokee turban. He talks to the Ross couple as he walks toward them. "Mr. and Mrs. Ross, have you heard about Chief Watts wiping out that murderin' Captain Sevier's cavalry. Our people took'em. We're finally standing up for ourselves." John watches with intense interest. "What happened, Mr. Fourkiller?"

Jack turns to answer. Mrs. Ross intervenes." Mr. Fourkiller, please don't talk about those things around John. Things are bad enough without encouraging our children to make war."

Mr. Fourkiller looks like a small boy that had just been scolded. "I'm sorry, Mrs. Ross, I didn't know John was here."

Mr. Ross goes to his son. He kneels before him while Mrs. Ross fills Jack's order in the background. John's father explains to his son. "Right now both sides rush to win and control. They fight time as much as each other to survive.

John tries to understand. "Are the Whites trying to kill us?"

His father replies, "Yes, John. We must stay away from the fight and speak for peace to help stop this killing for land by the White's and killing to extract justice by the tribes. The killing of any race, by anyone, is wrong. The times we live in will be over someday and we'll all have to live with what we did."

John is curious. "Yes sir, but you are white and our people don't harm you."

Mr. Ross looks at his son with understanding. "Because I am a man of peace, son, and I have the heart of a Cherokee. I always treat others as I wish to be treated. Forgive your enemies, John. That's when the healing starts. Do you understand?"

John nods his head yes and continues his quizzing. "You fought once."

John's father patiently replies, "That's right, John. We must fight sometimes to protect our family. I still fight in my own way, but peace is always first, if it is at all possible."

John Ross appears very mature in his childlike answer. "Yes, Father. Treat others as you would be treated."

Mr. Ross smiles and hugs him with a new respect. "That's my boy."

John has learned a valuable lesson this day, but it doesn't help what is going on in the Cherokee Dominion. Jack Fourkiller looks out the window. "Well, look at this. Chief Watts himself."

John's father goes to the door. He turns to John. "John, you and your mother stay in here."

Mr. Ross walks outside. John runs to the window and looks outside. His father shakes hands with Chief Watts and greets the other warriors with a wave. The Chief and Mr. Ross walk to the side of the Trading Post. They enter a side door that lead to a room under the Post. Ten warriors enter behind them.

Outside, warriors bring up ten pack animals. The Chief exits with his men carrying rifles and ammunition and they load them on the pack animals. A seven-year old boy runs to Chief Watts from the corner of the building and the Chief smiles very big and picks him up. They talk and the Chief puts the boy down.

John has moved to the Trading Post porch. "Hey, Talmidge Watts."

Talmidge looks proudly toward John. "John Ross this is my Uncle." Chief Watts smiles at John and at his favorite nephew.

John nods. "You want to play stickball?"

Talmidge is all for it. He and John move to the field across the road from the Trading post with the sticks and ball. The boys begin to play the game.

Eventually all of the pack animals are loaded. John's father comes out of the room and shakes hands again with the Chief and watches as the war-party rides out.

The Chief and warriors ride past John and Talmidge. Talmidge waves with enthusiasm. John watches and studies the group. Talmidge turns back to his friend. "I'm going to be just like my uncle."

John says, "He is a real warrior. I think I will fight someday too."

John's mother yells from the store's front porch. "John go home and get your father's horse and bring back the pecans that are in the barn." John waves to let his mother know he heard her. He and Talmidge start down the dirt road and in a few minutes they are passing an old Cherokee farmer's property. There they see three men beating him, the men unhook his mule from the plow in the open field and start to ride away on their horses with the mule in tow as the old man falls to the ground. Out of nowhere The Ridge appears with two warriors. He rides past the white men and hits one with his battle club and then the next before the men can defend themselves. Another warrior grabs the third and wrestles him to the ground from his horse. Ridge and a warrior bring the bleeding men in front of John and Talmidge. The Ridge greets them. "John Ross and Talmidge Watts, two fine warriors. Did you see these men attack grandfather Crittenden?" They nod yes.

The warrior checking the grandfather comes to Ridge. "He is dead."

Suddenly Ridge jerks his tomahawk from his belt and slams it into the top of the white man's head nearest him. Blood spatters across John and Talmidge as the man wilts to the ground and jerks in the throes of death. The Ridge says, "John, you kill this man. Ridge points to the second man. The man begs. "Please don't kill me boy, please."

Ridge jerks the tomahawk from the dead man's head and hands it to John. "Kill him, he killed a fine grandfather worth ten of him."

John hesitates, looking at the frightened man. The Ridge waits. He finally, very gently, takes the tomahawk from John and then slams it into the side of the next man's head. He falls to the ground dead. Ridge looks at John. "It is all right young one. You are a man of peace. We need you there. You need not kill."

Ridge turns to Talmidge. "Do you want revenge for the Grandfather? Talmidge shakes his head no. The warrior next to Ridge swiftly cuts the killers throat from ear to ear. The man falls shaking and bleeding to death. Ridge looks at his men and says, "Leave them here as an example to others."

Ridge and his men mount up. He says, "John you and Talmidge take the mule and these no goods horse to the Grandfather's widow. Tell her what happened here and tell her we will bury him in his field."

Ridge yelps, and they ride away. John and Tallmadge go about rounding up the livestock.

# CHAPTER NINE

## CHEROKEE NATION

### 1798

### WAR TAKES THE BEST AND THE WORST.

The battles rage on in Cherokee Territory. October, seventeen-hundred ninety-eight the strong and determined Chief Watts shows his Cherokee People's new strength with his well-trained and organized warrior/soldiers. They are proficient in the tactics of guerilla Warfare and are a force to be reckoned with. Watts and his men finally have provided the Cherokee Nation with a barrier against encroaching settlers and the U.S. Army throughout their land. He is a strong enforcer against new settlers and everyone in the region knows it.

A conflict has arisen between the Cherokee and the owners of Gillespie's Station, a new trading post encroaching on Cherokee land. The trading post appears more like an army fort than a trading post, but the need for security in this time of violence is more important than a good looking storefront. Watts and a party of one hundred Cherokee and Creek warriors prepare to assault Gillespie's Station, intent on serving a final eviction. The Ridge checks his horse and weapons. The Ridge could be simply referred to as Ridge, but out of respect he is called, The Ridge meaning he is one of kind. John and Talmidge sit on a nearby log. The Ridge mounts. Talmidge speaks up. "You want me to go."

Ridge smiles and advises kindly. "Your job is to watch and become wise in battle. Do your job."

John smiles at Ridge knowing the outcome. "What about you John are you about ready." John shakes his head no. Ridge smiles, "some day." John nods yes.

Chief Watt's men position for the pending attack and Ridge joins them. Suddenly Captain Sevier and Sergeant Prince with a hundred men emerge from the brush line of the forest exhausted from their earlier campaign and the trip. They are weary looking as they ride toward Gillespie's Station. Chief Watts hand signals his warriors to wait. Then the sergeant and his rear guard break out of the forest following Sevier's troops. He signals other of his warriors closer to the enclosure to move. The soldier/warriors inch closer and closer in the seclusion of the thick forest and underbrush.

The massive gates of the trading post fortress open for Sevier and his men. The troops move inside and in a moment the rear guard enters. As the last man moves inside Chief Watts gives the word. Before the doors can be closed, all of the Cherokee and Creek warriors charge into the Station, taking it and Sevier's men by surprise. Only a token resistance is met from the captain's troop while the rear guard is killed almost immediately. The warriors fight hand to hand with the soldiers and civilians. The Cherokee and Creek Indians wield light weight, thin and very sharp tomahawks, large hunting knives and red battle clubs that are very effective against sabers and excellent for this close-in combat. These hardened war veterans overtake the station as quickly and effectively as any seasoned Army troops.

The reserve Cherokee forces complete the overrunning of the Station and finalize the mission by destroying the last resistance. In the aftermath almost all of the people are dead, including soldiers, settlers, women and children. Cherokee chief, John Watts, walks through the battle area with a minor chief leading their horses behind them. "I am sorry to kill to keep our land and freedom. These things belong to all. Many brave people died today. Most appalling are the women and children killed in this horrible battle. Such a senseless waste over land and pride."

The Minor Chief is remorseful. "We must let it be known this cannot be. But the whites are so ruthless. We must defend our own people."

The two men mount their war-Horses and start to ride out when they see Captain Sevier, Sergeant Prince and two young soldiers' with their hands tied behind their back waiting to be executed. The Ridge steps before Sevier ready to cut his throat with a long and very sharp bone-handled knife. Chief Watts looks them over. "No Ridge. Do not harm them. Let them go to tell the story about what happened here. The killing has to stop with someone and someplace. This is the one and the place. Go and turn them out."

The Ridge nods and signals other warriors to help. They get the soldiers to their feet and eject them from the Station with their hands still tied behind their backs. Sevier and his men walk on. Chief Watts and his minor chief ride out of the Station. A young Cherokee warrior attaches a parchment letter to the front post of the entrance with a hunting knife. The stealth warriors ride into the forest and fade from sight.

A half hour later, a detail of U. S. Army troops rides slowly and cautiously into the battle-torn Gillespie's Station. Outriders swiftly search and canvas the area to be sure there are no attackers left. They see massive destruction and bodies lay everywhere.

The Top-sergeant at the head of the troop sees the letter. He rides to the post and removes it and gallops back to the Captain and a Federal Inspector riding with them. "Captain, I found this on that post over there. Seems that these Injuns want to apologize for unintentionally killing the women and children."

The Captain reaches for the letter while surveying the area. "I'll take that, Sergeant."

The top-sergeant complies. "Yes sir." But the "yes sirs," are wearing thin on all the troops in the territory. The veteran soldiers are tired of watching their officers run them head long into situations that many feel are morally wrong.

The captain looks at the Federal Territorial Inspector who is riding with them to investigate just this type of carnage, a lesser public official being escorted through the Cherokee Nation. "It's signed by four chiefs. One of them is John Watts, the new Principal Chief. It says they remind us of the treachery in killing Chief Abram and Tassel at the fort."

The inspector sympathizes on this delicate political subject. "Both sides are speeding toward a collision course of victory or defeat at horrible prices. It's a marathon to just survive. Only time will tell this outcome."

The captain agrees. "The Kirk incident was an unfortunate mistake, but these continued killings solve nothing."

The inspector reflects. "It seems killing has become our way."

The captain reads on. "They add, when you move off the land, then we will make peace. I wonder if Washington will even try to make this peace."

The official says, "This bloody combat is far from over whether Washington wants peace or not. The people are just carrying it forward."

The captain nods. "It will be a long time, I'm afraid." He catches a glimpse of somebody in the underbrush. "Top Sergeant, send two men to check that movement in the brush. Troops make ready to defend against the unknown." All of the soldiers take their rifles from the saddle scabbards and make ready. The officer draws his pistol and stands by waiting and watching.

The Sergeant gives the order and two of his best soldiers ride toward the location. The two troops move their horses through the underbrush and into the forest. Suddenly one the soldiers sees something. "Over here."

Just as suddenly Talmidge Watts runs from hiding into tall grass, then through the forest. The soldiers barrel through the forest after him. They stop. "It's a kid, let him go." The lead trooper is little more concerned now about his decision. "That's an Indian kid." Then the other soldier sees Sevier and his men walking. "Look, survivors." They ride to them, dismount, and offer them canteens of water while untying their hands. "What the hell happened?" ask a soldier.

Sevier looks at them calmly, rubbing his wrists. "Hell on Earth."

The lead trooper turns toward the captain and his company of men. "Come on, our company is here. We'll take you back to the fort." They all walk together back to the Station.

Talmidge lies behind a large fallen log breathing hard. He hears a noise. "Psst, psst!" Talmidge looks around. "Psst."

The voice whispers louder. "Over here."

Talmidge can see John hiding in the undergrowth. He quietly goes to him. "Boy that was close."

John says, "Talmidge Watts, you nearly got us caught. We shouldn't have followed your uncle anyway."

Talmidge quickly replies. "It wasn't my fault. I don't know how they saw me.

John is not going to let him off so easy. "If you hadn't run, they wouldn't even know we were here. We could have been killed."

Talmidge is insulted. "Are you saying I was scared and ran away?"

John Ross replies, "Yes you were and almost got us caught and maybe killed. Then your uncle would have come for us. You know the rest."

Talmidge relents saying, "Yeah, you're right, I swear that it'll never happen again."

John sees his friend is hurt and tries to console him. "Talmidge, a person isn't always perfect."

Then behind them Pushmataha and his men stand silently. Talmidge and John turn slowly to look. Pushmataha kneels and speaks. "Your friend is right." Talmidge nods a little.

John stares. "You are Pushmataha the Choctaw Chief. You're famous."

Pushmataha says. "Go home now, Chief Watts will be looking

for you."

Pushmataha and his men are contract soldier for the U. S. Army and are only on duty when contracted for a campaign. The Chief knows he may suffer the consequences of his actions if he and his men are confronted out here in the woods by a superior force, before he has a chance to explain to Army General Headquarter and clear himself. Pushmataha also knows the boys need to be safe because they will be shooting on sight for being Indians.

The boys acknowledge and hurry to their horses. They quickly ride for home. The mighty Pushmataha signals his men to attack the unsuspecting soldiers. The battle rages and Sevier is in the fight again.

# CHAPTER TEN

## CHEROKEE NATION, TRIBAL COUNCIL HOUSE

### 1799-1806

### THIS IS OUR HOME!

Seven years later, after many confrontations over land between troops of the United States Government and the Cherokee Nation, President Thomas Jefferson signs legislation called the Georgia Compact. The Compact opens the way to take more land than ever before.

This Federal legislation sets up an irrevocable, hostile situation between the Cherokee Nation and the State of Georgia. The Georgia politicians have learned to make war with laws, not guns, all at the expense of the Cherokee Nation.

John Ross remembers only too well the Georgia Compact. "Over the years the Cherokee people had changed so much. They tried again and again to deal with the White culture peacefully. The White Government's continued to take our land, no matter how much we changed or complied."

John Ross continues, "By this time in Cherokee history, our people began to dress like the White Man, use their mannerisms and some of the wealthier Cherokee began to own slaves. I could not believe our people had succumbed to these European life styles. Considering how much we cherished freedom, to take slaves, to take freedom from another, was a contradiction within our way of life. To

106

those who did not believe in slavery it was an abomination."

"The Cherokee finally complied in every manner to show their willingness to get along. The tribal members paid taxes to the Federal and Local Governments. They were loyal citizens of the new country. However, the closer the Cherokee Nation came to complying with the policies, the more helpless we were against the power of the United States Government. There was always a contemptuous attitude from local Federal Officials. The Officials focused on making policies to destroy the unity of the tribe.

The once united and powerful Cherokee Nation is slowly and deliberately being dismantled by the United States. All of the fighting and U. S. troop movements against the Cherokee are focused in the heart of the Cherokee Nation. To add to the problems, the Cherokee have political troubles with factions of different tribal bands going their own way in defiance of Council laws. A division of power in the homeland had begun in eighteen hundred and five."

A secret midnight Cherokee Council meeting is underway inside a bark-covered assembly house, lit by kerosene lamps.

The flames release a dark almost black vapor as they burn. A proper murky note for this night. The Council of twenty Cherokee Chiefs and Council Members talk about a northern Cherokee Village Chief named, Doublehead.

John Ross is now a twenty-six year old adult and a new member of the Council of the Cherokee Nation. He sits with his friend, Talmidge Watts, also a new Council member, waiting for the meeting to start. These young men are well liked and both aspire to high post in the Tribe. They have become respected Council members and an influence within the Council.

Talmidge whispers to John. "John, I don't know about this."

John frowns. "We have got to stop this treason. If we don't stop it now, it'll get worse."

Talmidge says, "This could cause a tribal war between the bands, that's the last thing we need."

John replies, "Talmidge, we are helping not destroying. We build our Nation."

Talmidge nods. Chief Vann, the new Chief of all Cherokee stands. "It is voted unanimously, by this Council and this Principal Chief, that Chief Doublehead is sentenced to death for the act of treason for selling Cherokee Land without Council approval. Our most trusted warrior, The Ridge, as is our tradition, will be given the honor of executing the guilty man."

The Principal Chief proudly smiles and looks at The Ridge, a young stocky warrior. He stands and confidently acknowledges his chief. Chief Vann is anxious to get this politically unpopular deed out of the way. "Ridge, you will choose someone to help and carry out your duty. This execution is to be carried out tonight!"

The Ridge looks around the room. The fireplace lights the member's faces like mysterious beings. Ridge smiles slightly as he scans past his friends, John and Talmidge. "As the Council orders, so it will be."

Chief Vann adds a footnote. "This race for survival between us and the White Government still exists. Time is counted by the moment in this war of elimination. We must rid ourselves of all like Chief Doublehead who corrupts and weakens us. We now fight for our very lives." Ridge's expression shows his agreement.

Chief Vann ends the meeting by saying, "Go and carry out your poor duty."

The Ridge is a full-blood Cherokee and politically he is now going against the other full-bloods who are an influential faction of the tribe and like to be consulted before the Council acts on this type of business. The Ridge has always been loyal to this Council because he believes times are changing and someone has to compromise in order to eventually have peace inside the tribe. The Council now consist of both mixed-blood (White and Cherokee) and full-blood (All Cherokee) members. Decisions are hard to come by in this group, but today they all agree and The Ridge is reconciled to his unfortunate duty. He turns and walks out of the Council meeting.

Talmidge and John Ross excuse themselves and follow The Ridge outside. The Ridge's image is visible standing beside his horse. He pulls a rifle from its scabbard and checks it to be sure it is loaded. He returns the high quality rifle to its place and puts on his tight fitting riding gloves. The Ridge takes his pistol from its holster and checks it. He returns it with an air of determination.

John and Talmidge stop next to The Ridge. John says, "I want you to know, I am behind you. Anything you need I will back you."

Talmidge concurs, "That goes for me too, Ridge.

The Ridge nods. "Good, I need friends like you. Everybody is afraid to commit these days."

Ridge mounts his tall and powerful sorrel horse and rides out.

John and Talmidge watch The Ridge ride from the Council House into the darkness. While they watch, Quatie, a very pretty young woman and full-blood Cherokee steps up behind them. "Talmidge Watts, what are you doing here with your snoopy friend?"

John and Talmidge jump from the surprise, and then catch themselves. Talmidge recognizes the young lady. "Country girl, haven't you heard?" We are Council members. Something you should know."

John is interested in this pretty Cherokee girl. "Who are you?"

Quatie is not very interested in this handsome and almost white Cherokee boy. "I am Quatie, who are you, White-Man?"

John tries to conjure up more maleness for his defense. "I am, John Ross, Cherokee."

Talmidge is put out by the whole exchange. "Let's go, John. She is pure trouble. You will never do anything she will not tell her mother about and then the whole world."

Quatie continues. "Where are you going?"

Talmidge laughs. "Aren't you nosey? We're going to see the little people."

Quatie retorts. "Joining the little minded don't you mean?"

John laughs. "Little people."

Quatie makes another point. "John Ross, you are White, you should not be here."

John Ross is totally insulted by the remark. "I'm not White, I told you, I am Cherokee!"

Talmidge is ready to go and very tired of Quatie. "I'm going. You coming?"

Quatie smiles. "Where you going, Talmidge Watts? You got a secret?"

Talmidge is quick to speak. "There's no secret, get lost."

John Ross and Talmidge walk to their horses and promptly leave. They ride a short distance down the street to the "Blue Goose" cafe and bar. They dismount and start inside.

John still has Quatie on his now one track mind. "Who is that girl?"

Talmidge smiles with a little pride. "She's my cousin and a lot of righteous trouble. She talks all the time and is bossy too."

John says about Quatie, "Kind of pretty."

Talmidge laughs. "Don't tell me you got it for her." Talmidge pats his friend on the back and they walk inside. "I feel for ya'."

The same night that John and Talmidge are reminiscing at the Blue Goose, The Ridge travels to pick up his help, a man named Sanders. As with many Cherokee he has no first name, his name is just Sanders.

The Ridge stops in front of a well-kept white-washed log home. He walks to the front door and knocks. In a moment, a mix-breed Cherokee woman answers the door. "Hello Ridge, come in."

The Ridge says, "Hello, Queen. Is Sanders here?"

Queen is not very friendly. "Yes." She turns her head and says, "Sanders, Ridge is here."

Sanders comes to the door putting his shirt on. He says, "Ridge, good to see you."

The Ridge is business like. "Could we talk, outside?"

Sanders looks at Queen then steps outside. "What is it," he asks.

Ridge delivers the Councils message with authority. "You are chosen by the Council to go with me for the enforcement against Doublehead."

Sanders is very reluctant and hesitates. "Ridge, I don't know about this. What did he do to be executed?"

The Ridge says, "He sold Cherokee land outside of Council law."

Sanders nods his head.

Ridge is forceful and full of authority. "It is an order, let's go."

Sanders does not want this but knows his duty to the tribe. "All right, but I am not sure about this."

Queen has overheard and butts in to save her husband from something she thinks could hurt them later. "This is not a good idea, Sanders. I don't like it."

Sanders is firm and knows his poor duty only too well. "I got to go, Queen. Go on in the house."

Queen huffs inside and glances back. "You better come back safe love. It's on your head Ridge."

Sanders turns to Ridge. "See what you did. Now I'm going to deal with that for a week, maybe longer."

Ridge smiles and pats him on the shoulder. "Sorry, like they say, can't live with them, can't live without them. Let's go, so we can get back by morning."

They walk to the barn for Sanders to get his horse. The Ridge says, "Don't worry you'll come back safe, love."

Sanders smiles at his friend. "You need to get married. Then you would understand."

In a few minutes' Ridge and Sanders are moving through the moonlit forest toward their solemn duty and a tragic national destiny.

As the Ridge and Sanders draw near, they slow the pace and ride toward the old wilderness tavern, "The Raven." They say it is Chief Doublehead's second home.

Ridge assures Sanders. "He'll be here."

Sanders is uneasy about the whole situation. "I don't know Ridge; the Council may be pushing this a little too fast."

The Ridge asks. "Sanders, are you afraid?"

Sanders is insulted. "Hell no, I just didn't expect to ever be chosen for a Council enforcement. I guess being your friend has its hazards."

The Ridge is relaxed with his duty and determined to carry it out. "It's up to us to enforce this law. We will do our duty and be home before morning."

Sanders doesn't like his poor situation. "I hope so, Ridge."

They ride past a small wood sided house sitting near the old tavern. A dimly lit kerosene lamp shows through a dirty window. Ridge and Sanders continue to the side of the tavern and stop. They get off and tie their animals to the hitching post. The two men quickly check their rifles and pistols and move inside slowly.

The Ridge looks around the ancient room. Twenty people, both Indian and White eat and drink from crude utensils. It gets quiet almost immediately. All of the rough looking men and women stare at The Ridge.

The Ridge spots Doublehead, a large and heavy Cherokee man, with long black, braided hair. Doublehead sits with the bearing of a chief staring at his executioner.

Two unsavory characters drink with Doublehead at his rustic table. They are caught by surprise when The Ridge quickly raises his pistol and fires. Doublehead is hit in the face under his right eye. He falls back then slumps forward bleeding.

Sanders is surprised by the abrupt downing of Chief Doublehead. He promptly raises his rifle and holds it on the crowd. "Don't anybody move! This is Tribal Business, stay out of it."

The Ridge is satisfied as Doublehead slumps on the table. Ridge cautiously moves toward him. Suddenly, Doublehead revives and unexpectedly jumps up. He runs past the Ridge and Sanders, almost knocking them down. The two recover and Sanders yells to The Ridge. "Get him; I'll take care of this."

Sanders scans the crowded room. "Don't move, this is ordered by the Council. Just stand still."

Ridge quickly runs outside as Doublehead bolts toward the small house next to the Tavern and runs inside. In a moment an old woman runs from the house and heads for the tavern.

The Ridge exits the Tavern in time to see Doublehead enter the house and the old woman passes by him. He walks slowly and methodically following a trail of blood toward the small dwelling.

Doublehead breathes hard. His wound bleeds freely. The heavy chief quickly looks around the bedroom and sees several old winter blankets stacked on a small single bed. He grabs the patchwork blankets and covers himself with them in a dark corner.

The Ridge enters slowly and cautiously and looks around the room. Ridge turns his back to the blankets and continues to scan the room. He suddenly turns and fires his rifle into the pile and pauses. Ridge draws his pistol and fires six more times. The blankets explode with rips and tears from the bullets blasting through the material. "You have been ordered executed by decree of the Council, traitor."

Doublehead burst from under the shredded blankets taking Ridge completely off guard. The profusely bleeding Chief Doublehead attacks The Ridge with a fierceness that only a man who knows he's about to die can muster.

Doublehead hits The Ridge hard with his fist, again and again. Ridge falls back after the blow. He regains his balance and attacks Doublehead. To his surprise Doublehead appears even stronger. The Ridge hits Doublehead. It does not faze the chief. The powerful Minor chief charges again. He gets Ridge in a headlock and starts hitting him in the head. Ridge breaks loose.

The Ridge instinctively jerks a tomahawk from his belt and hits Doublehead in the front of the skull as they collide. Doublehead's eyes get wide and he falls back on the floor, dead after eight bullets in his body and a tomahawk in the skull. Maybe they should have kept him as a front line warrior.

Sanders runs into the room out of breath. "What happened? He's, he's so bloody."

The Ridge breathes hard. "I hope this slows things down."

Sanders is wide eyed. "I'd say this stopped things for him."

The Ridge readily agrees. "Yeah."

Sanders turns to Ridge. "I hope we did the right thing, in our rush to dole out justice."

Ridge is ready to go home. "Let's go, his people will bury him."

Sanders and the Ridge quickly exit the old cabin. They hastily get to their horses and mount up. Before they hit their saddles a mob of twenty people are yelling obscenities and making threats.

The Ridge and Sanders urge their horses ahead as the mob tries to pull them from their mounts. Dust boils from the heels of the speeding horses as they move down the well-traveled tavern road.

Just as quickly, six riders are in the saddle, firing shots at The Ridge and Sanders. They turn into the forest and their horse's crash through the timberline lit by moonlight.

The Ridge guides his speeding horse toward a downed tree. He sails over it with ease. Sanders horse follows. They hit the ground on the other side and skin out through the dark woods. The men who are giving chase are heard slowing down and talking, seemingly lost in the dark. This day, is not lost in the dark, but is remembered by many in the Cherokee Nation.

John Ross sits quietly on a large log deep in the Cherokee forest near his favorite rolling clear stream. His friend Talmidge is close by. John watches the crystal water flow smoothly by.

Talmidge quietly walks up behind him. "John!" Talmidge ask, "Have you heard about The Ridge and Sanders?"

John looks toward Talmidge. "No, what happened with that?"

Talmidge sits with John and elaborates. "They killed, Chief Doublehead. It was really bloody. The Full-Bloods don't like it and they're mad at the new council. That means us. You and me, singled out."

John is interested and concerned. "I don't get it. I thought the Council spoke for all Cherokee people, mixed or full-blood?"

Talmidge says, "I guess not, the Full-Bloods are pretty damn mad about a whole lot of things. My father says it's not like the old days. We now fight the White Government and ourselves."

John says, "We have to do everything we know to survive. Every moment counts from now on."

Talmidge replies, "I don't know. All I know is my uncle says we did the right thing and I believe him."

John says, "We've got to do something. This will probably cause Quatie not to like me anymore, either."

Talmidge looks around. He sees Quatie standing at the edge of the trees in her white cotton blouse and dark prairie skirt. She looks like an exotic painting. Quatie smiles at Talmidge discretely. She continues to quietly watch from the shadow. Then Talmidge realizes he hadn't answered John. "Yeah, you're probably shot out of the saddle on that."

John still doesn't realize Quatie is around. "Shut up, you're the one with the problem. Any decent woman would be afraid to be seen with your homely ass."

Talmidge asks John a question hoping he will say something embarrassing for Quatie to hear. "So that's why you're way out here insulting me, mopping around, over her. You're whipped. She's got you on a leash."

John says, "What?"

Talmidge gives up, he's ready to leave. "Well, I gotta go. White-blood or not, we're friends. Chin up, eagle beak. Quatie's pretty reasonable."

John grins. "Thanks, Talmidge. At least I have one friend."

As he watches Talmidge walk away John notices Quatie standing in the forest. She smiles broadly and walks to him. He stands and smiles. Quatie walks into his arms; they embrace and kiss that special lovers kiss. They are so in love nothing else matters. The only thing they notice is each other.

The two of them stop, keeping their faces very close together. John is serious, but what a time to think of politics. "Quatie, have you heard about the tribal split over, Chief Doublehead?"

Quatie nibbles on his face. "Don't worry about me. I love you,

John Ross. I see no color. Our people must learn to love each other no matter what the blood."

John stares affectionately at Quatie. "I love you." He says.

She giggles and hugs John as he holds her face in his hands and pushes her Raven black hair from her face. He looks into Quatie's passionate dark eyes and kisses her pouting pink lips. John is in love. He kisses her again with more passion. John and Quatie drop down to the lush grass floor of the forest. They continue to kiss passionately. Quatie White cotton blouse is open enough for John to see her swollen cleavage. He can hardly control his hunger for her. He kisses Quatie harder, with more passion than he has ever felt. Could this be it, the day? He begins to rub Quatie's well-formed and voluptuous breast. She returns his kiss with deep, deep passion and stops. John is almost shocked by the sudden closure on his lust.

Quatie looks into John's blazing eyes and smiles with a completely controlled charm. "John, you will have to marry me first. Then we can do what we want."

John's eyes show surprise, then calm. He doesn't know what to do. John wants to persist and crash passionately ahead. But he doesn't what to upset Quatie and loss her. Then he decides. This decision is special. John blurts it out. "All right, I love you. I want to be with you always."

From the corner of John's eye he sees a horse's legs. He and Quatie look up. Three crude White fur trappers sit on horseback grinning down at them with brown crusty teeth. The lead trapper laughs as he speaks. "Go on there boy, take her. We'll wait."

John is firm as he and Quatie stand. "What are you doing here?"

The second trapper speaks up. "We's passin' through. You want that woman or are ya leavin' her for us?"

John stands his ground as Quatie draws back behind him. "We don't want any trouble just leave us alone."

The trappers dismount. The third trapper grabs Quatie. John tries to defend her. The second trapper pulls his huge hunting knife and hits John across the head with the handle. "Don't make me cut ya, boy. I need this woman."

John glares up from the ground at the cruel trappers. The Leader takes Quatie and drags her toward the woods. John gets up bleeding from his hair line and is knocked down again. The second trapper kicks him over and over. Quatie screams for John. John breaks free and jumps up. He hits the second trapper. The third trapper is on him beating John within an inch of his life. The second trapper kicks John more when he hits the ground again.

Without warning The Ridge blasts from the thick forest on his stout war-Pony. He slams his battle club into the face of the leader and blood spatters everywhere. Quatie's face is covered with the residue. She grabs the dead man's knife and runs behind The Ridge.

Ridge is quickly on the other two trappers. He runs the third trapper down with his horse. The screaming man is trampled under the powerful war-pony's sharp hooves. John stands and hits the second trapper. The Ridge speeds past and slams his battle club into the second trappers head crushing his skull. He falls to the ground dead.

Quatie is on top of the third trapper. She thrusts the wide bladed hunting knife deep in the weakened trapper's chest. John, The Ridge, and Quatie stop and look at the destruction. Quatie begins to cry. The Ridge rides past John and pitches him the battle club. "Learn to use it. There will be more."

Ridge looks at Quatie. "Take care of your woman."

The Ridge rides on and as his horse gallops across the opening it appears he is one with his powerful animal. As John turns to Quatie, she embraces him. John worries about his friend, the ever loyal Ridge.

It didn't take long for the results of Doublehead's death to surface. Back in New Echota, a large group of upset Cherokee have surrounded The Ridge and Sanders. The people are afraid things have gone too fast, and these two's presence fuel the fire. Enemies of the Council push the mob to frenzy. "Murders! Killers! Red-apple." The Red apple term was often used as an insult. It meant Red man on the outside and White Man on the inside.

Muffled protests filled the air. The crowd grows and becomes violent. The Ridge tries to explain the action, but the people continue to protest and form this growing angry mob. Ridge is finally able to calm them for a moment. He starts to talk, but the crowd will not listen. The men in the front grab Ridge and Sanders. Suddenly, John Ross and Talmidge are between them.

John yells out. "Stop this. STOP! I am John Ross, a Council Member. I am one of the reasons The Ridge and Sanders were ordered to execute Chief Doublehead. I am sorry for his family, but Doublehead was guilty of treason. He damaged our Nation by selling property he had no right to sell. There is no doubt! He sold Cherokee land, your land, to a greedy Land Company. To men that are our enemies. He did this in spite of Council Orders. Tribal law is clear, no Cherokee land will be sold, ever, under the penalty of death! The people he sold our land to are the very people that lobby in Washington, D.C. for laws that take our land and have soldiers kill us. The Ridge and Sanders are not your enemy. They are your protectors. They are your salvation."

A man yells out from the crowd. "Maybe you're the guilty one?"

John is very firm in his stance. "Maybe I am. But these men are not. What I am guilty of is protecting you and your property. It is time to end this. We are in danger, due to men like Doublehead. Ridge and Sanders are loyal Cherokee."

Another man yells out. "Let them go!"

The Ridge steps beside John. He wants to explain and have his say. "I am, Ridge. This is, Sanders. We defend your Nation willingly with our own lives. I do not take any life casually. I am a warrior of the Cherokee Nation, loyal to the Nation. I march only to defend." The Ridge is on a roll and continues. "Not only have I defended our nation against aggression, I defend against treason. The treason that rots the very soul of the Cherokee and eats away at our roots. It allows others to take our homes and our very lives. Follow your leaders, so we may overcome this great power that has us in its grasp."

He scans the crowd. They are silent. The Ridge is the master speaker and leader this day. The crowd starts to disburse. John, Talmidge, Ridge and Sanders walk to the Blue Goose Cafe and bar.

The elderly John Ross continues his story to Cal. "After the enforcement, we still were united from time to time, during special situations, but never again completely."

"Within two years the Creek Nation, our northern neighbors, had finally had enough of the White Government meddling in their affairs."

A Creek war-party of four hundred first rate warriors, sit on war-horses watching a U.S. Army encampment full of activity. All of the tribes in the region have been abused by Government policies. The policies always allow the settlers to encroach on Indian properties and all Indian Nations have suffered the same fate. But the Creeks finally and totally are in full rebellion. They declare war against the United States of America.

The old Cherokee Chief's eloquent story brings the four

hundred Creeks to life. They abruptly charge the army encampment, killing all of the garrisoned troops. The U. S. Army sent General Andrew Jackson to command the field action against the Creek Nation. Such simple words for death and destruction.

The Cherokee Nation can see disaster coming and it has a name, Andrew Jackson.

John Ross has become a strong leader and a well thought of Council Member, trusted in times like these. All of the praise seems a million miles away now. He has other things on his mind, they are Quatie.

# CHAPTER ELEVEN

## CHEROKEE NATION, QUATIE'S HOME

### 1813-1814

### LOVE IS IN THE AIR.

John is solemn is his telling of the past. "That day with The Ridge was the last time my friend and I agreed on the direction of the Cherokee Nation." John takes a drink of water. He lets his eyes fall as he praises him. "The Ridge had a good heart and he wanted only good for the Nation, but I felt he did not understand the motives of the White Government. Ridge favored them and their decisions to move us from our land. Some say he and his family were paid for their favorable opinions, but I believe he was just misguided. This Government wanted absolute control of the land and us out of the way. They wove lies to cause internal strife just like the split between Ridge's faction and the Council. They took full advantage of any and all weaknesses."

John looks at Cal and shakes his head. "The Ridge became further involved with his relatives that adamantly wanted the tribe to move from the territory believing the promises of prosperity. They opposed me and the Council at every point. The Council's position was clear they did not want the tribe to be moved knowing there would a great possibility of a loss of property and life. The White government promised money and land, but our experience had told us this would change. The differences finally deteriorated to a power struggle between the Council and the Ridge faction."

John smiles as he changes his train of thought. "With all of the turmoil I still had Quatie on my mind. She was just a girl then and we had become serious about our feelings for each other. I dearly loved her. She was so pretty and innocent with the spirit of a wild horse." His face lights up as he tells Cal about his true love. Cal envisions John as a young man in his late twenty's. He rides a beautiful black horse he had just purchased from a local horse trader at the trading post. He stops at the front of a small, properly-kept log home, the home of Quatie and her Cherokee family. He dismounts and ties his horse. John has been seeing Quatie for more than seven years now. He has become mature enough to be interested in making their love a permanent situation.

Quatie walks from the house to the yard, closer to John. She is coy and flirtatious. "Hello, John Ross, what brings you out here?"

John tries to be casual about this big moment, but he is nervous. "I saw your family at the Trading Post and thought I'd ride out. I've wanted to talk with you, and..."

Quatie banters, a little more. "And what, did you want me to see your new horse?"

John can't wait. He blurts it out. "Well, I, ah, I think we should go ahead and get married. We've waited long enough. I love you."

Quatie sweetly holds John's hand. There is a long pause while Quatie looks at John's face and eyes. "I love you too, John. I know our differences in blood will cause some family problems and tribal gossip. But, I love you no matter what is said and yes we have waited long enough."

John is impatient waiting for his answer. "Well, when do we do it?"

Quatie looks at him. She kisses John on the cheek and uses her beautiful smile to tease him. "Well, next week I guess."

John's face is instantly covered with a large smile. He holds Quatie and looks closely at her. "Good, I thought you were going to say next month."

Quatie continues her flirtatious grin. "Anything good is not completed quickly, but a week is good."

John is happy. He smiles. "You were worried about our blood, but a Full-Blood can marry a mixed bred. There is no reason we can't be happy." He smiles. "I'm one-eighth and proud of it. We can pull our families together, I think, maybe." He smiles again.

Quatie lovingly gestures an agreement knowing there will never be a problem for John in that realm.

John reluctantly makes a confession. "Quatie, the White Government's army is calling Cherokee men into the army by order of the treaty our Council signed. We have agreed to fight with them for peace with us. Some peace this has become. I have been commissioned an officer, and Talmidge is going too."

Quatie is surprised. John promptly finalizes the statement. "We can't wait a week. Let's get married, tomorrow."

Quatie is still surprised. She is overwhelmed by the speed of it all. "John, you should have told me earlier. Have you thought about this, you will be fighting our Creek Brothers?"

John is sincere and pleads with his love. "Quatie, the Council has ordered it. We have a treaty with the White Government."

Quatie has become somber. "I don't know, John."

John appeals to her. "Oh Quatie, I must go. I want you with me for the rest of my life. Don't you see I have to move fast, besides I need to gain skill in their Army to help our own nation?"

Quatie understands and wants to marry John, but she is thinking about the problems with they're not-so-understanding families. "All right, John Ross, but you deal with my family and yours." He smiles, and Quatie hugs him.

After a very busy day of telling family members and getting the preacher, Quatie and John are on schedule to be married the next day.

By ten o'clock in the morning carriages and coaches roll toward a white-washed rural church and John and Quatie's impromptu wedding. The church is picturesque sitting deep in the Cherokee Nation near the Ross family trading post. All is going well and so far nobody is angry, at this point an excellent accomplishment for John Ross.

A high white steeple crowns the small church, surrounded by large shade trees. Loud organ music rings out from the usually quiet little church.

Within an hour Talmidge is playing the Wedding March to a full church of Cherokee friends and relatives. Suddenly he breaks into a show tune. The stern Full-Blood Cherokee preacher cuts his eyes toward Talmidge and Talmidge goes back to playing the Wedding March.

Quatie stands in front of her immediate family, twenty Full-Blood Cherokee. She is dressed in her favorite white lace dress holding a bouquet of beautiful local yellow flowers. Quatie peers at John lovingly.

Both families huddle in the rear of the church. Quatie's family solemnly stares at John Ross' family across the aisle from them, not in anger, but sheer exhaustion of getting prepared for this event.

John is dressed in his full dress blue, U. S. Cavalry Uniform with Second Lieutenant bars shining on his shoulders. He looks at Quatie lovingly. The two families take their seats.

John glances at Quatie's father. He is stone faced. John looks at Quatie's mother she is the same. John smiles at them. Quatie's father and mother turn the corner of their mouths up slightly in a tiny grin and just as quickly it is gone.

John steps forward to meet Quatie in the isle. He decides to be friendly to her family. John looks over at them. They all smile, almost in unison.

Quatie steps closer to John's side and kisses him on the cheek. They turn and walk down the aisle as Talmidge wildly plays the Wedding March. He's more absorbed in his music than the wedding.

Quatie looks at John and whispers as they walk. "My father likes you."

John is amused by her optimistic statement. "I could tell by his genuine smile."

Quatie and John stop in front of their full-blooded Cherokee preacher. He looks at them sternly and suddenly breaks into a huge grin. John and Quatie look at each other. Their eyes are filled with love.

The organ music gets louder. Talmidge, the Cherokee Beethoven, plays on. The Preacher cuts his eyes toward Talmidge. The organ gets quieter. The Pastor starts the service. "Dearly beloved..." His voice trails off as the organ music plays on.

John glances around the room at all of his friends and family. The preacher is speaking to him, but he does not hear. Quatie elbows him.

The preacher finalizes. "Do you take this woman for your lawfully wedded wife till death do you part?"

John smiles and looks lovingly at Quatie. "Yes. I do, forever."

The stern preacher looks at him. "I do is enough."

Quatie smiles as she listens to the preacher speak to her. "Do you Quatie, take John for your lawfully wedded husband, till death do you part?"

Quatie smiles. "Oh yes, I do."

The preacher rolls his eyes at the sound of oh yes. "I pronounce you man and wife. John you may kiss the bride."

John pulls Quatie to him and kisses her deeply. He continues to kiss her until there is an uncomfortable feeling in the air. The preacher gently pulls them apart and says, "All right plenty of time for that at home. Go home."

John and Quatie smile and turn leaving the church. Talmidge begins to play a show tune as they move. The preacher discretely waves at Talmidge to change the tune. Quatie and John continue outside past congratulating friend and family to an awaiting buggy. They jump in and John drives away.

## CHAPTER TWELVE

## CREEK NATION, BATTLEFIELD, UNITED STATES OF AMERICA,

### 1813

### A PROMISE MADE MUST BE KEPT.

John Ross can still hear in his distant memory the sounds of Talmidge's organ music at the wedding as they blend with the sounds of an ongoing battle far off in the Creek Nation. He misses Quatie more than he had imagined he could. John is a striking symbol of a Cherokee soldier in full battle gear. He moves quickly across the battlefield toward blasting canons and rifle fire. Men's war cries fill the air, marking the reality of brutal combat in the Creek Nation War.

Cal Chase can see the colorful images of the Creek War and General Andrew Jackson leading a company of Union soldiers into battle. John Ross continues to color Cal's thoughts. "When General Jackson arrived, he had demanded the Cherokee Nation choose sides.

Jackson declared there would be no neutrality in this battle between the United States of America and the Creek Nation and there was none. The full backing of the United States Government, is promised if the Cherokee troops join General Jackson's expedition, whatever that means. The Council's promise to fight, as stated in the treaty, hangs over the Cherokee's head; they made a promise and they will live up to it.

To comply with the treaty, the Cherokee Council sent token troops including John Ross to comply with their agreement, but finally they were pushed into a new amendment to the treaty. The new version states they must fight with all of their available warriors. It is said Jackson took it on himself to make the amendment and enforce it by intimidation. These actions taken by Jackson and complied with by the Cherokee Council forced an honoring of the old treaty of friendship between the two nations at the expense of all the Cherokee people. The Cherokee's good faith is trampled again.

John remembers that day at General Jackson's camp. He is young and an honorable United States Army Officer in command of six hundred uniformed Cherokee Union troops. John recalls, "The Cherokee Union soldiers campaigned in many battles with General Jackson, were he picked me as his Adjutant."

John Ross and Andrew Jackson ride toward the command post tent at the final battle of the Creek war. John has just been put in charge of all Cherokee troops. His Cherokee soldiers and supplemented white troops have surrounded the last of the Creek warriors.

The Creeks make a stand behind heavily fortified earth embankments surrounding them like a fort. John and the General dismount and go inside the Command post. John sees his old friend, The Ridge. "Ridge has been promoted to the rank of Major in the United States Army."

He was in full uniform, walking into the Post tent. The Ridge spoke to the General and me for a moment. He hurriedly took a map and left. "From the day he was promoted, he liked his new name so well he changed it on the spot. Thus, he was forever known as Major Ridge. After that day I never saw him again."

Across the battlefield twenty-four hundred White U.S. Army troops and six hundred Cherokee cavalry troops are poised for battle against one thousand of the Creek Nations fiercest warriors.

How times change. The Cherokee must fight their once good neighbors, in a war not their own. A treaty, a piece of paper creates a situation where one friend wars against another. How important a paper is. A word is given, a word is kept.

The Creeks continue to dig in and fortify their positions. They are well supplied and have some of the best battle-hardened warriors in the fight. They have all of the advantages in full measure, except one. They cannot be re-supplied. Creek War Chiefs post their top marksmen along all of the skirmish line walls. The time is tense. The battlefield is quiet.

Then, out of the blue, a Creek War Chief walks from the fortress under a white flag flanked by two towering warriors. Sevier now a lieutenant Colonel and the old Cherokee nemesis sits his horse with the ever loyal Sergeant Prince nearest to the War Chief. Sevier rides forward. They speak for a moment, and he rides to John Ross, standing with his troops, and Talmidge.

Sevier relays the message. "They want to talk to you, Major Ross. Don't make me think you're not gonna fight, or worse, be a turncoat."

John looks at him with disgust. "Remember your place, Lieutenant Colonel. You are not in charge of this Cherokee force."

Sevier grins. "No, but I do have the rank." Sevier returns to his position, watching.

John and Talmidge mount up and ride to the Creek chief. They dismount and shake hands with him and his warriors. In the distance General Jackson watches intently. He turns to Sergeant Prince, standing nearby. "What the hell is he doing?" The sergeant just gives a blank stare. "Don't know, sir."

John looks at the Creek chief with compassion for his plight. The chief speaks to John. "John Ross, honored Council. Talmidge, it is good to see you are well. We are honored that you meet with us. I know our tribes have said the words that we are enemies after so many years of friendship, and I know the General has forced your people to be against us. I ask you why you have chosen to fight our people this day?"

John softly speaks to his cultural brother. "I have not chosen this day to fight. This day has chosen us. Our destiny is here."

The Creek chief looks deep into John's soul. "Fight with us, brother. We will defeat this cruel general and win the day."

Thunder rolls in the mountains miles away. John and Talmidge look toward the sound. John is solemn. "This is our day of reckoning. We cannot."

The Creek chief is brief. "One of us has a wrong to right."

John looks at his friend, Talmidge, for support and then at the chief. "The Cherokee have given their word to the White General. It cannot change."

The chief is proud and considerate. "I respect your word, even though it is against us."

Talmidge is very sad. He speaks up "I am sorry, my brothers. This is not our way. We are trapped in fate."

They all shake hand in arm. The Creek retreat to their

fortress. John and Talmidge watch them go. Talmidge can't contain his emotions. "We have betrayed our brothers of the land, today. We are the worst of the worst."

John speaks with authority as he turns and walks leading his horse back to his troops. "We gave our word. We will fight."

Talmidge follows while thinking. "Yes Sir! We will fight and kill our own kind for our enemy. I will do it. I don't do it for them. I do it for us and our precious honor, and because of our precious word."

Suddenly, General Jackson hastily rides beside John. He speaks down to him as he walks. "What the hell do they want?"

John looks up. "Peace and honor."

The general is angry. "Major, you tell me directly what their intentions are."

John is firm. "They intend to fight and give no quarter."

General Jackson's words cut at John with a targeted threat.

"Major, if you are holding anything back I will not court martial you. I will have you shot. Do we have an understanding?"

John looks up with disgust. "We do."

General Jackson speaks as he rides on. "Go about your duties."

Talmidge is completely disgusted. "He's a ruthless son-of-a-bitch. Let's mount up, get our troops and kill him for the Creek people. Then cut the top of his head open and piss in it."

John tries to maintain his dignity. "I would like to personally shot him between the eyes. But, we have given our word as a nation to fight with him and it will be so."

Talmidge chuckles, "Well, as a man, I'd like to kick his ass and still piss in his evil skull, but I would settle for the bullet between his cruel eyes."

The two old friends walk to their ready troops. John looks at Talmidge sincerely. "You speak very good English, for a mad Indian."

Talmidge smiles as they walk. "In English or in any other language, greed and power-hungry asses like him are all the same. Power at anybody's expense."

As John and Talmidge reach their troops, the first shot is fired and the fight for survival begins. The Creek lay down a barrage of heavy gunfire, powerful enough to not allow the U. S. troops to move.

John helps Cal see that day. "I positioned my Cherokee soldiers in a defensive live along the rear of the Creek fortress for the battle. I was nervous and proud that day, proud of my people for their honor and bravery. My replacement as Adjutant to General Jackson was Sam Houston. I think both the General and I were happy to be away from each other. He had become so callous and ambitious."

Sam walks past the Cherokee troops on his way to the Command Post. John and Sam greet each other and speak for a moment. Sam excuses himself and departs.

John's sad commentary continues. "That day was a day to never be repeated. My Cherokee troops could not attack the Creeks flank because the river ran across the back of their bunker protecting them and laying down a gauntlet for us. They were well-fortified front and rear. The Creek warriors position appeared impregnable. I decided we had to stop the stale mate."

John Ross waits in anticipation with his Cherokee soldiers across the river from the rear of the fortress. His eyes scan for an opening to attack or a weakness to charge. The Creek stronghold stands firm, still fighting the rest of the U. S. Army in the front of their fortress. They have given no quarter to all attacks.

John continues to scan the area. He suddenly jerks his jacket off and dives into the river. John swims hard for the opposite bank. Creek warriors just two hundred yards away lay down a barrage of rifle fire from their rear position, cutting the top of the water around John. He churns the water harder, getting close to fifty Creek canoes on the other side. Talmidge sees what is happening and yells for the Cherokee troops to fire at the Creeks trying to kill John. The Cherokee begin to shoot and the Creek have to take cover.

John finally gets to shore where the vacated canoes sit. He dodges bullets and pulls the two nearest canoes into the river. John begins to swims back toward his men between the canoes for cover to stay out of sight.

Another barrage of rifle fire screams around him. Cherokee soldiers are shooting back. Seconds later, Talmidge dives in to help his old friend. John's soldiers hastily help him and Talmidge out of the water. When his feet hit the dry ground, John, yells out an order. "Take these canoes and some more men, bring the rest of them back. We'll attack the rear soon as we get all of the men across and in position."

Talmidge smiles at John and yells out. "Yes sir!" He gives the orders to cross and has a rifle unit lay down rifle fire to protect his men. He turns to John. "I'd follow you to hell, my Brother."

John is a little more cheerful in his grim statement. "You may have, my Brother."

Talmidge pats him on the back and goes to his men. More men

are in the canoes starting across. The Cherokee Rifle Company keeps a steady barrage of rifle fire covering their comrades. Within minutes hundreds of Cherokee soldiers are crossing the river in canoes and swimming along side. The first troops to cross fight the rear flank of the Creek Fortress. As the last canoes hit the shore, the Cherokee reinforcements charge the weakened rear position.

Creek warriors are now forced to fight two fronts.

They are unprepared for the forceful attack to their flank. General Jackson coolly observes the battle from the Command Post. He sees his opportunity made by John Ross and the Cherokee troops. Jackson turns to Houston. "Sam, take the reserve troops and hit'em with all you've got.

Houston quickly answers over the raging battle. "Yes Sir." Sam rushes out of the Command tent looking toward two sergeants waiting nearby. "Get the Reserve troops ready."

The sergeants acknowledge. "Yes sir! Yes sir!" They hurriedly leave.

Houston pulls his saber and walks toward the battlefield preparing himself mentally for battle.

Across the river the Cherokee and Creek warriors fight in full hand to hand combat. Cherokee troops are engaged in twenty different pitched battles over a ten-acre plot. Talmidge moves toward the front of the fortress along the side of the furious raging battle. He wants to open a hole for the front troops to get inside.

From out of nowhere, Talmidge is hit in the shoulder by an arrow. He turns to the side in pain. Talmidge can see a Creek warrior reloading his bow. Their eyes meet. The warrior throws his bow down and charges with a tomahawk in hand.

Talmidge has dropped his rifle and there is no time to retrieve it. He breaks off the arrow from his shoulder and jerks out his hunting knife to defend. The warrior is on him. They clash with a thud, Talmidge's small knife against a modern metal tomahawk.

The warrior slashes again and again with his razor sharp axe. Talmidge backs away, more and more. He yells out. "Stop, Talon. I don't want to hurt you." The warrior is a family friend of Talmidge's people.

Talon yells out. "Die, you traitor."

Talmidge ducks away from Talon's advance. His friend slashes again and then closes in. Talmidge is forced to defend himself. Talmidge is cornered and is about to be killed. As Talon raises his tomahawk for the killing. He exposes himself to a knife thrust by the wounded Talmidge, who thrust his knife deep into Talon's chest. Talon is mortally wounded. His friend falls into Talmidge's arms.

Talmidge kneels holding his friend's body as he lowers him to the ground. Talmidge cries over his old family friend but has no time to think. He kindly lays his friend's head on the ground and hurriedly leaves, to complete his sad mission.

Talmidge has made his way almost to the front position along the fortress' dirt wall. He can see Houston standing in front of his formed troops. Sam gives the battle command. "CHARGE!"

Houston and five hundred men charge the front barriers of the Creek fortress. Houston charges up the hill to penetrate the front fortress. He presses his men forward to enter the stronghold. An arrow hits him in the front thigh. Houston flinches and continues to fight with saber drawn. A Creek warrior charges him with a bright red battle club. Houston blocks the impact and counters with a deathblow from his saber. Houston turns. Talmidge comes up behind him as he fights another Creek warrior. Talmidge kills the Creek warrior, saving Sam. Sam yells to him. "Pull the arrow out!"

The disoriented Talmidge can't believe his ears. "What?"

Sam counters a blow from another Creek warrior and

runs him through. He yells over the battlefield noise to Talmidge dodging bullets nearby. "Pull the damn arrow out it's killing me!"

Talmidge grabs the "dam" arrow. Sam waits and watches for attackers. "Do it."

Talmidge is a little anxious, he breaks the arrow off and pushes it through Sam's leg and out the other side. Houston winches from the pain and slashes another attacking Creek warrior. Talmidge dodges and the Creek falls on the battlefield. Shots ring out as another warrior attacks Houston. Houston is hit in the shoulder and forearm on the same side. He grabs his saber with the other hand and slashes the charging Creek brave. The falls dead. Talmidge shoots another attacker charging Houston's back. Houston smiles a thank you. They both turn to defend. The battlefield is suddenly quiet. Sam looks across the massive sea of bodies and sees John Ross kill the last Creek warrior with his pistol.

Ross and Houston's eyes meet. There is regret in their gaze. The battlefield is strewn with over one thousand Creek Nation warriors killed, and forty-four White and Cherokee soldiers dead. Hundreds of wounded troops and warriors are moaning and struggling against their injuries. A thousand Red Creek Battle Clubs mark the place of their brave owner's last stand.

A small narrow stream passes through the camp flowing pale red with courageous men's blood almost completely dammed by dead Creek warriors red battle clubs. As the rushing stream swirls along its wandering path, it forms small patterns that look like rose buds. Talmidge remembers how much John loves roses, particularly red roses reminding him of Quatie. He will never forget this day of blood. Talmidge watches John and Sam and thinks back on his childhood with John for just an instant, as he scans the killing field covered with bodies, young and old. The sight overwhelms him. He puts his saber away with a clang and sadly walks away. Sam is curious and turns to him. "Soldier, what's your name?"

Talmidge keeps walking as he speaks favoring his shoulder wound. "Just another damn Indian, sir."

Sam watches him go, not saying anything. John recounts his sinking feeling that day. "It was a sad day for me and my soldiers. Talmidge was especially affected. He never got over it. We sped toward another obscure freedom in league with an indifferent and arrogant General Jackson and a federal government bent on using us up and taking our land. So much death and destruction for so little gain! How could man do to this to man? Needless as wars are, our people developed an unwanted glory in that battle. We were known as a formidable force and honorable people."

General Jackson rode through the battlefield surveying the hard fought victory and gloating. John continues. "Something happened to him that bitter day. Maybe it was the meeting I had with the Creek chief or maybe it was just his run away ego and lust for power. From that time on, the General hated all Indians, particularly the Cherokee, and he proved it at every opportunity. Within a few months, the race for our valuable land was on again led by Andrew Jackson. Now, there is a new urgency in the air, just to survive. We wanted to escape the White-Man and he wanted to kill us. It had become a war of genocide. A war to be won, either in the courtroom, or in the battlefield and I don't think either side cared which. The words of the day were live or die for the moment. The bitterest atrocity was on our troops march home."

John recalls for Cal an appalling scene of U. S. soldiers attacking yet another Cherokee town immediately after they had helped the army defeat the Creek Nation. The troops were in the process of killing every living thing in the friendly settlement. They also set about burning the people's homes and destroying their winter food sources. The mission of the U. S. Army was still genocide to all Indian people no matter what the name of the tribe. The aged John's tone is thoughtful and sad. "Because of the color of my peoples skin, the soldiers were ordered to attack our homes and families. They didn't know or care that we were the United States soldiers that fought side by side with them. These troops have left a wave of carnage on as many friendly villages as they had on their enemy. What the Territorial Army missed the outlaws got in the absence of the men of the villages. The soldiers were simply told Indians are Indians. Our people were caught in a quagmire of deception and bad military decisions prompted by greedy politicians."

A few short months later after the total surrender of entire the Creek Nation, the Cherokee soldiers are finally going home from a hard-fought war with a heavy heart. John and Master Sergeant

Talmidge Watts ride at the head of a column of three hundred Cherokee U. S. Cavalry soldiers. In the distance Talmidge can see a large column of billowing gray smoke rising high in the blue sky. He turns to John. "That's the Jumper Band village."

John is quick. "Let's ride."

Talmidge directs the troops, and they ride full bore toward the burning village. John slows the pace before entering the small village. "Talmidge, form a skirmish line." Talmidge immediately gives the order, and the Cherokee troops form for battle. They move slowly into the smoldering village. They come upon a line of about two hundred mounted white union troops. They watch a dozen of their soldiers fight with ten surviving warriors of the Jumper Band defending their families.

John quickly responds. "Rifles ready."

Every man in the veteran company of Cherokee troops readies his rifle aiming at the white Union soldiers. Every man, red man and white stops. They watch John for the next move. To John's surprise Lieutenant Colonel Sevier is the commander of the white-troops. He moves forward from his Company of men and confronts John. "What's the meaning of this, Major?"

John is angry and holds back nothing. "Colonel, you are on Cherokee soil, a nation friendly to the United States of America Government.

The Colonel is uncaring and laughs. "Hell Major, Indians are Indians, and they hate the army."

John rides closer to the Lieutenant Colonel, only he and Sevier can hear. "Colonel, I am Indian, Cherokee Indian. Remove your men immediately, or I will give the order to execute you and every man that sits a horse under your command."

Sevier looks at him sternly. "Major, you being an Indian officer is not gonna cut anything with my men or the brass. So why don't you just get on out of here, and let this be."

John glares at the colonel. "This blood is on your hands." He draws his service revolver and cocks it pointing at Sevier's face.

Sevier immediately reacts, staring back at John. "A Company, skirmish line, rifles ready."

The white troops immediately move into position ready to fight. The scene is set for disaster. John stares at the Colonel. The Cherokee of the Jumper Band about fifty men appear from behind a log building and quickly fix their rifles on Sevier and his troops. Talmidge watches intently. He glances toward his troops to be sure they are ready.

Sevier doesn't move. He cuts his eyes toward the Cherokee Jumper Band with rifles pointed at him and then to the three hundred ready Cherokee Union troops. "What's your move, Major?"

John continues his cold stare. "I hate to do this Colonel, but I am going to shoot you."

The Colonel smiles. "I believe you would." His eyes roll toward his troops. "Stand down." Sevier's well-trained troops put their weapons down.

John continues to glare at Sevier. "You and your men get out of Cherokee Territory. If you linger, we will hunt you down and kill you to the last man as you have done to these people today." John lowers his pistol.

Sevier pauses for a moment then nods and rides toward his men speaking as he rides. "Column of two's, guide on me." Sergeant Prince signals the men and they form a column and follow the Colonel out of the village and into the dark forest. The Cherokee, both citizen and soldier keep their rifle trained on the exiting soldiers until the last man is out of sight.

John gives the order. "Steady your rifles." The whole village relaxes. John looks toward Talmidge. "Talmidge, move them out."

Talmidge gives the orders for the soldiers to form and

move out on the trail. Talmidge follows the Cherokee troop. John watches for a moment. A village elder walks to John. "Thank you, brave warrior. Will you seek revenge?"

John relaxes. "No, I'm afraid it would just make matters worse, and we would get no satisfaction from their commanding general.

We must learn to defend against all comers. I am sorry for you. I will send people back to help."

The elder pats him on the leg and walks away. John rides on to catch up with his soldiers.

# CHAPTER THIRTEEN

## CHEROKEE NATION, JOHN ROSS RURAL ES-TATE

### 1814-1836

### HOME SWEET HOME.

John looks at Talmidge as they ride. "Well, we made it without being killed."

Talmidge is happy about his home coming. "We sure did. Who would have thought it, home again? "

John is still thinking about going home but realizes he has urgent business to attend to. "Cut a dozen men loose to help the people in the village."

Talmidge gives the order for his best, the first platoon, to help the ailing people. The willing Cherokee soldiers and their sergeant exit the column and ride back to the smoldering village.

A few hours later, John halts his column of troops at the crest of a sprawling hillside that overlooks his scenic rural home. John pats Talmidge on the shoulder. "I'll see you soon old friend, don't be a stranger. Release the men when you get to town."

Talmidge nods and rides on with his anxious troops in tow. John waves, turns and rides to his lonely looking house. His beautiful two story southern home shows the need for a few repairs. John smiles and realizes war takes many tolls from the living as well as the dead. His well-used blue uniform is dusty and worn. He moves his horse anxiously to the front of the house looking it over. John dismounts, ties his mount and continues to look. The beautiful Quatie walks from the corner of the house showing six months pregnant. John sees Quatie and hurries to her, at the same time she sees John and runs to him. They meet and kiss wildly. John stops and looks into Quatie's eyes. "Oh God, I missed you." He kisses her again and again.

Quatie pulls him closer, she kisses John deeply and passionately while she cries. Quatie stops and looks at him. "I was afraid I'd never see you again."

Quatie stops and looks down at her belly and rubs it with her hand. "Say hello to daddy, it's been a long time since we have seen him."

John smiles and lovingly rubs her stomach. Quatie is pleased. She smiles and pushes her windblown Raven black hair from her face. Quatie kisses John again. She looks at him with pure love. "I'm so glad you're home."

John can't hide his joy. "I am too, Quatie. We can finally be a family." John looks at her pregnant stomach and pats it. "You are the most fertile woman I know."

Quatie playfully hits John on the chest. "I'd better be the only woman you know, every time you come home I get pregnant."

John smiles and looks at Quatie. "Well, I'm home and you're already pregnant." Quatie laughs, she kisses John with glee.

They walk toward the front porch with their arms around each other. Quatie pinches John on the butt as they walk. John looks at her and smiles. They are a family again. Voices are heard in the distance. John and Quatie turn to see two wagon loads of people rolling toward their house. John can see his mother and father. Mr. Ross stands in the moving wagon. "Hey, soldier, I thought we'd drop in. Didn't expect to see you here?"

John waves to them. The wagons stop next to John and Quatie. Mr. Ross says, "We came by to take Quatie and the baby to a cook out at church. Guess we'll do it here." Mr. and Mrs. Ross get off the wagon with the rest of the people. They both hug their son and daughter-in-law. The relatives and friends pay their respects. John is a happy man, he is back home with his family.

The group begins to set up tables and start cooking. Quatie stays close to John. Food is being laid out on the table and smells of home cooking is in the air. John relaxes on the porch with his wife and father. John and his father go to visit with an old aunt sitting nearby. A young boy takes John's horse to the stable. Mr. Ross looks at John. "We kept the place up pretty good. Looks like we could have given it a coat of paint before you got home."

John is happy and doesn't care. "It's all right. I thank you for what you did. I'll take care of everything now."

Mrs. Ross looks over at her son. "What are you going to do Son?"

John is in thought. "I don't know, Mother. I guess I'll work at the store or something."

His father says, "I'm sorry, Son, we don't have the store anymore. The soldiers burned it."

John's face is filled with sadness hearing about his childhood workplace and all the fun times he had there. "Sorry, Father, no matter, we'll make it."

Mr. Ross is strong and supportive. "That's right, Son, we'll make it just fine."

John looks toward the fire and the cooking food. "That fried chicken sure does smell good."

John's father stands. "Come on, let's get the preacher and start the service. Then we can eat some of that fried chicken, like big ole pigs."

They all move to the front yard. Quatie puts her arm around John's waist. Red roses grow surrounding the porch and line the walkway through the yard.

John looks down at the roses. "I love roses, red roses because they remind me of you."

Quatie smiles as they walk. "Me?"

John replies. "You my love. Just you."

The family Preacher that married John and Quatie has gathered his flock. He welcomes John homes and starts the sermon. "Let us pray. Dear Lord, we are so glad John has come home with all of his brave men. Please save and protect those Brothers who fell in combat, to honor our Nation. Thank you Lord for this day. Amen."

The Preacher begins his message. "Today, we welcome our brothers home. Today we start anew. Let us go forth with love and goodwill." The preacher smiles and looks around the group. "And... let's eat." They all laugh and move to the picnic area. The ladies have set a fine table and the food is heaped high on every plate. Home, home again. It is always good, no matter how large or small.

John Ross day dreams about he and his families future. He visualizes a new Cherokee Council meeting in progress. Long lines of Tribal members file through to speak to the Council and cast their votes for a new Principal Chief of the Cherokee Nation. "I did act on my dream and campaigned hard for months, and was elected. I couldn't believe I was now chief of all Cherokee. Me, Principle Chief of the Cherokee Nation."

This election started a period of prosperity, and divided the Cherokee Nation further at the same time. Since John was one-eighth Cherokee, most of the Full Bloods resented his election, but by this time in their long history a majority of Cherokee people were part white and they didn't care about degrees of blood. The people just cared about saving their nation. With only that they began to prosper and build.

Unfortunately the ailing nation still struggles to survive against the growing United States Government. It is imperative they move forward with all haste and become stronger, to stop the genocide of the Cherokee people."

John fondly remembers a little red schoolhouse being built. "In a short time, under my leadership, the Nation built eighteen more schools. I felt education was a better weapon than a gun."

"The great Sequoyah made a Cherokee alphabet that caused

communication to be better and easier for our people than ever before. With his printing press, he printed in both the Cherokee language and English. That press advanced our people on two levels. Culturally it made us proud, and our communication level doubled."

"We developed a National Cherokee Constitution. The Constitution unified us and stated our people's autonomous rights. It declared sovereign rights to our lands and a government for everyone in the Nation. The constitution gave us a legal leg to stand on in the courts of the growing new nation we struggled with, the United States of America. As things had commonly gone for the Cherokee since the colonization of our country, the new rights didn't last. Andrew Jackson was sworn in as President and we had hell to pay. Our old enemy that we fought so hard for was elected in the year eighteen-twenty-eight to his first term and in eighteen-twenty-nine he gave the first state of the union address. President Jackson stated he favored expansionism, which equaled in political jargon, taking more Indian lands for white commerce. Not just Cherokee, but all of the tribes. Jackson was genuinely arrogant and ruthless in his endeavors."

"I sent a Cherokee Committee to see President Jackson. They were instructed to stay until he could have an audience with them. I can't tell you how many times that poor aide of his covered for Jackson by walking from the President's office shaking his head, no. Just after the President's State of the Union Address, Jackson proceeded to push the Indian Removal Act through congress. It was brutally apparent he intended to get rid of his loyal friends, the Cherokee. He was severing all ties with his administration without saying a word to the people he was hurting. This removal act put all Indians off their land and further west to the new Indian Territories called Oklahoma. We tried many more times to see President Jackson but he never would open his door. He simply plowed ahead on his destructive path with many followers, particularly the greedy trading companies and land barons. Jackson made it plain he didn't like Indians."

"We had many northern sympathizers, but that was not enough. The states were given wide powers through the Indian Removal Act to take our land. Along with using laws, some Georgians formed ruthless radical groups to force the Cherokee from their land. Jackson's support and his new law gave many greedy Georgian an unwritten mandate to push us out of the state. On one terrible day ten Georgia horsemen dressed in white sheets and hoods rode through a Cherokee-owned farmyard. They set the house and barn on fire with torches and stopped in front of the house ready to kill anyone who tries to escape. Screams are heard from inside the blazing house. No one will come out. The locals called those raiders Pony Clubs. The Cherokee had once called them friends and neighbors."

# CHAPTER FOURTEEN

## STATE OF GEORGIA, RURAL JAIL

### 1836-1837

### LAW EAST OF THE MISSISSIPPI

Another side effect of Jackson's policy is the assault on the Cherokee's National Newspaper Office. A group of men break into the Indian Advocate Newspaper Office in Georgia. Talmidge rushes in to stop them. Three men have turned over the press and scatter papers over the office. He fights with the gruff and rustic Sheriff Freddie Wallace and two deputies. Three more Cherokee warriors enter and subdue the Sheriff and his men at gunpoint. They are at a standoff.

John Ross walks in. "What's the meaning of this?"

Sheriff Wallace is snide. "We got confiscation papers. I'm takin' this here newspaper by order of the State Judge, over in Atlanta. So, just back off there, boy."

John is amused at the ignorance of his adversary. "Sir, you are under arrest, by order of me, John Ross, Principal Chief of the Cherokee Nation. You have trespassed onto Cherokee Nation sovereignty. Your judge has no power in this sovereign nation."

The sheriff is pushy and arrogant. "What the hell you talkin' about?"

John speaks to him with full authority of his nation. "This is another country sheriff, you have no power here. Take them to the border and eject them. If you come back, you will be in our Cherokee

Nation jail for a very long time."

Talmidge smiles at the sheriff and green toothed deputies and mocks them. "Go on git, boy."

John cuts a look at Talmidge for being unprofessional. Talmidge straightens himself.

The sheriff is angry. "I'll be back."

The warriors take the sheriff and deputies out.

"They finally did confiscate our newspaper with the help of the United States Federal Government. That paper was the only link of true communications for all of our people and a valuable tool for us. Jackson and Georgia's plan of removal is working only too well."

John reminisces about his old hero, Major Ridge. "Major Ridge has become rich and powerful. He got involved with John Ridge, his son and Elias Boudinot. They began negotiations with the U. S. Government, without Council approval, to remove our people to the new Indian Territory. The three men signed a treaty with the government. It is said the government paid them. Any one of these acts is treasonous according to tribal law. We knew the Major Ridge, John Ridge and Elias Boudinot treaty as the Dirty Papers. The Ridge must have known that he was committing the same type of offense that had lead to his execution of Doublehead."

It was said by some, that Major Ridge uttered to himself, after signing the Dirty Papers treaty, "I have just signed my death warrant."

John tells Cal the problems created by that treaty. "This agreement gave the United States Government what it most needed, the ability to legally get rid of us once and for all, with no exceptions. Some of the Ridge faction went ahead with little record keeping, but it was about five thousand. The remaining Cherokee were rounded up and imprisoned in stockades, under the command of General Winfield Scott, a robust older man. The Cherokee never believed the U. S. Government would round up tax paying citizens and put them in stockades for no good reason, but they were lucky it was General Scott at least he was humane. The split between Ridge's people and mine was so severe that they offered no assistance during the imprisonment or on the way to the new territory. A small exception was made when we did finally arrive."

The entire Ridge group is now in the new territory and things have quieted down. A mature John Ross sits in the living room of his southern home thinking about the "Dirty Papers," and holding a book. He is comfortable in his favorite red-leather wingback chair, dressed only in his black canvas pants and knitted cotton under shirt. John's home is in excellent condition now and well kept. The theme is southern with a few Cherokee artifacts around the room.

Quatie walks down the cherry-wood stairs. Her dress is casual, a simple white skirt and blouse, but Quatie's grace is always present. Her long black hair flows over her shoulders and frames her smooth bronze face. John looks up to see her. "Are the boys at your mother's?"

Quatie smiles lovingly at with her husband. "Yes, both of them, you are stuck with me my love. Being alone with me has its benefits."

John smiles. "I can't think of anything I'd like better than being with the woman of my dreams."

Quatie smiles seductively. "Keep talking, it will probably get you anything you want." Quatie sits beside John looking at him lovingly.

John moves closer and kisses her with that same old passion. "Oh, I want this beautiful woman."

Quatie smiles and kisses him back, softly and slowly. "How bad."

John becomes more playful and aggressive. "Bad."

Suddenly the front door is kicked open. A large dirty man wearing a Sheriff's badge and holding a shotgun rushes in. John and Quatie scramble to defend themselves. The sheriff hits Quatie across the forehead with the barrel of his shotgun. She falls backward to the floor. Her blood splatters across John's face as the sheriff hits him with his fist.

Quatie tries to regain her senses while lying on the hard floor. Blood drips from her head and runs down her pretty face. The sheriff jerks the dazed John to his feet. He hits him again and again while he is still dazed and puts a pair of crude handcuffs on his wrist. "I'm Freddie Wallace, 'member me. I'm residin' sheriff of this here county, and I got orders to pick you up and put you in jail, Mr. Big Chief John Ross."

The statement shocks John. He screams out at the backwoods sheriff. "What the hell is going on? This is Cherokee land."

The bold sheriff is very crude and abrupt. "The Governments movin' you Injuns, and you're first, big chief."

John pleads to help Quatie. "Let me take care of my wife!"

Sheriff Wallace is unconcerned. "She'll be all right, chief. Let's go!"

Sheriff Wallace pushes John toward the door. "This is my home! You are on sovereign Cherokee land."

The Sheriff is snide. "Not for long, big chief. Ole' Andrew Jackson's makin' sure of that." The Sheriff pushes John again.

John turns and yells. "Quatie, are you all right?"

Quatie rises weakly from the floor. "I'm all right, John!"

John sees Quatie's bleeding face. He goes Crazy and attacks the scruffy sheriff. John hits Wallace and throws him against the wall. The sheriff takes another set of chain handcuffs from his belt and hits John across the face. John is dazed. Sheriff Wallace pushes him backward and hits him with his fist. "Go on, git!" John is still on his feet, Wallace hits John on the chest with his shotgun butt and knocks him completely out the front door. John skids across the porch and takes a roll on the grass outside. Quatie moves weakly getting into a position to see John. "I'll get help, John."

Wallace's green-teeth deputy waits on his underfed horse with pistol drawn. He holds two horses for John and the sheriff. "Hell Sheriff, old Mr. Big Chief don't look so tough to me."

Inside the house Quatie struggles, attempting to stand. She

staggers to the doorway. Tears well up in her eyes as she watches the brutal Sheriff and John. If Quatie had only known her future in another part of the Indian Nation, she would have left that moment for any place but this place and would have never come back. John sees another opening as he attacks the Sheriff. He and Wallace fall to the ground and the deputy cackles as John and the sheriff fight. They are on their feet and John hits him again. The Deputy can see his boss is losing so he fires his pistol in the ground near John. John stops and looks at the deputy who tries to be funny. "Hold on boy. Cain't have ya hurtin' my employer there."

The sheriff is huffing and puffing from the fight. "It's about damn time, idiot Yahoo!"

The sheriff turns to John and hits him as John awkwardly tries to defend himself with his handcuffed hands. "Get up big chief and get on that horse, and if ya try to run, I'll kill ya on the spot." They all mount up and ride away. Quatie cries while watching from the window.

Across the Territory not far from John's house, in a remote wilderness Army camp, called Hinasee Garrison, Georgia, soldiers build eight huge log stockades. The giant stockades are designed with small sheds on the interior for cover from the weather and catwalks high on the walls for armed guards to hold Indian prisoners during the round up for the Indian Removal Act-a Jackson Federal project well underway. General Scott strolls by the newly built stockades with his Adjutant, Captain Cain. The captain is a picture of a soldier and cavalry officer. "You know Captain Cain this whole process is going to come back on us. We are making an unpopular history this day."

Captain Cain agrees. "I don't envy you, your position, Sir."

General Scott is remorseful. "I'd rather be beaten than inflict this on these people, but I'm a soldier and I obey orders."

Sevier, now a full Colonel still in the cavalry passes by with eighty troops riding under his command. He raises his hand for the column to stop. Sergeant Prince is still with him and is now a sergeant major. He shouts orders from the front of the column. "Halt." The

Colonel gets off his horse and salutes General Scott. The General and Captain Cain return the courtesy. "Sir, we're ready to start the round up."

General Scott dismisses the Colonel with a common order. "Carry out your orders, Colonel."

Sevier mounts his horse and rides to the front of the column. "Move 'em out, Sergeant Major Prince."

Sergeant Major Prince gives the order. "Move out, single column, yoo!" The Troop of eighty men rides toward the dark rolling hills. General Scott and Captain Cain watch them go and walk on.

The roundup of Indian Citizens is underway. Later that day Quatie is still in shock from the assault. She sits in John's favorite chair, near the front door of her home, putting medication on her head. Quatie is still dizzy and crying. She hears a noise and looks through the front window. Quatie sees the mounted Calvary Troop led by Colonel Sevier. They have stopped in front of her house, with twenty Cherokee prisoners on foot. Quatie is startled. "Oh, my God!"

She runs to the back door, jerks it open and runs into the arms of two rough looking soldiers. They grab her before she can exit. One of the soldiers says, "Where you going so fast, Injun?"

Quatie is dragged from the house and thrown in with the rest of the prisoners. She doesn't know it, but this patrol is one of many in the territory taking prisoners and driving them to the stockades. The patrol moves out. A half-hour later, Colonel Sevier and his men move onto a nearby plantation doing the work that suits Sevier so well. They ride into the front yard of the stately residence. A slave dressed in fine butler's clothes walks from the house to Sevier. "Hello sir, could I help you?"

The Colonel looks at him for a second. "Arrest him."

Two soldiers get off their horses and take the black man. "The rest of you men round up everybody on this plantation. It is Cherokee owned."

The slave tries to talk to the soldiers. "But master, I..." Sevier interrupts. "Take him to the barn with the others, until we have them all."

The soldiers enter the house and fields behind the house arresting Cherokee hired-hands and slaves owned by the Cherokee plantation owner. A soldier jerks and drags a Cherokee woman from the house past Colonel Sevier. She yells out at Sevier. "You animal, this is my home."

The Colonel has a cold look toward her. "Madam you were under orders to vacate your premises, you have not. This is the price you pay."

The woman screams out at him again. "This is my home, I worked for it and paid for it with my sweat! You have no right." The woman looks up and sees her children in the window inside her house. "My children let me get my children."

The Colonel is cruel. "Take her with the others."

Two soldiers roughly take her away. She bits and kicks all of the way. Another soldier follows dragging the young children toward the barn behind their mother as they cry for her. A Cherokee man, the husband and father, runs from the corner of the house. "Leave my children alone!" He runs toward the soldier with the children. The soldier pulls his pistol and fires, killing the man, in front of his children. The Cherokee woman also sees the incident and screams out, "You murdered my husband!"

She begins to cry and sits on the ground. The soldiers jerk the woman up and drag her to the barn. The children scream for their mother. Sevier stands by and calmly watches. Sergeant Prince walks beside the Colonel. "We have them all, Sir."

Sevier appears satisfied with a job well done, not considering the death of the Cherokee man. "All right Sergeant Prince, mount the men up and move the prisoners out. We'll head for the stockade."

The sergeant turns to the men. "Yes sir. You heard the Colonel, move out."

The soldiers move the prisoners out of the barn and force them down the road. They surround them with their horses as they go. Two soldiers in the background dig a grave for the Cherokee Man. The two children break and run between the horses and into the woods. A soldier starts to pursue them. Colonel Sevier speaks as he continues to ride forward. "Come back, corporal. Let them go."

The children's mother screams from the crowd of prisoners and struggles to get past a soldier's horse as he moves to block her. "Let me get my babies!"

Sevier keeps riding unconcerned. "Keep them moving, sergeant."

Sergeant Major Prince looks at the soldier blocking the woman. "Yes sir, keep her moving trooper."

The soldier draws his saber and raises it over the woman. She screams out in a crying rage. "Go ahead you murderer!"

A slave woman grabs her and pulls her back. "Come on Miz. Vandell, let's go, the children will be all right, come on now." They keep walking, the woman bellows and cries as they walk.

The little cherub faces of the children watch from behind an old rotted log in the forest. They see the soldiers and their mother getting further away. The children cry and scream, but they are afraid to follow. "Mamma, Mamma, come back."

The soldiers keep the prisoners moving as they fade out of sight over a distant hill. The hardnosed troopers drive and push the prisoners to move faster down the rough dirt road. Quatie ambles in a daze on the heavily wooded trail. She suddenly notices her aging mother and a few other relatives have been taken prisoner. Quatie moves from the rear of the column to the front to be with her fraught mother. She puts her arm around her as they walk. "Are you all right, mother? Where are the babies?"

The old Cherokee woman has a large cut across her face and a beaten hopeless stare. She looks at Quatie. Quatie holds her closer as they walk. "Oh mother, what have they done to you?"

The old woman pats Quatie as they walk. "When I saw the soldiers, I sent the boys to your cousins house. They took them ahead to the new territory away from all of this."

Quatie smiles holding back tears. "It will be all right, we just have to stay alive until we can get away or get to the babies."

In the background Sevier gives orders to a sergeant. "Sergeant Norton, Take a few men and pick-up those stragglers up by Thornton fork." The sergeant acknowledges and rides away.

The prisoners continue to walk like the living dead, exhausted on their feet, almost in a trance. Quatie's eyes fill with tears of fear and emotional pain while she marches next to her fatigued mother.

# CHAPTER FIFTEEN

## CHEROKEE NATION REBELLION

### 1837

### LET US FIGHT FOR RIGHT.

Chief Ross remembers another capture that didn't go as well for the intruding soldiers. In another part of the Cherokee Nation Sergeant Norton, a troop platoon leader assigned to round up Cherokee and his men arrived at the stockades and were quickly dispatched to do their duty. "All Cherokee were not submissive. An old Cherokee man named Tasli, affectionately called Charley, was seized very early at his farm along with his wife, a brother, his three sons and their families by Sergeant Norton's troops." From John's vivid description Cal imagines how it must have been that brutal day.

Later in the day Tasli-Charley's family and a few other prisoners that are arrested by the soldiers along the way, are pushed and prodded across a small rolling plain of vetch and clover bordering the thick forest of the rolling green foothills. The huddled mass is on their way to the bleak stockades of their veiled enemy, the United States Government. The ten armed cavalry soldiers command a loose guard on the small group slowly moving through the short grass leaving a flattened trail like an emerald billboard marking the way. Old Charley moves along slowly. He watches the soldiers as they beat and push the tired Cherokee to go faster. A troop prods Charley's old wife with a saber to speed her along. Charley starts walking faster and stops beside each Cherokee man.

Tasli-Charley speaks softly and quietly to the men in their native language, as he moves from one to the other. He speaks to the last Cherokee. "We must resist. Join with me and when I signal, take the soldier nearest to you and disarm him and keep the weapon. We will escape."

Charley continues speaking in Cherokee to the men. The soldiers don't realize what is planned. Charley moves back to his wife to assist her. The soldiers continue to strike and prod the slower moving prisoners. Charley looks around. He sees he is clear to attack. Charley signals the others. Each Cherokee immediately jumps the nearest soldier, pulling him from his horse. They take the soldiers weapons. Some troops have one and two Cherokee on them, fighting. The Cherokee women help the old and children get away into the woods. Charley yells out to the fighting Cherokee. "Do not kill, we only want weapons and to escape."

A sudden shot rings out breaking the rustle of the fight for freedom; Charley looks in the general direction of the sound. The leader of the group, Sergeant Norton, falls from his horse, dying. He is shot by accident while a Cherokee warrior wrestles with a nearby soldier for his rifle. The Cherokee fighting with Norton breaks the dying soldier's fall and lays him on the ground softly. Charley yells out, "No, no, do not kill!"

The remaining soldiers are almost immediately disarmed and sent home down the grassy trail like coddled pets. The Cherokee rapidly take the cavalry horses in hand and armed with the soldiers weapons, they mount up and ride into the dark forest with their families anticipating their immediate future. The soldiers finally begin to regroup after the Cherokee are out of sight and begin to talk about what to do while walking to the stockades. The bold Cherokee people that escaped that day rapidly became known as the Eastern Band of the Cherokee Nation.

The Eastern Band found refuge deep in the hills of the Carolina's and never left their sacred lands. Along the way, a white United States Cavalry Colonel came to the Eastern Band and over a long period of time became their friend and a citizen of the Cherokee Nation. He began to train his fellow citizens, the Cherokee, just as he had trained many soldiers before. The colonel did not give his name, only to be known by his army rank. This Cherokee citizen Colonel kept training and teaching his new nation to keep them strong and free. The new Eastern Band army of warriors forwarded dispatches to the commanding officers of the occupying U. S. Army stating that they wanted to live on their lands free, peaceful, and undisturbed. However, if war came to their land they would fight under the command of their new military leader.

The Colonel made them a force so formidable they were simply ignored. The politicians and generals didn't want any more trouble than they already had. This campaign had grown into a brew of bad decisions and dissention in the ranks of the military and politicians. As time went on the citizenry in the Eastern United States were concerned about the federal and states governments actions in the south and voiced their opposition through protest and in the ballot box. Now the Eastern Band is about to become another political embarrassment by being led by a U. S. Cavalry Officer and there is always the possibility of the U. S. Army being defeated by them. They are simply forgotten for the political moment.

Sergeant Norton's tired and beaten soldiers stumble toward the fortified front gates of the first stockade in late afternoon. The Stockade Gate Guard yells out from his high perch, "Men approaching on foot."

Twenty regular stockade guards go to their defense post inside along the wall of the giant stockade. Their small heads can be seen above the top of the stockade's huge log wall from outside. The sergeant of the guard yells out for more information. "Can you identify, private?"

The Gate Guard yells his best guess from the perch. "Sort of looks like soldiers, if they are, they're torn to hell."

The sergeant takes his cue from the new information. "Open the gate! Stand ready to defend." The gates swing open and Norton's exhausted soldiers stumble inside feeling much safer.

The tired soldiers stop as the gates close directly behind them. A crowd gathers around the men. Sergeant Prince pushes his way through the crowd. "What happened?"

An exhausted corporal speaks up. "We were bringin' in a bunch of stragglers, and all of a sudden they jumped us, took our weapons and killed Sergeant Norton."

In the background the log gates open again as Colonel Sevier and General Scott walk through the opening. Sergeant Prince comes to attention. The General booms with authority. "What happened here, Sergeant Prince?"

The sergeant confidently relays the information. "The corporal informs me that his detail was overpowered by Cherokee prisoners and Sergeant Norton was killed by one of them. The prisoners escaped into the mountains with the troops' weapons and horses."

General Scott turns to Colonel Sevier. "Colonel, it will be impossible to get them out of there in any timely manner. Dispatch word, by one of the warriors, that if the leaders will come in and talk with us, we can work something out."

The Colonel offers a promotion gathering answer. "Yes, sir."

The General warns. "Be sure and handle this right Colonel. We don't need more trouble."

Colonel Sevier attempts to curry more favor with the General by his answer. "Yes, Sir, I will see that no further problems are caused by these animals."

General Scott recognizes Sevier's poor attitude from many years of promotion seekers polishing their faces on the back of his pants. He recaps his order. "Not my meaning, Colonel. Correct your attitude and make proper arrangements."

The Colonel recognizes his possible career shortening statement and corrects it for the moment. "Yes, Sir, I'll take care of it."

General Scott is abrupt. "Time is short. I want these Indians moved as soon as possible without delay. The sooner we do this, the sooner the conflict will stop. Clean it up, Colonel."

Colonel Sevier's facial expression is agreeable while he nods his compliance. General Scott glances around the area, turns and walks back toward the headquarters tent as quickly as he came.

Sergeant Major Prince steps beside the Colonel as he speaks. "Sergeant Major, we need to show strength now by taking a strong stand against the bastards that killed our man out on the trail. But, for now, as the general said, send word out, if the Eastern Band men that escaped will come in, we'll work this problem out."

Just behind the Colonel, Quatie and her family members mill around just inside the stockade gates with thirty to forty other prisoners. Twenty more Cherokee are being moved into the stockade by ten mounted cavalry guards. As the Cherokee prisoners clear the entrance, the troops disperse and move back outside the gateway. Quatie turns to look toward the departing soldiers, but the gate slams shut with a bang before she can get a good look. Quatie comes to the realization of where she is and scans the dreary stockade, looking at each weary person and their families.

Quatie and the new prisoners disperse and melt into the masses already inside the fortifications. Quatie's mother makes her way to the bulky log wall and sits alone as Quatie sadly watches the panorama of bereavement.

A close friend recognizes Quatie under her dirty face and haggard look from the long journey. The friend yells out. "Quatie is here. Quatie is here!" Everyone gathers around her and starts to mumble and talk about how the chief's wife is being treated and how bad the conditions are inside the stockades. A guard near the gate watches and decides it is getting dangerous and starts to move up to the catwalk ladder on the wall when three warriors grab him. He shoots one in the leg and the other two begin to beat him. Two guard on the catwalk shoot near them trying to stop the beating. The beating continues, and the guards take aim again, this time to kill the warriors. Quatie quickly steps between their aim and the warriors yelling at the Cherokee men to stop. All is calm for the moment. She goes to the soldier and gets him to his feet as the warriors stand near waiting for the worst. The soldier above hold their aim to kill. She helps the beaten soldier move outside the gate as two guards open it and take him. Quatie silently and quickly goes to the warriors and pushes them into the crowd. "Go now, this is not the time." She kneels beside the wounded warrior while the guards hold their aim on her and the Cherokee man. She checks his wound and tears his shirt to make a bandage. Quatie wraps it around his bleeding leg. Two women come from the crowd and take him away to the wall. Quatie looks up at the guard and waits. They hesitate and then lower their rifles. She walks on into the crowd. Quatie continues to look around the area. She can see an Army Officer enter the gate and talk to the catwalk guards. Quatie continues to scan the area and sees a weary, beaten people, torn and bleeding. She says to herself, "Why do they treat us so? Can it really be their greed that brings such great misery to so many?"

Back in the territory, Sevier's soldiers still search for Cherokee stragglers. Colonel Sevier and his troop approach a small picturesque southern style farm owned by an up and coming young Cherokee couple, Ethan Sringwater and his wife, Mary. Ethan works in his whitewashed horse stables while singing to himself. He is an average man with a good build and a handsome face. His dark skin shines with sweat as he works quickly in the warm barn. The sunlight shines through the back window of the small barn creating ribbons of yellow lights across the dirt floor while Ethan brushes one of his two strong gray horses that are tied in their well kept stables. A horseman's shadow ripples past the window cutting through the daylight casting a shadow on the dirt floor. Then another and another passes by. Ethan looks up and casually walks to the barn exit. He sees fifty mounted cavalry troops gathered around the front porch of his small white farm-house. Three soldiers are already on his front porch. Ethan walks briskly toward the brazen troops.

Colonel Sevier and Sergeant Major Prince are still mounted on their horses and in command of this wilderness force. The sergeant major speaks to the three men on the porch. "Corporal Conroy, you and Taylor stay here and bring these stragglers in." Corporal Conroy and Private Taylor acknowledge by nodding. The Colonel looks toward two others soldiers. "McGuire, Paine stay here and help them."

The Privates spout out those tired words of the U. S. Army. "Yes Sir." "Yes Sir."

Sevier gives an order with his usual overbearing tone. "Move'em out, sergeant major!"

Sergeant Major Prince is mechanical in his commanding compliance. "Move out, column of twos!" The remaining forty-six troops turn and form a double column. They move out on the forest trail with the Colonel and Sergeant Prince leading the way.

Ethan is still walking quickly toward the soldiers on the porch. The men suddenly realize he is coming. Corporal Conroy pulls his revolver. "That's far enough Injun, stop right there!" The corporal looks at Paine and McGuire. "Go get'em and tie him up."

Ethan stands in place and watches. Corporal Conroy yells out again. "Don't even think about runnin', blanket-ass. I'll drop you before you get two feet."

Private Paine and McGuire walk toward Ethan. They grab him and push him toward his house. Ethan's wife, Mary, walks out the front door. Her fragile girl-like frame glows in the sunlight. Mary's pretty brown eyes scan the scene. The soldiers are startled and so is she. They quickly point their weapons at her. Mary's pretty child-like face scowls with fear. She speaks out. "Ethan, what's going on?"

Ethan consoles his precious wife. "It's all right, Mary, don't be afraid. Go back in the house."

Her beauty takes the rude corporal's eye. "Well, hello here. You better stay right there woman." Mary is worried. Fear covers her face.

The corporal is cocky. "Tie him to the porch post right here."

Private's Paine and McGuire tie Ethan to the sturdy white porch post while Private Taylor looks on. Paine doesn't like the situation and speaks up. "Corporal, we're supposed to take these people in, what the hell are you doing?"

The Corporal intends to intimidate the Privates to have complete control. "Shut your mouth, I'm running this show and don't fur git it!" He grabs Mary by the wrist. "Just as soon as I take my pleasures with this squaw, you can take her anywhere you want."

Ethan is visibly upset and very angry. "Leave her alone!"

Private McGuire chimes in. "Corporal, you're asking for trouble!"

Conroy is arrogant. "Well you Injun-lovers stay out of here or I might just put the hurt on ya."

Private Taylor worries. "Corporal, this just ain't right."

The corporal is dreadfully tough. He uses a final intimidation. "I ain't above shootin' ya fur sassin me, asshole!"

The three soldiers are disgusted. Ethan struggles against his ropes.

Corporal Conroy pushes the fragile Mary toward the front door of the house holding her petite arm tight. He stops and looks at Ethan. "Don't worry, she'll still want ya when I'm done." He laughs like a jackal, making Ethan pull hard against his cutting ropes.

The Cherokee man stares viciously at the crude corporal. Private Taylor is totally fed up with Conroy, but also intimidated. "Get on with it, I want to get the hell out of here."

The other soldiers get their horses and walk them to the barn. Ethan feels a loose knot on his rough ropes, he begins to work it loose. Corporal Conroy pulls on the frightened Mary to move her into the house. She claws her fingernails into the doorsill. Conroy twists her arm harder and shoves her. She will not let go. The corporal turns and hits Mary hard with his fist in the mouth splitting her lip. The blow stuns her and knocks her inside the house. Mary's mouth bleeds. She screams against Conroy as she comes around.

Mary cries hard and screams more as the Corporal rips her lightweight dress off during the fracas. Conroy throws her down on the hard oak floor near the fireplace and rips the rest of her clothes off. He lustfully tears at her delicate sculptured nude body. She squirms beyond her normal strength to get away. Conroy hits Mary hard again across the face. Mary whimpers from the sharp pain, then relaxes and gives up her struggle.

Corporal Conroy unbuttons his pants and crawls on top of her. She screams again with a renewed struggle in a last effort. The corporal grabs her long silky black hair and pulls her head back to the floor trying to hold her in place. He settles down on her and tries to kiss Mary's injured mouth. Mary moves her head frantically trying to avoid his caress.

The three soldiers are settled in the horse barn relaxing, just waiting, when they hear the corporal scream. All of the privates run to the farmhouse. Private Paine speaks while he runs. "I knew it, something bad would come of this!"

Paine is the first through the door. The other two are right behind him. They abruptly stop. The Corporal's body lies in a pool of blood running from his head. Ethan stands over him holding a stick of firewood with a look of remorse on his face. Ethan and Mary's small baby cries and screams in the background.

Mary lies on the floor, naked and badly beaten, she curls up and cries harder. The soldiers just stare at Corporal Conroy's body. Ethan kneels beside his wife caressing her and turns to the soldiers. "What has brought us to this?"

Paine is stunned. He just shakes his head. "I don't know. I just don't know."

Out in the Cherokee Territory, Colonel Sevier still drives his men hard to grab as many Cherokee prisoners as he can. The colonel will not be outdone. He must impress General Scott for that ever present rush for more rank and position. It's late evening and beginning to get dark as Sevier and his men move along a new forest trail leading to the stockades. They come upon a remote well-made log house hidden in the camouflage of huge trees growing in front and around it. Sevier would have missed the house entirely if not for smoke coming from the chimney. The colonel moves his tattered group toward the house. He stops his assembly of two hundred prisoners in front of the cabin and stares at the quiet residence. A middle-aged heavy-built Cherokee woman and three young children from five to nine-years-old come out of their cozy little cottage to see the troops and prisoners. Sevier screeches out a tired order. "Take them, Sergeant Major!"

The sergeant lets those familiar words roll from his tongue. "Yes, Sir." Prince rides his strong horse to the house. He speaks to the kindly woman. "You and the children join the others ma'am."

The good-natured Cherokee woman is shocked. The pleasant smile fades from her kind face, she does not understand. "Why, what have we done?"

The sergeant draws his cavalry saber with the brass-knuckle bow and lion's head pommel that looks much to noble for this poor deed. "Let's go, NOW!"

The woman wants to stand-up for her rights. "I cannot, we must wait for my husband! Besides this Cherokee land, you have no authority here."

Sergeant Major Prince doesn't want this, but in his mind he knows he must obey. "Let's go lady, I don't want to hurt you. All Cherokee are ordered removed to the new Indian territory."

The Cherokee lady runs for the forest with her children. The sergeant charges his cavalry horse in front of her and knocks her down. He turns the horse and faces her. The children return to her as she gets up. The woman's children surround her. "Get goin or I'll take your head off if I have to." Prince rides closer and holds the blade of his polished saber close to her kind and decent looking face.

The startled motherly woman begins to cry in fear and disgust. She bows her head while her young children support her by holding her arm and hugging close to their strong mother. The polite Cherokee lady regains her faculties and walks with her weeping children to the group of waiting prisoners.

The long dusty trip back to the stockade is exhausting. Supplies are short and prisoners have neither water nor food on the trail. The troops drive them harder hoping to save time and get back to the stockades before they start dropping out.

Sevier's down-trodden prisoners arrive past midnight. The colony of imprisoned has swollen to four hundred. The colonel and his men herd them to the nearest designated stockade. "Open the gates! Prisoners comin' in."

The large log double-gates open in the stockade wall. Tired soldiers drive the exhausted prisoners inside. Colonel Sevier sits on his worn-out horse and watches. The colonel glances at the sergeant major mounted next to him. "Sergeant, bed the men down. We'll start again in the morning."

The sergeant major replies asserting his military and moral duty. "Yes, Sir. I'll need to hold a few men to feed and water the prisoners."

The Colonel's statement comes cold. "Leave them, Sergeant Major. We'll have it done before we leave in the morning."

The sergeant respectfully objects. "But, Sir."

Colonel Sevier is firm. "Sergeant! This is a battle of the fittest. If we don't do this now, the truth of this is someday we could be the ones in their stockade or hung by our balls from a tree. It's about survival. You have your orders."

The familiar words ring out with little meaning from a regretful sergeant major. "Yes, Sir!"

The sergeant turns his horse and rides to the exterior of the stockade. The gates close as his last man exits. He stops to speak with the men. The colonel rides past and listens and watches the sergeant as he speaks to the troops. "All right men, bed your horses down and get some rest. We're on at dawn!" He waits but does not dismiss them. The colonel rides away.

Sergeant Prince waits until he is out of earshot. "All right let's do it. Water'em, then bed down."

The soldiers dismount and go to the water well. They pick up wooden buckets and begin to carry water to the prisoners inside the stockade.

Inside the dark stockade hundreds of new prisoners sit around the stockade walls. Soldiers stop and let them drink from their water buckets. Soft cries fill the air. Across the prison many low conversations are heard muffled in the darkness. Thankful eyes watch the soldiers move on.

An unrecognizable Cherokee man is dragged into the stockade on foot with a bloody rope tied around his raw and bleeding wrists. He stumbles and falls as the shadowed soldier that pulls him stops and gets off of his sweating horse. The soldier cuts the thick rope loose and rides out.

The man weakly gets up and begins to move to a dark corner of his new prison. Hardly anyone notices, it is just another event in this bizarre episode of military commitment on behalf of its government. The cruelty has become unnoticed commonplace behavior. Prince offers Ethan a cool drink as he and his men begin to leave the stockade. Ethan, who is oblivious to his surroundings, automatically takes a drink but his mind thinks only of Mary and their child. Ethan, who does not know what has happened to them, begins to wonder the stockade as in a fog. Prince looks on for a moment, then he and his tired men leave past the armed post guard's silhouetted against the bright sky. The massive gates close behind Prince, and he looks back for an instant as more guards move along the catwalks high above the prisoners.

Many whispered conversations overlap as the people below the silhouetted guards communicate their pain and fear. "Mamma I'm hungry." "What are they going to do with us?" "Oh God, how could this be happening?"

Quickly it is dawn and workmen are hard at work building ten more Stockades, to maintain about a thousand Cherokee prisoners. About ten thousand more Cherokee prisoners should complete the removal. Their thumping hammers set the cadence for the day. General Scott's men waste no time in the round up this early morning.

Three more cavalry companies herd groups of three and four hundred Cherokee prisoners into the holding areas.

Sergeant Major Prince and five privates ride aboard a large freight wagon drawn by huge draft horses carrying water in slat sided barrels banded together with iron rings and slabs of salt-pork in wooden crates headed for the stockades. The soldiers are tired from their activities in the stockade just a few hours before. Prince and his men drive through the secured gates and into the middle of a horde of hungry people. Prince stops the big wagon and gets off with his men following. He yells out to the Cherokee. "All right, everybody line up, it's breakfast time."

Sergeant Prince turns to his soldiers. "Cut about a half a hand size of that salt pork, and one cup of water. We gotta stay on the move, hurry it up." The five privates acknowledge and go about their work.

Three of the privates cut the sides of pork with huge butcher knives and the other two serve water. Two Cherokee get their meat and water, a third steps up to get his. The private looks at the meat for a moment. He sees an unsalted corner with maggots in it. He simply cuts it off, throws it on the ground and keeps serving.

The private on the opposite side of the wagon cuts his dirty hand with the sharp butcher knife. He yelps from the pain and bleeds. The trooper has no medicine so he sanitizes his hand by wiping it on the salt pork in spite of the pain of the salt in his wound. He keeps serving. The Cherokee are so weary, they don't even notice. The Indian prisoners just move on through the line.

Sergeant Major Prince hurries the Cherokee prisoners. "Come on, hurry up. We gotta get back to the railhead, if you want to eat again!"

The exhausted prisoners settle down around the rough walls of the stockade after they are served. The women slowly feed their hungry children. The proud mothers and fathers can only watch and wait for the babies to fill their stomachs waiting for a few scraps for themselves trying to remain strong. Quatie sits against the rough stockade barrier. She feeds a small orphaned female child. Edna, an old Cherokee woman comes to her. "Quatie, you need rest. I will feed the child."

Quatie is overwhelmed, but feels compelled to feed

and medicate all of her people. "There are many sick people. Go ahead and feed this child, I'll give the medicines. Is the herb bag here?"

Edna admires Quatie. "Yes, I have it here. You are the best of us, save yourself, so you can help later. It will get worse."

Quatie stands and takes the herb bag. She pats Edna on the shoulder for the compliment. The young child cuddles up to the old woman and relaxes. Quatie looks at the orphaned child lovingly and runs her fingers through the little girls long black hair thinking of her own sons. "Take her with the other children when you have finished. Talmidge's wife is taking care of all the orphans until we find their parents."

Edna nods. Quatie walks away to medicate the wounded. The old woman calls after her. "Get rest!" Quatie nods and moves on.

Quatie comes to a tattered man sitting in the darkest corner of the stockade. Quatie looks closer and stops beside him. It's, Talmidge. He holds his bloody arms and hands close to his broad chest. She kneels down beside him and pulls at his bloody hands to see. "Oh Talmidge, Let me see. I'm so glad I found you. I want to help you. I found out Victoria is with the orphan children."

Talmidge nods and sits silently. Quatie pulls his hands and arms to where she can see them. She flinches from the gory sight. Talmidge's wrists are almost cut to the bone from rope burns. He says, "I'm all right, take care of the others."

Quatie smiles and pulls fresh herbs from the medicine bag. She begins to put them on his tender wounds. Talmidge pulls back slightly from the sting. Quatie continues to doctor him and console her friend with soft words. "Cousin, you are a strong warrior, we need you healthy to help the others. Besides, I need you and John needs you. You are our best friend."

Talmidge is concerned for his people and his friends. "What have they done with our chief?"

Quatie worries but tries to hide it. "He has been taken away, but I know John is trying to help. We'll just have to wait."

The fierce warrior comes out from inside Talmidge. "Time has run out. We must fight now. They will kill us by the hundreds every day just letting us die from disease. Soon there will be no warriors to fight."

Quatie wants to keep things together until she hears from John. "You're right, fight to help keep our people alive until we can get justice. We are not people of war. We are people of peace and love."

Talmidge admires her strength. Quatie finishes doctoring him and stands. Talmidge is thankful. "Thank you, you are strong and give a lesson to us all." She smiles and walks toward another injured person.

Talmidge yells out. "If they have hurt John, there will be war."

# CHAPTER SIXTEEN

## STATE OF GEORGIA, RURAL JAIL

### 1837

### LAW EAST OF THE MISSISSIPPI

Sheriff Freddie Wallace uses his shotgun barrel to prod John along the dark forest foot-trail leading to the jail. They stumble toward the front door of the backwoods building. John's hands are still secured by ancient handcuffs. His face is bruised and swollen from his beatings. John trips and regains his footing. The sheriff hits John hard in the back with his shotgun butt. "Git on in there, stinkin' half-breed."

John stumbles through the door of the filthy jail but remains standing. He stands in the middle of the run-down jail's bleached wood floor. The grinning green-toothed deputy gets up from his homemade desk. He holds a large bone-handled hunting knife glaring at his new prisoner. John stares at the strange deputy with a cautious eye. The sheriff's gravel voice intervenes. "Go on and git them cuffs off."

The harsh deputy is the same backwoods-country hillbilly that was at the Cherokee newspaper office. "I's thinkin' of just skinnin' his carcass or maybe scalpin' him alive. You know, just fer how he treated us at the newspaper. That's purty ill-mannered."

The sheriff is just plain mean and stupid, but he follows orders. "Put him in jail, he'll get what's comin' to him when he goes to the stockades with old General Winfield Scott. He's a big man, accordin' to them soldiers that came by."

The deputy looks at John and says, "I hear the Injuns call him Principal Chief of all of 'em. Hey, he's famous, ain't he?"

The Sheriff is more direct. "I call him principal murderer of good Georgians. But there ain't nothin' we can do 'bout it, this time."

The deputy takes John's handcuffs off and pulls him by the shirt through a rustic doorway and into the hall of the jail cells. The site in the cell, directly in front of John, shocks him. The Deputy grins showing his big green teeth as he speaks. "What's wrong, Mr. Big, ain't you never seen a hanged Injun before?"

The deputy opens the rusty jail door. An Indian man hangs from the rustic rafters with a hangman's noose around his neck. He has been there for several days. The man is bloated and turning black from decomposition. John gags as he is pushed inside the compartment with his dead cell-mate. The almost cross-eyed deputy looks cruelly at John. "Enjoy your company there, big chief. Maybe suicides the ticket. Like your outlaw buddy there. If you're lucky that is." The repulsive deputy laughs.

John can't hold back. "You murdered this man! You disgusting scum!"

The Deputy laughs. "You're full of that uppity talk ain't ya?"

John is disgusted. "At least I can make a sentence."

The deputy turns to Ross. "Watch your tongue there, Injun. We don't cotton to you people nearly as much as our darky slaves and you know what happens to them when they talk back."

John is out of control, observing this revolting crime.

"You are the lowest form of life on earth. No, you're just stupid."

The deputy is unfazed. He walks out sporting a silly grin. "Well, if you survive your little stay with us, the soldiers'll be here in a couple of weeks to get ya. Till then, you and your friend can play checkers or somethin." The deputy slams the hall door.

John looks around the jail. All of the other jail cells are open and vacant. The entire area is filthy. He stands and walks to the bars. John look's sadly at the hanging corpse. He sees something in his tightly clenched fist. It's a glint of metal. John glances down at the lock on the jail door and then looks back at the glimpse of metal. He goes to the body. John grimaces from the stench as he pries the corpse's hand open. He takes a key from his fellow Cherokee. John turns and tries it on the jail door. The key turns and the door opens. John smiles and turns to the dead man. "Thank you, Brother."

He exits the cell and quietly walks to the back door. John tries the door it's locked. He moves to the front and looks through into the sheriff's office. He scans the room. He sees the big hunting knife lying on top of the desk and the sheriff's shotgun leaned against the same desk. He hears the sheriff excuse himself and waits patiently.

The sheriff slowly walks to his run-down shack a hundred and fifty yards away. John figures the sheriff is far enough down the road by now. He burst into the room and knocks the deputy out of his chair with his fist. John grabs the shotgun and points it at the yapping stunned deputy. "Don't shoot me. Don't shoot." Then John takes a thin bladed hunting knife from the desk. The deputies eyes get big, and he gets quiet.

John grins. "I won't shoot you, unless you force me, and I really hope you do, moss mouth. Get in the jail."

The deputy reluctantly moves into the jail cell with the corpse. John looks at the bloated dead man. He cuts him down and makes the deputy help him wrap the poor man in a blanket while holding his gun on green-tooth. John is sorry for the Cherokee man. "I'm sorry I have to leave you like this." He turns to the deputy. "You know, deputy, we Cherokee have a saying, "There are three sources of knowledge". I can tell you, you're not one of them."

Green-tooth is angry. "You ain't gonna get away with this, but hell, if you gotta leave me in here, give me somethin to breath through, the stink is awful."

John locks the jail door. "I may not get away, but you'll be here with my rotting friend to enjoy every savory aroma. Oh, I'm sorry, I forgot, you're ignorant. That means you are going to be here with the stink for along time. I just hope they take the right stinker when they come for you." He walks outside. John throws the shotgun and keys into the bushes and disappears in the dark forest. He blast through the deep woods breaking limbs and knocking leaves from the trees as he tears through the undergrowth. The Sheriff has heard his coon hounds bark and looked out the window to see John running through the woods. The over confident sheriff is caught totally by surprise. "That Injun got away, damn it."

He walks outside and takes his shabby no-name brand hat off. He throws it on the dusty ground. "Deputy Hogg's got some serious explainin' to do."

The Sheriff rushes inside the backwoods jail. He walks to the deputy sitting in the jail cell holding his nose. "You dummy, you let him go."

The deputy is glad to see his hateful boss. "Sorry, Boss. Git me out of here. The stank is dismal. The bastard surprised me."

The perplexed sheriff notices the smell has elevated from the body since John and the deputy moved it. He holds his nose to avoid the harsh odor. "Bein' able to open a pocketknife would surprise me about you."

The Sheriff unlocks the jail door with his set of keys. "Let's go!" They move through the office and grab a couple of shotguns from the gun rack and rip through the front door after John.

John has been running hard for an hour. He slows the pace and moves slower along a riverbank. John can hear dogs and people breaking through the undergrowth of the forest in the distance. He turns and crosses the shallow river. A few steps into the river and shotgun blasts ring out. They break the water next to him. John moves faster. He doesn't want to be caught by the ruthless Sheriff and his dull Deputy. Shots ring out around John again. The simpleton twins laugh and talk as they shoot at him.

John reaches the opposite riverbank. He scurries up the overgrown bank and disappears into the woods. The sheriff and deputy cuss and fire their weapons at the vacant woods. The sheriff laughs and yells out. "Run boy, run!"

The deputy grins. "Look at him go. Lickety split. "
John hears them laughing as he moves quickly through the thick woods. His breathing is labored as he blazes a difficult trail. Chief Ross runs hard for another two hours. He finally slows down and begins to walk. His side bursts with pain from running so long. John can hear the night creatures singing their song. He smiles as he walks. "What are you so happy about, Mr. Owl? You could be somebody's breakfast by morning." John sees a light in the distance. He walks toward it.

In a few minutes, John is close to the light. It's a busy wilderness tavern and John needs food and a horse. He is quietly happy about his find. John stops and quietly watches from the edge of the woods. Two drunken men come out, get on their horses and ride away. Then a Troop of four soldiers rides through the area and stop next to the Tavern. A Corporal dismounts and goes inside for a few minutes. He comes out with two bottles of whiskey. The corporal remounts and they ride away. John is relieved. He moves to the tap house.

John looks through a dirty side window. The boondocks bar is full of rustic individuals and frontier types. He's trying to decide what to do with no money and looking like he just got out of jail. They would probably know he's on the run right away.

John watches a drunk stumble out. The drunk notices him. "Hey, how are ya?" John nods. "Come on, let's take a ride toward home and have a drink." The drunk pulls a pint bottle from his pocket and takes a long drink. John smiles. The drunk puts his bottle away and gets on his waiting horse. "Come on." John gets on a horse next to the drunk, and they ride away.

The next morning, the two horses stand in a coral, and John sits on the front porch of the drunken man's house eating a biscuit. He stands and looks through the window at his sleeping friend. He steps off of the porch and walks toward a distant valley. John leaves the horse behind, he doesn't want to be known as a horse thief.

Later in the day John sits by a bubbling stream watching nature go by and collecting his thoughts. Suddenly a soldier yells out from a ridge above him to more troops riding up-stream from John. "There's one of'em. All of the soldiers ride at full speed toward John. He jumps up and runs as hard as he can go. A cavalry man bears down on him. John stops and turns. He screams and runs at the horse a few feet away bearing down on him at full speed. The horse bolts to the side and dumps his rider. John moves quick to the horse and grabs him as he passes. John swings up on his back and rides away. The rest of the troopers arrive too late. John is out of sight and out of danger for now. The worst of it, John had to take the troopers horse.

The next afternoon John arrives at his home. He waits in the tree line surveying the area. He sees Union soldiers camped around the front of his house and a white couple with six small children moving in. John contemplates for a moment and moves on.

The next day John stops at a watering hole to let his horse drink. He dismounts and gets down on the ground to drink from the pool. A wagon with white settlers comes around the corner. "Hey, there's the breed everybody's lookin' for."

The farmer pulls his rifle and fires at John. He hits a rock near him. John turns for his startled horse, but the horse breaks away and runs. Chief Ross is trapped. He stops and gives up as the farmer pulls his pistol out ready to fire. The farmer looks him over from his high place on the wagon. "Don't move breed. I'm comin' down there."

John stares at him. The farmer's wife tells the overweight homesteader to be careful. He stops in front of John, rifle drawn. "You don't look like no Injun bad man ta me. What they want you for?"

John answers. "Because I am Cherokee."

The man is confused. "Is there a bounty on Indians?"

John shakes his head, no.

The farmer doesn't want anything to do with him if there's no money involved. "Well, git on out of here. I ain't gonna hurt ya." John is a little surprised. He turns and walks away.

Five days later John is desperate for food. He stalks a wild turkey on foot and without a weapon. At the same time he grabs the bird a gray wolf grabs it from the other side. John holds on, the bird squawks and the wolf growls while he tugs on the wild fowl. John is disgusted having to fight everybody and now nature. He lets go of the immense bird and yells at the wolf. The startled wolf lets go of the turkey. The large feathered creature flies away. The angry wolf stares at John. He turns away and urinates on a bush before he trots away. "Same to you." John turns and walks through the massive stand of timber.

In a few minutes he comes onto an army camp setting at the foot of a valley, below him. Soldiers mill around the area going about their daily chores while guards walk the picket line. John is frustrated. He knows the region is full of soldiers looking for him and other Cherokee. John moves on. Late that afternoon John walks across a small open field. Suddenly from out of the woods five men wearing white sheets and hoods ride him down. They circle John with pistols drawn.

The leader nods at two of the men. The two men get off their horses and grab John. They roughly put a hemp rope around John's neck with a hangman's noose already tied at the end of the rope. The hooded men bind his hands behind him and get back on their horses. They lead John to a tree by the rope around his neck. The man with the end of the rope throws it over a strong limb. The leader speaks to John. "You got anything ta say, breed."

John looks at them with contempt and disgust. "Go to hell you murdering bastards."

The rider wraps the rope around his saddle horn and pulls John off of the ground. John struggles against the rope. He bows his neck hard for strength to keep from breaking his neck and to breath. The rider ties the rope off on a branch and they all ride away.

John kicks and struggles as he chokes. Suddenly the sound of the rope being cut is heard and he drops to the ground. John opens his eyes slowly, coughing and choking. He sees Sergeant Major Prince standing over him taking the noose from his neck. "We got here just in time, Chief Ross." He helps John get up. "Come on, let's go."

John rolls his eyes and weakly gets up. He is stressed further than he has ever been. John takes a deep breath and closes his eyes for a moment to recompose. He appears to be in prayer. A soldier brings a horse for John. Prince takes the horse. "You're lucky. We found this horse on the trail or you'd be walking."

John feebly shakes his weary head, the horse is the cavalry horse he had lost earlier. Prince cuts his chafed hands loose. They all mount up and ride back toward the stockades. The intense search for John's people is still underway by many infantry and cavalry units. The vigilance of finding Cherokee prisoners to take to the stockades has not let up. The sun sets over the stockades while Colonel Sevier brings in another group of two hundred prisoners. General Scott watches with Captain Cain. The strutting Colonel leads the slow-moving column past his commanding officer. His troops herd the Cherokee prisoners into the rustic log stockade.

Sevier turns and rides beside the general. He salutes and reports. "Sir, the last of them are being put in now. The count's around seventeen thousand. We'll be ready to start the removal to the Territories anytime after tomorrow."

General Scott is pleased, a low death count until now and all of the Cherokee are in place for the removal. "Very good, Colonel."

The Colonel continues his report. "Sir we had a soldier killed by a Cherokee man. We're holding him in Stockade Two."

This is not very good news for a smooth running operation and General Scott wants information. "Give me a full report?"

Colonel Sevier tries to make it routine. "The Cherokee claims a soldier was molesting his wife. They got into a fight and our man was killed."

The General wants to get to the bottom of this black mark on his operation. "Were there witnesses?"

The Colonel wants to dispose of the matter as quickly as possible.

"No sir, the three soldiers assigned with the dead man were not with him when it happened. The only witness was another Cherokee and you know Indians when it comes to protecting their own."

General Scott is unconcerned with gossip, he just wants the facts. "Is this man in custody?"

And that familiar phrase pops up. "Yes Sir."

The General wants this to end. "Do whatever it takes to get these people on the trail and end this disaster."

Captain Cain speaks up. "Time is short. Winter is coming."

The General does not appear to care. "We are not wintering these people." The Colonel agrees. Captain Cain nods.

General Scott feels it is a small issue and can be handled by his subordinate. "Just handle it, Colonel, today."

He complies with fervor. "Yes sir, right away." Colonel Sevier salutes and rides away.

The Colonel likes his new power. He rides like a strutting peacock through the gates of stockade number two. The stern officer stops just inside and gets off his spirited horse. Sevier looks at Sergeant Major Prince. "Sergeant, bring me the prisoner."

Sergeant Prince complies. "Yes, Sir." He turns to a guard. "Bring me, Ethan Springwater."

Two troopers go to a dark corner of the stockade and pull the well-guarded prisoner to his feet. Ethan is bound and gagged; dried blood covers his face from the beatings he has gotten while in the stockade.

The guards drag Ethan in front of Colonel Sevier. He looks at the sergeant and crows out an order. "Is this the man that killed, Corporal Conroy?" Sevier is playing the role. He's more than officer material; he's bound for politics.

Sergeant Major Prince goes along in a half-hearted manner. "Yes sir, that's the man."

The Colonel enjoys this pretension a little more. "Put him on the wall!"

The sergeant major is surprised. He watches as the stockade

guards drags Ethan to the log wall. A third guard drives a spike high in the wall, high enough to hook the prisoners rope bound hands over the rusty spike and leave him dangling in the air. The two husky guards hoist Ethan up and hook the ropes binding his hands over the spike leaving him hanging.

The ruthless Colonel watches smugly. The high burning campfires and the full moon illuminate Ethan's weak and bloody body hanging from the spike, it appears almost biblical. In contrast, the same flames dance over Colonel Sevier's stone face causing it to appear almost demonic.

He yells out another command. "Get ten Indians and ten troops with rifles and pistols."

The sergeant articulates those familiar words to comply. "Yes sir." He turns toward the fortress guards. "I need ten riflemen with pistols ready, now, let's go, let's go!"

Private Paine rushes to the sergeant. "Sergeant Major Prince, I saw the whole thing, that man was protecting his wife. The Corporal was beating and raping her in front of his child for God sakes."

Sergeant Major Prince is more worried about keeping his rank than saving the Cherokee man's life. He knows an order is an order and the Officers can sort it out later and not at his expense. "Private, unless you want to spend the next thirty days muckin' stables, you'll shut up. The Colonel won't like this."

Private Paine doesn't care, he persist. "But this ain't right! There's a man's life at stack."

The Sergeant realizes this conversation is getting too loud and taking too long. He will end it before there is another ordeal. "Private, I said shut your mouth, that's an order. I'll take your behavior up with Colonel Sevier when this is over. Get back to your post."

The Private is disgusted. He walks to the rear of the crowd of soldiers. More soldiers come in from outside the stockade gates and the guard shack. Ten soldiers gather and Prince positions them. The sergeant informs Colonel Sevier. "We're ready, Sir."

The Colonel pursues every inch of his new power. "Get the ten

Indians."

The sergeant turns to his troops. "Get ten bucks up here, on the double!"

The ten soldiers grab ten Cherokee men at random. Colonel Sevier shouts another order as they gather the men. "Line them up facing the prisoner."

Sergeant Prince looks at his men. "Do it!"

The ten Cherokee men are lined up firing squad style, facing Ethan. The arrogant Officer yells a strange order. "Give the Indians your rifles."

The soldiers hesitate. The Colonel is not happy with the hesitation. "Now!"

The soldiers give the ten Cherokee their rifles. The stockade guards stand ready as Sevier continues. "Now gentlemen, this is how it works. The Indians will get into firing positions. On my command, they will execute the prisoner with ten bullets in his body. If this does not happen, Sergeant Prince, your men will execute the ten Bucks. All of them."

There is silence as everyone contemplates this show of indifference. The Colonel brakes the silence. "Firing positions."

The Cherokee men in the firing squad hesitate. The soldiers cock their pistols and point them at the back of each of the ten Cherokee' heads. The Cherokee men raise their rifles and aim them at Ethan hanging on the wall. The riotous Cherokee prisoners in the crowd are held back by Stockade guards. They start to rumble and yell out to the soldiers and Colonel Sevier.

Quatie pushes her way from the crowd of Cherokee people and confronts the overbearing Colonel. "Stop this, it's insane!"

Sevier looks at her angrily. "This is an execution for murder, stand back or you'll be next on the wall."

Quatie yells out at the Colonel as she struggles against the guards. "It's wrong! This is murder!"

Sevier ignores her. "Sergeant!"

The sergeant turns and yells to the troops. "Company A, rifles ready, on the double!"

A column of soldiers moves into the stockade between the firing squad and the crowd of Cherokee being held at bay. Talmidge pulls Quatie back as the soldiers close in. Quatie desperately yells out again. "Murderers, you'll pay for this."

Sevier looks at her with disgust, then surveys the area. "Fire!"

A split second of silence and then a volley of ten shots break the silence. Ethan's body jerks as bullets rip into him and finally, a dying gasp as he wanes. The Cherokee firing squad is sad and looks down at the ground while they lower their rifles. Ethan's wife with their baby in her arms screams out in grief and defiance.

Quatie quickly goes to Mary and holds her while the baby screams. Tears run down Quatie's cheeks. She looks at the Colonel defiantly. Their eyes meet in separate states of defiance.

The Colonel glares at Quatie then looks away. Mary screams out and cries into Quatie's shoulder. "Ethan, Ethan!" She goes to her knees crying. Quatie is reminded, that could be John on the wall or maybe it has already happened. The soldiers stand firm as the crowd has a pushing match with them. Sevier looks at the crowd and speaks to his sergeant. "Bury him."

Sergeant Prince yells out to his men. "I need a burial detail!"

Colonel Sevier bellows. "Sergeant Prince." Prince looks at the colonel. "The Cherokee shot him, let them bury him."

Sergeant Prince makes the usual compliance. "Yes, Sir." He turns to the soldiers. "All right, have the bucks bury him. Come on, let's go, get him off the wall."

Colonel Sevier swaggers out through the stockade

gates, while in the background, Ethan's body is taken from the wall. The Cherokee people do not move. They simply watch with disgust and tears. The Colonel casually walks out. Murmurs are heard as he leaves. The crowd's dialogues overlap as they yell at the strutting Officer. "He was innocent. Murderer! Savage!"

Outside the front gate of Stockade Number Two, Sergeant Prince walks quickly after Colonel Sevier. He yells out. "Colonel." Sevier gives him an indignant look.

The sergeant corrects. "Sir!"

The Colonel's power is riding high, he looks as if he were dictating from a throne as he speaks to the sergeant. "What is it, Sergeant Prince?"

Prince walks close and speaks quietly. "One of the Privates at the killing says the executed man is innocent. I got him quiet, but he could be trouble."

Sevier spits out another profound statement. "Lock him up for the night. See if anyone else sees it his way, we'll transfer them out at dawn to another stockade."

At that point, the sergeant wishes he could go with Private Paine. He salutes and walks to the back of the stockade, looking for Paine.

Sergeant Prince finally rounds up the Private and discovers McGuire agrees with him. They both are jailed and held for a few days. As promised the colonel transfers them to another stockade. Out of his way and silenced.

Two post guards come for Privates Paine and McGuire. They are up early to be taken to their new duty station. The guards escort Paine and McGuire to their waiting horses. "You Injun lovers are gettin' transferred for kissin' up to the them blanket-asses."

Paine is insulted. "No, we got transferred for being honest."

The guard laughs. "Honest as the day is long. I've heard'em all."

The soldiers all mount up and ride out toward a distant stockade. They ride past a wooden rack with two Indians and a soldier tied to it with their backs exposed. A guard is flogging them for some unknown punishment. The soldier was probably derelict in his duty in some way, and the offending Indians always set a good example to keep the other prisoners in line.

One of the guards looks over at the Privates. "Must of stole some food?"

Paine and McGuire shake their heads as they ride. The young

soldiers pass another detail of working Cherokee men. They dig a long trench, a hundred yards long and chest deep.

Near their own stockade, Paine and McGuire pass a burial detail of two Cherokee digging a grave for another executed Cherokee man. They watch silently while thinking how sorry they feel for the Cherokee people.

One of the burial detail Cherokee speaks to a soldier. Before the Cherokee can get out of the grave they dug, the soldier hits him with a rifle butt. The two privates turn a blind eye to the scene and ride on.

In a few minutes they arrive at the front of their new home. The gates open, and the exiled Privates ride inside with their two armed escorts. The ambitious Colonel Sevier had already extended his method of execution.

"Tasli Charley had heard of General Scott's promise and voluntarily came in with his brother and two eldest sons to resolve the problems associated with the escape and Sergeant Norton's death. But the mold was set against all Cherokee."

Privates Paine and McGuire ride into their new duty station with the post guards in tow. A group of three hundred Cherokee gather inside the sparsely populated prison. There the familiar execution style was again. Ten Cherokee are lined up with rifles and ten soldiers behind them.

Tasli Charley, his brother and two sons stand, tied to the wall, in front of the Cherokee firing squad.

Private Paine can't believe the rerun he is seeing in front of eyes. "I don't believe this, these officers have gone crazy."

Private McGuire feels sorry for the Cherokee men. "They're probably no more guilty than that other poor devil."

They stop and listen. The guards stop beside them. A Lieutenant with the same career-building style shouts an order. "For leading the rebellion that resulted in the death of a United States soldier, it is the order of the area Commander, Colonel Daniel Sevier, you be executed by firing squad. "Sergeant, carry out the order."

Charley yells out to his people. "Never surrender, Never give up."

The sergeant looks at the young Lieutenant. "Yes sir." He turns to the Cherokee firing squad. "Fire."

The Cherokee firing squad reluctantly fire their weapons. Charley, his brother and two sons hang from the wall, dead. Tasli Charley's Eastern Band, however, lives on in the Cherokee hills of Indian Territory.

## CHAPTER SEVENTEEN

---

## CHEROKEE NATION, HINASEE STOCKADES COMMAND POST

### 1838

### A BITTER TRAIL OF TEARS.

Finally, after a long time in isolation at a distant stockade, Chief John Ross has made his way to the Command Post of General Scott. John is hopeful he will be able to insert his waning influence to stop the atrocities.

John and his guards stop their horses at the Post Commander's front door. His hands are bound with crude ropes. An obnoxious guard speaks to John. "Just stay on your horse, Breed."

General Scott's guard speaks to the lead soldier. "What do ya want Trooper?"

The guard is abrupt. "This is the breed chief everybody's lookin for. We had him over in Stockade Seven. The General wants to see him."

"Wait here." He goes inside the Command Tent. John Ross watches the entrance for a few moments. General Scott's Guard walks out. "All right, bring him in."

John's guard pushes him off his horse with his foot. He hits the ground hard. "There he is. All yours." The two Guards take John's horse and ride away into the darkness.

The General's guard helps John to his feet. "Those idiots. Come on. You sure don't look like any Indian I ever saw. You're awful white." The guard cuts his ropes loose.

John confirms his race. "I am Cherokee."

"Well good for you. Come on in."

The Guard escorts John inside the Command Post. Kerosene lanterns light the tent. General Scott sits behind a field desk with Captain Cain next to him. Colonel Sevier sits nearby eating and talking with Sergeant Major Prince. They all stop and look. The Guard stands beside, John. "Your Indian, Sir."

General Scott is cordial. "Thank you, corporal. That is all, resume your post."

He answers with that familiar compliance and leaves. "Yes, Sir."

General Scott gestures to a chair and gets right to the point. "Please, Principal Chief Ross, sit down. I understand you feel this action is illegal and unjust?"

Sevier stops eating and glares at John. He and Prince then continue to eat.

John Ross remains standing. "That's right, General. I am here to protest the brutal treatment of my people and the murder of an innocent man, Ethan Springwater. A man that simply was protecting his family from harm and his wife from being raped."

The General is more firm in his statement and less cordial. "I don't know how you know these things since you haven't been here. But if I were you Chief Ross, I'd guard my words. Murder is a very strong charge. We too have lost. We lost two troops to your people, in separate incidents."

John Ross is equally as firm in his rebuttal. "General Scott, the Cherokee are real people. They have been in the stockade for months and many have died from disease due to poor sanitation. We have feelings. We cry when our people die. We hurt when injured. Your State and Federal Governments have taken our freedom, our farms and plantations, our newspapers, our businesses, because White politicians wanted them for profit. Where's the justice in an eviction of convenience? A taking, because another wants what you have or an execution of convenience to quiet the adversary."

General Scott is frustrated, he simply chooses to terminate the conversation. "I don't worry with the politics of it. I carry out the orders."

John has a warning tone. "You should worry, general. It could be your family someday under a different general or a different government."

General Scott wants to end this conversation so he doesn't have to defend his indefensible position. "Your protest falls on deaf ears, Sir. We will remove the Cherokee to Indian Territory tomorrow. It is August now and if you don't get stated you'll be caught in November and December in those jagged hills in Arkansas and if it rains your situation will be much worse than now."

John sees he has lost his appeal, before he asks. He tries to get a concession that will help. "Sir, winter is coming, our people do not have clothing or food to make such a journey."

General Scott is persistent. "Chief Ross, your people will be removed under the provisions of the Indian Removal Act to the new Indian Territory, get your people ready to travel. We will not waste another day."

John pleads for his people. "Please general, reconsider. Allow my Minor Chiefs and me to supervise the removal. If we must go, let us take ourselves, at least we may forage along the way. I pledge to you we will go without incident."

General Scott hesitates for a moment and answers. "I will take your word, John Ross. Remember time is short. You must leave tomorrow without delay or all of your people will be caught in the dead of winter."

John is thankful for this small concession. "Thank you, General. We will be ready by tomorrow afternoon. I know many of my people will die on this tragic journey. But that is the albatross your government and Andrew Jackson will bear." He starts to exit the tent. "I have a last request, would you assign someone to help me find my wife, Quatie?"

Everyone is silent. General Scott watches John go. "Guard, take Chief Ross to Lieutenant Marshall and instruct him to find Chief Ross's Wife."

The Guard enters. "Yes, Sir."

The general is solemn. "Also, show Chief Ross around the stockades and help him find his chief's and make sure he gets supplied for his trip."

"Yes, Sir." The Guard leaves.

"Why would a man, only one-eighth Cherokee and wealthy to boot want to deal with a bunch of savages," asks the general.

Captain Cain understands John and is compassionate for the plight of the Cherokee people. "Because he's a leader and a man of honor that loves his people. Very rare in these times, Very rare in deed."

John rallies his people. They begin to line-up the large cargo wagons and get them ready for loading. The work horses and riding horses are checked over to be sure they are ready for the trip.

Meager supplies are loaded on the wagons, including beans, rice, flour and related staples. The fever of being free again catches on and everyone pitches in to help. The wagons are loaded in a few hours and the task of taking a census is under way by a group of Minor Chiefs. The Census will be used to account for the people and their properties on the trail and at arrival in the new land.

The Chiefs and John work through the night getting ready for the journey. Chief Ross wants to stop the immediate suffering at the hands of the soldiers and Indian hating officers. By the next afternoon they have had a chance to get a little rest and are ready for their long and fruitless journey. Thirteen thousand men, women and children are ready to leave.

John watches his people pack the last of their meager belongings. Sixty waiting freight wagons are staged and ready to move out. The Cherokee have gathered and are ready for the mass exit. Talmidge walks with John. "We are ready. You will lead the last group. We are going in phases of one thousand to keep the people organized and spread out on the trail to avoid congestion."

John is preoccupied with finding his wife. "Good, good, did you find, Quatie?"

Talmidge smiles. "We have, Bob Lowry is bringing her."

John smiles. "Such an English name for a Full-Blood Cherokee. Talmidge, have you heard anything about my sons?"

Talmidge smiles. "Yes they are safe in the new territory."

John smiles. "I can't wait to see them."

Talmidge nods and becomes sincere. "I think we make a mistake taking English names and their ways."

John reluctantly states what he knows is now the bitter truth. "No, they are now the wardens of this land. We must be as they are but retain our heritage, or we will have nothing and be nothing."

Bob Lowery, a jolly and robust Cherokee Man carries a bedroll as he walks with Quatie. She sees John and runs to him.

John turns to see his wife. She runs into his open arms. They kiss wildly. Quatie looks at John while he holds her in his arms. "I missed you so. The soldiers came on us like locust. I had no time to let you know where they were taking us."

John only hears his heart. "I thought I had lost you forever! What would I do without you?"

Quatie holds her lost love. "You'll never find out. We'll be together forever."

"Let's never be apart again, Quatie."

They embrace and kiss. John and Quatie continue to nuzzle and kiss each other. John is now forty-eight years old and Quatie is forty-five, the years have been good to them. They are in good health and still in love. Quatie becomes serious. "We must be strong for this journey. I don't want to lose you again.

John is confident. "We will make it."

Talmidge takes the bedroll from Mr. Lowery while they chat in the background.

John lovingly puts his arm around Quatie. They watch their

people move out on the first stage of their journey. They are loaded with only a few belongings and twenty odd camp dogs following the wagons.

Talmidge kisses his wife and child and watches them walk with the others in front of his wagon. He moves to his freight wagon already stage to move out with the group. Talmidge throws his bedroll inside, gets on board and drives his team of horses down the trail with the rest of his people. Mr. Lowery follows the wagon on foot.

A cold wind blows over John and Quatie. Quatie shivers and John draws her closer. She looks up at him. "I need to see my sons, take me to them."

He smiles. "I promise you will see them. I miss them too."

Talmidge yells back to John. "We will pick the rest of our supplies at Rattlesnake Springs, Tennessee then on to Oklahoma."

John nods and watches him move away.

Three horsemen sit on a ridge above the Cherokee's exodus. The men are General Scott, Captain Cain and Colonel Sevier. They watch with a feeling of relief. The General has an afterthought. "Hell is a place on Earth."

The Cherokee people soon realize this bitter path is truly a "Trail of Tears" as they travel to a new land that has been opened up for them in a place some call Oklahoma. The groups move slowly over across a long trail, across rough mountainous country crossing Georgia, Alabama, Tennessee and Arkansas and finally into Indian Territory bordering the west side of Arkansas. They have been on this harsh trail consisting of wagon ruts and sometimes cutting their own roads for almost six months, burying the dead every night. It is Early January, somewhere in Central Arkansas, the weather is cold and the winter rains have started. Cruel reality has set in. The caravan of Cherokee freight wagons travel slowly through a mountain pass. It is dark and a few of the wagons haven't reached the top of the mountain yet. The warriors have organized a security force to fend off robbers and gangs, but these warriors are more often used to help keep the wagons moving by getting them out of holes and deep ruts. The hard rain continues to fall causing wave after wave of water to roll down the trail. The people walk along the narrow mountain trail shivering from the rain and cold. The horse teams struggle to make it up the slick trail.

Mary walks with her child beside the heavy supply wagon still thinking about Ethan and grieving, keeping her footing as best she can. Abruptly the wooden wheel on the supply wagon breaks off and falls on Mary and her baby as they walk. The wheel knocks another woman and two children off the slippery bluff into a deep canyon. Screams are heard until they are abruptly replaced by the thuds of their bodies hitting the bottom.

Talmidge who was driving the broken supply wagon luckily wasn't hurt when he was thrown from the driver's seat to the floor of the wagon. He jumps down from his wagon and runs to check Mary and her baby. The baby is dead and Mary is waning. Talmidge cries as he places the infant to the side and covers his little face with a blanket. Quatie having seen what happened runs to his aid. Talmidge continues to check Mary as she gasps for breath. He says with a remorseful cry, "She's dead, now her whole family's dead!"

The Rain is almost blinding. Quatie puts her arm around him and says, "I know, Talmidge. I'm sorry, but we must get help. Don't slow down, we've got to get to the mountain top or it'll be a month through this mud."

Two people stop to help. Others struggle past on foot in the background not realizing what has happened in the heavy rain. Talmidge is almost crazed with guilt and pain and shouts, "The White Government caused this." Thunder and lightning roll across the sky.

Quatie consoles him. "I know, I know. I guess our land was more valuable than our lives."

Talmidge's grief shows like a light in the dark. He stands as eight more Cherokee men gather around the wagon. A man yells out. "Grab the wagon, and heave. Talmidge, you pull her out from under the wagon."

Talmidge positions himself to pull. The Cherokee man yells. "Heave!"

The men raise the wagon. Two others raise the wheel that was half way under the wagon. Talmidge pulls Mary's crushed body from under it. Quatie tenderly puts her hand on the dead woman's forehead as Talmidge picks her up in his arms. Quatie takes her hand from Mary's face, she says, "You're better off, Mary."

Talmidge lays her on top of the canvas-covered supplies in the wagon as the men drop it back to the ground. He looks at Quatie with tears in his eyes. "There are no blankets to cover her."

Quatie knows she must be strong and show her old friend that strength. "I know, Talmidge, but we must get to the top. If we hesitate now, we'll never make it to the new land."

He acknowledges and pulls tools from under the wagon seat. He yells out over the rain to the waiting men. "Somebody help me with this wheel." A Cherokee man grabs the tools and starts to work. The other men raise the wagon and Talmidge puts the wheel on a large threaded stem that holds the wheel in place. The man with the tools puts a new bolt on the stem and hand tightens it. The men let the wagon down and the man with the wrench tightens the bolt on the stem.

Quatie shivers and walks on as the cold rain pours over her. The first group of wagons have made it to the top and set up a makeshift camp in the nearest clearing. Wagons are pulled into a circle and a large piece of canvas over the center creating a shelter.

Hundreds of makeshift tents have spouted around the mountain top. Some are simple blankets over tree limbs, all with people huddled together, trying to stay dry and warm in the cold.

John walks across the grounds toward the wagons. He turns as he feels Quatie's presence. She walks up the trail with twenty stragglers. Quatie turns to look at them and shout encouragement. "Come on you can make it!"

John rushes through the mud and rain to Quatie. He moves past six men digging shallow graves. Bodies lie around them waiting for burial.

John stops in front of Quatie. The stragglers walk past. Quatie looks at him, then at her people and continues to encourage them. "Get under the cover, I'll be along to help in a few minutes."

Quatie turns back to John. Her eyes have dark blue circles under them and her face is pale. Quatie's lips quiver. "John."

John has the look of alarm on his face. "Oh my God, Quatie, what has happened?" He embraces her. "Let's get you someplace warm."

John walks with Quatie looking for an open spot, out of the driving rain. They walk past the wagons where people huddle under them. All of the spaces are packed and their clothes are soaked. John supports her while he looks as they walk. John and Quatie pass by the last wagon, Edna yells out. "John!"

John looks. He sees Edna with three children and an old man. She holds all of them huddled under a blanket. Water pours from the wet blanket. All of the people around them sit in mud.

Edna speaks to John again. "John, take Henry." John and Quatie walk closer. Edna cries. "Take Henry to the grave site, he died, he just died. Be gentle, we'll take Quatie and you when you get back."

John feels he has been blessed by this small gesture. "Thank you, Edna. I'm sorry about, Henry."

John pulls Henry's body from under the blanket. Quatie shakes as she takes his place. John tries to comfort Quatie then leaves with Henry's body. "I'll be back, Quatie. I'll be back."

John puts Henry's body over his shoulder. He carries him to the gravesite and drops poor Henry in an open grave filled with water. John tries to push mud in over his body but he has no shovel. John is frustrated and makes a final, futile effort to push more mud into the grave with his bare hands. John stands and walks almost defeated back to Quatie.

Quatie sits on the wet ground and shivers uncontrollably from the cold. She hears a young girl crying from the pain of a difficult pregnancy. Quatie looks around and sees the young girl trying to have her baby in the confined quarters. People are cramped in around her; wet, cold and crying.

Quatie weakly crawls through her people to get to the suffering girl. She stops in front of the young woman. "I'll help you."

The pregnant girl welcomes Quatie. She cries and gasps for breath while Quatie comforts her. "Just relax."

Quatie feels under the young woman's dress and finds the baby's head crowning. Two old women hold the young woman's back and assist her. Quatie begins to direct the young woman's birthing. "Help me, your baby is coming. Push harder."

The birth mother pushes hard. "I'm trying, I'm trying."

Quatie smiles weakly, thinking of her own son's births. "There it is."

Quatie pulls a screaming baby girl from under the young woman's dress. She, as is Cherokee tradition, bites the birth cord to sever it from the baby. Quatie smiles triumphantly. "It's a girl!"

The new mother smiles weakly at Quatie. "Someone get a blanket and dry the baby off." Says Quatie.

A young boy gives Quatie his coat for the baby. He shakes from the cold. The two old women lay the baby down and cover her with the boy's coat.

Quatie lifts the baby and lays it on the young woman. The old woman speaks. "I will take the baby, she is gone and the baby's father is dead."

Quatie looks at the old woman, then at the young woman's body. Quatie echoes an involuntary statement. "A life for a life."

The men begin to remove the young woman's body. Quatie watches with a glazed stare as they take the young woman away. She shivers violently from the cold.

Quatie moves back to her place. The others look at her through hollow exhausted eyes. John sees Quatie, she shivers and coughs. John takes his coat off and puts it around her. He embraces her. Quatie speaks softly to her husband. "John, I'm afraid, I feel cold and hollow."

John holds her tighter. "It'll be all right. We'll be in the Territory soon, and get you back into good health. Hang on, just hang on."

John is afraid for Quatie. Tears roll down his cheeks while he silently holds his dear Quatie closer. Babies and young children cry in the dark and cold background. John knows it is imperative that he shows strength and set an example for his suffering people. He doubles his effort to not show a vulnerable side.

It's a bitter cold night and impossible to stay warm. All of the wood is wet. There are no campfires that night. All they do is try to stay alive.

Finally the sun comes up and it stops raining. John wakes up still holding Quatie. A few people are milling around trying to prepare for the day. They are working at getting campfires going but it is a difficult task, especially in the morning's raw cold.

John shakes Quatie and tries to wake her. "Time to get going, Quatie. Come on, Honey! Wake up. Quatie!" John turns her face and looks at her. Her eyes are closed and her face is cold. He puts his cheek close to her mouth and nose to check her breathing. John is shocked. "Oh Quatie, Dear Quatie." John openly cries. He holds her tight and mutters. "God, why must we suffer so?"

The people begin to notice John and look at him. John picks up Quatie and carries her past his people to the mass grave site. They are sad and they feel his pain. He stops at the grave and lays Quatie tenderly on the ground and fixes her wet hair.

John stands and grabs a shovel sticking in the muddy ground. He starts to dig. Talmidge steps beside him. "Let me help, John."

John looks at him. "Thank you, Talmidge. But we have others to consider."

John stops and looks back with Talmidge at the other people standing in front of twenty more graves. A gust of wind cuts through the forest behind John. He turns and looks. The wind whisks the dew drops off the winter tree limbs. As the drops touch the ground, a blanket of glittering silver light floods the forest floor around Quatie's body.

Everything appears frozen in place. John's anger is gone and he feels a peace. He will never forget the horrible things that have happened to him and his people, but at least he can deal with it now. A sense of a presence comes over him as he looks at the scene. He feels someone or something is there he just doesn't know what. A large bald eagle flies low overhead and shrieks.

Quatie's mystical, windblown image comes into focus as it rises from her body. John watches with reverence. He hears Quatie's voice. "John, I love you."

He continues to look toward Quatie's image and call her name. "Quatie."

Talmidge, not seeing Quatie, thinks John is just grief stricken. He puts his arm around his friend John trying to console him.

Quatie's image dissipates as John watches. He hears her soft sweet voice. "I'll always love you, John." The powerful eagle flies over John again, soaring lower near him. It shrieks, then soars into the low clouds.

He looks at Talmidge's sad face. John looks back at Quatie's grave site and decides his mind is playing tricks on him. He glances toward his people as they go about taking care of their families. Talmidge consoles John by putting his hand on John's shoulder. John wonders if he actually saw Quatie's loving image appear where the eagle disappeared into the clouds or was he just hallucinating in his moment of grief. Thunder rolls through the clouds. He feels her spirit connect with his. John gazes back at the camp. Ten people carry their dead to be buried near his beloved Quatie, the first lady of the Cherokee Nation. "I will come back for you dear Quatie and put you in a better place."

With this sad memory the old chief becomes lost for a moment then continues his story to Cal Chase. "Women of the Cherokee Nation were honored counsel. We valued and respected their opinions. They gave us great strength in the best, and the worst, of times. My beloved Quatie was that and more, and I did come back for her and gave her a proper burial at the Mount Holly Cemetery in Little Rock, the Capital of Arkansas."

The rest of the trip is as bitter as any other part of it; food is short, the weather is freezing and harsh reality has set in. Two more months pass and they finally arrive in the new Indian Territory.

Even though it's cold, the new Territory is inviting and there are no Indian hater's. The lush valley's and winter grasses stretch for miles and crystal clear water is plentiful. They were finally home!

# CHAPTER EIGHTEEN

## NEW CHEROKEE NATION, OKLAHOMA TERRITORY

### 1839-1861

### RESURRECTION.

Five thousand, of the original thirteen thousand Cherokee Citizens survived the "Trail of Tears." The new arrivals pray for their new home and hope their fate is better. The newcomers relax for a moment in this lush valley of the new Indian Territory. They are thankful to be alive and hope this is a safer place. Two wagons are left and little food. John stops his column beside twin bubbling springs. The exhausted people gather around as they straggle in.

John walks past Edna. She reaches out and touches him. Two young women support her. John turns. "Is this to be our new home, Chief Ross?" Thunder rolls in the background and crackles in the hills.

John smiles and replies, "Yes Edna, you may rest now."

It thunders again. "John, you remember the omen, it's not over yet."

One of the young women puts a blanket over Edna's shoulders. John smiles and kneels beside her. "Rest now. There is no omen for our people, the thunder only warns us to be cautious on this new land."

Edna is direct. "Rest will not help this worn out old woman. I feel my end is near. I will meet the others soon."

John reminds Edna of her own strengths. "You are strong and you have survived a trip that many young could not."

She says, "I am glad our people have come from the fighting and greed of our old home to this new land, but we both know I am too weak to live. So, I ask you to watch over my grandchildren. The babies have no mother or father, you are the only one that can be sure they will have a family."

John realizes how realistic Edna is in her request. "I will Edna and God will be with you."

The three children, ages, two, three and five years old play in the background. Edna is encouraged as she looks at John standing there watching her grandchildren.

John walks a few steps to a nearby wagon. He gets up on the bed of the carrier and stands. John waits for the last few stragglers to walk in. He begins to make an important   speech inspired by Edna. "Cherokee, you have survived a treacherous Trail of Tears. We will rebuild our Nation starting today."

"Our Nation has many orphans, young and old, from this bitter trail and the wars. They are our heritage and the seed for the roots of a new Nation. Take them in and care for them."

"The greed of the Georgian Government drove us west to this land called Oklahoma. In driving us here they have killed more than half of our people."

"Don't despair, we have come to the end of our poor journey. The Ridge group has arrived before us, and they will help you settle. Don't hold back, even if we disagree they will help you. We are all Cherokee. We settle here! Our Nation will survive."

John Ross looks around, he sees the two springs bubbling from the ground making a stream that runs into the forest. "We will call it Tahlequah, two is enough. Yes, Tahlequah. We will build a great capital city, here in this new land. Our people have waited a long time to be free and independent, to live free from fear and want, to be Cherokee and live the Cherokee way. The time is now. Our city will have Government, industry and banking, but most important of all, freedom."

"Start your farms, build your buildings, a new way of life has begun for you. We have been on a race for survival. That time is over. We have now a more urgent time and we must press forward."

"We will build better. We will manage better. Our new Nation will be more than ever before. We must be victorious in our new Promised Land. Let us pray for our future!"

John puts his head down. The people join John in prayer. "Dear God, bless our people. Help them through their many tribulations. Bless them in their hour of need, amen."

John looks up and smiles. "You are the blood of my blood, brothers and sisters."

The Cherokee cheer as loud as they can in their weakened state. John gets down and starts

unloading the wagon. In a few minutes John feels a chill as he looks toward the nearby forest. He sees a shadow ripple past a tree in the forest.

John hesitates then walks past his people, blind to their existence, and into the forest.

He continues to walk and look. Suddenly a large Horned Owl flies past, surprising John and turning him toward a small grassy opening in the forest.

John steps into the opening. He is uneasy. "I feel you all around me, Quatie. I can hardly stand it, I miss you so much."

John's eyes are filled with tears. He hears a faint roll of thunder. He ask, "What does this mean? If it is you show me, give me a sign." The gray sky gets brighter. John's eyes search the clouds and he sees a beautiful white light sculptured in the image of Quatie.

He hears her voice. "I love you, John. Don't cry for me, I am home. I wait for you my love."

John looks on with tears running down his face. "I am so sorry, Quatie. I miss you so much."

A gentle breeze blows over John as Quatie speaks. "Be strong my husband."

Quatie's image brightens. John is desperate. "Quatie, I need you."

Her image fade as she speaks her last words. "I am here for you my love."

John looks almost frightened. "Don't leave me."

Although he searches for her, John knows Quatie's image is gone. He stops and composes himself, not sure of what has happened. John speaks to himself, hoping it is really Quatie and she can hear. "I don't know if that's you Quatie or my imagination. If it's really you, please give me a sign."

John looks and waits believing in his feelings, but nothing happens. As he begins to leave sunbeams break through the clouds. John feels a renewed sense of confidence and walks back to camp.

Old chief Ross reminisces to Cal. "You know, in those days, I felt so good about our people and their future. But, as the city began to build, our people remembered their past."

John recalls the beginnings of a bustling city. A small municipality of five buildings and the people are busy constructing six more new buildings. John then says, "But, they were thirsty for revenge against The Ridge faction for signing the Dirty Papers treaty. A group of Cherokee went to John Ridge's home."

John paints a fresh vision for Cal, how it was that brutal day. A group of twenty Cherokee wearing black hoods ride to John Ridge's home. They dismount and quietly surround the house without John Ridge being unaware anyone is there. He is alone in the house, his family having gone to visit his mother.

Two men burst through the front door with their pistols drawn and order John outside. He knows why they have come. "Have you come to kill me for signing the treaty?" The two men nod their heads; yes. "I signed it to save our people," says John. The men push him through the doorway and outside.

They drag John to the middle of the front yard and surround him.

Two other men push him to his knees. A third speaks to him. "For treason against your people, you are ordered to die for your crime."

John Ridge is erect on his knees. "I have done nothing wrong. All that I have done is for you."

He is brave. John looks up to them not for mercy, but for justice. "You are wrong about me. I forgive you." First one then another of their knives stab him; eventually he is stabbed more than twenty times. A brutal assassination. These men wanted to send a powerful message about acting outside of Council rule. The secret organization mounts up and rides away. John Ridge's body lies crumpled on the cool ground soaked in his own blood. He gasps his last gurgling breath, and it is over.

The old John Ross comments to Cal. "A secret organization killed him for treason. I understand this group felt they were protecting the Cherokee Nation from any further destruction, like the trail of tears. Many thought I had this done, but I do not condone assassination. The angry group felt that the men that signed the Dirty Papers Treaty to remove us, had killed the Cherokee people as if they had taken a gun to our heads. But John Ridge's death was not enough to pay the full price. They wanted more blood"

A different group of five men wearing the same black hoods rode many miles into the country to find Elias Boudinot working in his yard. They ride through the yard and surround him with their horses, pistols drawn. Three men holster their weapons and get off of their horses. Elias looks at the men. "What do you want?"

The front man answers. "You have committed treason against the Cherokee Nation."

"I have done nothing against the Nation."

Elias tries to break and run. The three men draw their hunting knives and stab Elias to death. As Elias drops to the ground dying he gasp his answer to his executioners. "I am guilty of nothing."

A man looks down at him. "You killed half of our Nation when you signed that treaty." Elias slides to the ground and dies.

John continues. "The group sends more agents to dispatch the

200

last man." While he speaks, he envisions the execution of his dear old friend.

Major Ridge moves slowly down a wooded country trail on horseback. He is going to visit an old friend in the next town. Major Ridge can hear unusual noises in the forest; he tries to observe their origin inconspicuously. He stops at a small shallow stream that trickles across the road to let his horse drink. Major Ridge is suspicious. There is too much noise and too much movement in the forest.

Major Ridge again sees movement in the forest. He draws his pistol and scans the woods. Out of sight five hooded gunmen steady their rifles each aimed at Ridge. Suddenly everything is eerily quiet. Major Ridge cocks his pistol. His eyes search for movement. Shots ring out from the thick woods. Major Ridge is hit five times in the head. He falls into the stream, dead by the assassins bullets. The last deed of revenge is done. Major Ridge had predicted his own demise at the Dirty Papers treaty-signing.

The Ridge did not show up at his friend's house where his brother waited for him. The friend and his brother split up to find him. The next morning Ridge's brother, Stan Watie, found his shattered body and took him to the local grocer/merchant and undertaker. Major Ridge's body then lies in state in a side room, off the General Store.

Major Ridge's rich and influential beloved brother stands over him. He is dressed in an expensive suit that shows the trappings of his wealth. Many people of the town gather to see Major Ridge. They stand around waiting and watching.

Stan Watie looks up from his brother and yells out. "I'll pay ten thousand dollars for the killer of my brother." The crowd is silent. They ignore him. Stan angrily walks out. The most powerful warrior of the Cherokee Nation is gone forever. The sound of thunder rolls through the mountains.

John tells Cal how this irreversible act affected his Nation. "This political revenge set the stage for the split of our people. Stan Watie hated me because he thought I was responsible for his brother's death.

He was rich and powerful. Stan lobbied everybody that would listen to join him against me and the Council."

"I went to a friend that had supported me many times, old Sequoyah. He joined me and started making speeches all over the Nation to heal the hurt and unite us again."

"His bold support through our new Cherokee language
newspaper kept the peace and advanced the effort daily. Sequoyah was truly a great man and he loved his people."

John remarks about white settlers building homes near the new Cherokee Capitol City. "As we progressed, White Settlers began to build near our thriving Capital City. We didn't fear their encroachment, because we had decided to make commerce of it, instead of the traditional land grab of the Whites. We sold property to the most trusted ones.

Due to the revenue from this and other land sales, construction of many Cherokee Government buildings was possible. We developed our Nation on a Democratic scale and built a building for a Supreme Court to handle Cherokee Nation legal affairs."

"We soon needed more housing for our legislative branches of Government. Two long log cabins were constructed. "These were the houses of Government for the Cherokee representatives. Our National Government was fashioned after the United States legislature.

Soon we found that outlaws gravitate to prosperity and with laws come the need for prisons. We built the Territorial Prison in eighteen-forty-eight, and prosperity was at a high."

John looks back to the last jewel in the crown of the
Cherokee Nation. He can see the construction of more Tribal Offices. "And of course we needed offices for National Diplomacy and a Treasury."

"By eighteen-fifty-nine, Cherokee farmers plowed many fields and raised bumper crops. Large plantation houses sprang up, busy with people working the fields. Cherokee ranchers grazed cattle on the plentiful grass, and every industry progressed on high."

"As the industries grew, a community began to grow. People built beautiful homes in the suburbs of the Capital city Tahlequah. As the Capital grew, it established several Cherokee national office buildings like the Supreme Court, The territorial prison and a treasury. It was not long until private retailer's sprouted businesses in the heart of the Capitol City. Commerce was growing everywhere. We then named the affluent suburb of our capital, Park Hill, bedroom community to get away from the hustle of the busy capital city and a retreat for the more affluent Cherokee families. Park Hill had beautiful white southern homes, and that style of architecture influenced other buildings. This southern style of architecture was carried over from our life in Georgia, just a little piece of our ancestral home."

A new manicured dirt street landscaped with red roses marked the main business and residential boulevard of the community. The tailored street was lined with new wooden sidewalks and vegetation. A small, elaborate bank distinguished the center of the city, marked by a proudly worded sign, "Park Hill Bank, Cherokee Nation."

John Ross walks across the main street of Park Hill toward his new home. Stan Watie and a group of twenty Cherokee soldiers from his private army stop him midway. "Ross, you are responsible for my brother's death and I mean to have him avenged."

"I assure you Stan; I had nothing to do with it. Major Ridge was my friend."

"If I find out otherwise, I'll come for you."

"You come, it'll be a mistake."

Stan and his Cherokee soldiers continue down the main street. John walks on. He remembers his home and city. "In Park Hill people walked the streets proudly and safely. It was a beautiful community, and I was not going to allow it to be destroyed by rebels. The Cherokee Nation was alive again and Park Hill flourished."

"There were National Balls, and social affairs. Success was everywhere, and the people were happy."

Trouble looms in Stan Watie's anger and suspicion. His

actions create political conflicts with the Ross faction and Cherokee Council. Stan's private Cherokee Army of two hundred has grown to one thousand, outside of Council Rule. Watie rides everywhere flaunting his power. The real reasons were not yet apparent.

John Ross continues in contact with the Cherokee people. He often speaks from a podium in front of the new Capitol Building to groups of Cherokee Nation citizens, red and white. Talmidge is still a close friend that lives just down the street from John in Park Hill. John tries hard to keep them united at these rallies. His old friend Sequoyah often speaks with him in support of John and the unity of the Cherokee. The Nation is gaining strength.

John rushes his people to succeed. The race is on to build the Cherokee Nation back to a powerful force, an entity to be reckoned with. All of these things in hopes of being able to reside in peace.

Unfortunately by eighteen-sixty-one, a Troop of Union and Confederate cavalry had clashed near the Territory and the Cherokee Nation was being pulled into the Civil War of the United States.

The Cherokee desperately want to avoid another war. They have been in a state of war for the last one hundred and fifty years and their new lives are finally good.

War has broken out all over the South, and is moving toward the Indian Territories. The Cherokee are determined to remain neutral, but Stan Watie and his followers threatened secession if the Cherokee Nation doesn't agree to support the Confederacy. Trouble boils and the old factions have surfaced again.

John and the Council petition the United States Army to protect them while they prepare to join with the Union. But there was no response and the Confederacy hovers nearby. The Confederate Army is ready to burn the Cherokee Nation to the ground if they make the wrong decision.

Stan Watie, being a wealthy slave owner, has always favored the South and his need for an Army is now apparent. Mr. Watie becomes politically stronger each day; the Confederacy promotes him to General in the Confederate States of America Army. The new General proudly rides at the front of a column of his new Cherokee

Confederate cavalry.

Pressure from the South grows stronger and the Cherokee Council hotly debates the choice: Union or Confederacy. Neither alliance is ideal, but survival is the name of this ancient game.

At every corner, Stan Watie applies political pressure with full support of the Confederate States Government. John Ross is finally pushed into a Confederate allegiance after many failed attempts by he and his Council to get Union Army support.

A few days after John's announcement of Confederate alliance. John looks out the window of the Cherokee Council meeting chamber located in the first floor of the Cherokee Treasury office. He can see Stan Watie riding at the head of his column of Cherokee Confederates. They stop, in formation, and General Watie dismounts. He walks toward the Council Chambers.

John turns to two more Confederate officers waiting with him. They exchange pleasantries and sit at the conference table with the Cherokee Council.

Stan Watie walks into the room. He smiles and nods to the gathering. "Gentlemen, I came to see history made this day." A Confederate Colonel sitting near John pulls out a chair for General Watie.

The Colonel turns to John and pulls the Confederate agreement from his leather dispatch pouch and lays it in front of John.

John hesitates. He looks at the Council, then to Stan Watie and the Confederate Officers. "This day is a day of bittersweet destiny for our Nation. I sign this under protest in the name of the Cherokee People." John Ross signs the allegiance to the Confederacy. A ceremony that he hoped would never be.

Clearly for John Ross and the Cherokee Nation the political die is cast. They must comply with the Confederacy. There is one hope. Maybe, the Cherokee Nation won't get involved. Most of the fighting is in the South. John can't help but think about the long overdue justice coming to those states that helped kill his people with the

"Removal Act." Justice is coming, and he for one is glad.

The renewed Cherokee Nation continues its prosperity during the brutal combat that rages throughout the South. They had reluctantly supported the Government that enslaves its own people. This was not the way of the Cherokee. But the alliance has forced the Cherokee Nation to admit that some Cherokee own slaves and are loyal to the Confederacy.

Even with all of the political disasters that had befallen John and his people, the beautiful Park Hill was always a refuge for him. It was his distant haven from the turmoil in his life, and it consoled his in the times he missed Quatie so much.

# CHAPTER NINETEEN

## CHEROKEE NATION, OKLAHOMA, PARK HILL

### 1861-1864

### BEGINNING OF THE END.

It's a late night in Park Hill, in the spring of eighteen-sixty-one. People in Tahlequah and Park Hill are jubilant it is like the Civil War is a million miles away. The war has just started and has had just a few conflicts, all in the Virginia area well over a thousand miles from John's people. So far the Cherokee have been left out of the fray, and John is glad.

A Cherokee Government Ball is in progress. Men are dressed in suits and Confederate Uniforms. Ladies wear beautiful ball gowns. Many Cherokee and White friends socialize while well-dressed waiters serve punch and champagne.

The ballroom is decorated with fresh roses cut from the streets of Park Hill. Discreetly, several shadows ripple across the large patio window that is lit from an outside plaza light. The shadows move past a set of double French doors as they continue to circle the building.

John Ross moves around the ballroom greeting guests, he is feeling good and looking good for man seventy one years old, talking with them and shaking hands. A large white woman stops John and offers her hand, which he takes and holds for a moment. "Chief John Ross, I just wanted to tell you how beautiful I think your community is."

John is ever the diplomat. "On behalf of my people, thank you. We have worked very hard to make Park Hill a place of beauty, a place of serenity and particularly a place in a nation that we can be proud of."

The woman loves to talk and after all, she is talking to the Head of State, which for the social circle she lives in, is quite an honor. "Park Hill is just wonderful, why just last week I was telling my husband, George, that's George Tuller, you know George. I'm Marie."

John gently interrupts trying to get away so he can make his diplomatic rounds. "It's always my pleasure to see you again Mrs. Tuller."

Mrs. Tuller is totally pleased by that statement. "Well, likewise. I'm sure. Anyway, I was telling George, how I had been through this territory when I was a child. Let me tell you, it was so dull and frightening. Nothing but wide open spaces, but you have certainly brought culture to the wilderness."

John Ross politely listens to Mrs. Tuller while she makes her lengthy speech. He looks past her shoulder for a moment and sees Talmidge motioning for him to come over. John does his best to be courteous. "Thank you again, Mrs. Tuller, we are very pleased with our entire community. Now if you will please excuse me, I see a bit of business I must attend to." John Ross hurries over to speak with Talmidge.

Marie Tuller turns to a group of woman standing nearby. She abruptly breaks into the conversation. "Such a nice man." The women appear confused as to who she means. Mrs. Tuller continues. "I mean Chief John Ross, but you know he doesn't look like an Indian to me, I think..."

John Ross strolls over to his friend and extends his hand. Talmidge takes it with an amused smile and a knowing look. "I see you've met Mrs. Tuller, I thought I might help you out."

John laughs. "Yes, I've had the overwhelming pleasure."

Talmidge thinks the woman is funny. "She's nice, but that woman can talk. She cornered me earlier. I'm glad, I'm Indian and don't talk much, you know." He laughs.

John smiles. "She and her husband have been friends to the Cherokee for a very long time. I wonder how?"

Talmidge grins and says, "I'd bet when she was a child, if they stuck her in a corner, she'd talk to the wall."

John smiles. "What do you need a wall for?" At this they both chuckle.

Talmidge says, "Well John, I must go. Victoria has come down with a pain in her head that, she says is from not eating, but I think it's the champagne. I just wanted to say good-bye before we leave."

John smiles at his old friend. "Take good care Talmidge, and say good night to Victoria for me."

They shake hands as Talmidge leaves. "I will John, good night."

John watches him go and is enjoying a moment alone when, without warning, fifty Union soldiers burst into the room from every exit with rifles pointed at the party guests. At first there is pandemonium; there are screams and expletives, there are couples who were separated from one another shouting each other's names; there are Confederate soldiers and officers, some wild eyed other more calm, and then there is John Ross standing quiet and erect in this sea of noise and confusion. As the guests hasten to quiet an aging Union colonel struts inside past the soldiers. It's Sevier. The crowd is silent wondering what will happen next. The colonel belts out an order. "Shoot anyone that moves."

Colonel Sevier looks around the crowded room and his eyes meet with those of John Ross. "Please Colonel," says John, "don't hurt anyone, take the soldiers and me. We're the only political people here. The rest are citizens of this community."

The Colonel, recognizing John says, "The ever popular John Ross, token White Chief of the Cherokee. I'm going to take your advice, Sir. You're just the man I am looking for." Then without warning, Confederate General Stan Watie pulls his Navy Colt revolver and shoots Colonel Sevier. The Colonel falls to the floor.

General Watie and two of his Confederate Officers exit through the French doors and onto the patio fighting their way past two guards with four Union soldiers in pursuit.

The entire ballroom is still. A Confederate officer suddenly pulls his revolver and shoots a Union soldier. The soldier falls to the floor, wounded. The Union soldiers having held their fire until now begin to shoot into the crowd. People run and fall from the rifle fire. John Ross falls to the floor wounded. The seven remaining Confederate soldiers pull their sabers and pistols making a valiant attempt to fight. They are cut down by Union rifle fire before they move from their tracks. People run and scream. In just a few seconds the ballroom become a scene of terrible carnage, and the smell of gun powder mingles with the smell of blood. To everyone's surprise, the Colonel staggers to his feet and yells out. "Cease fire, cease fire!"

Sergeant Major Prince picks John up off the floor. Blood trickles down the side of John's head. The Sergeant cocks his pistol and holds it to John's head. "Sir, Ross is secured."

Talmidge and Victoria are brought back inside the ballroom and held at gunpoint by guards. They watch from the crowd.

The Colonel favors his shoulder where he was hit by the confederate bullet. He looks at Prince and John. "Take him out and chain him."

"Yes, Sir." He pushes John toward the door.

The colonel shouts another order. "Sergeant Major!"

Prince looks back. "Yes, Sir."

The Colonel is weaker. "Take command, keep that Indian chained until you get to Washington."

The Sergeant uses that familiar delivery, "Yes, Sir."

The Colonel gives a final order in the form of advice. "You must hurry, we're in Confederate Territory and I'm sure they've heard the shots. Probably on the way now."

Prince understands, but is more concerned about the Colonel. "Yes, Sir, I'll get you a doctor."

Sevier gives him a very military command. "Just go, Sergeant,

I'll take care of myself. Go now!"

Sergeant Prince responds. "I'll get him there Sir."

The Colonel acknowledges and wrenches from the pain as he watches the Sergeant leave.

The Union soldiers drag John from the house, and put manacles with chains connecting them on his wrist. Two soldiers wrestle him up and on a horse. Three soldiers mount up, a fourth mounts and looks at the Sergeant Major. "We're ready, top-sergeant."

The sergeant looks at John's wound as blood tickles down the side of his face. "It's minor, you'll be all right."

Sergeant Prince mounts his horse. "Move him out, back to our lines."

He rides out. The four soldiers follow with John in tow.

The four soldiers in pursuit of Stan Watie have lost track of him, and his men and have returned. The wounded soldier and Sevier are put on their horses, the forty-five troops are mounted and ride into the darkness with Colonel Sevier in command.

Prince and his men with John fade into the distance headed northeast for Kansas. After a hard five-day ride through rough terrain, John, Prince and four Union soldiers stop at a hitching rail in front of a Kansas border railway station. This remote railhead is used for security, many miles north of Park Hill outside of Indian Territory. All of the men are exhausted and trailworn.

The Sergeant dismounts. "Step down, Mr. Ross."

As John gets off his horse, the sergeant directs his men to their duties. "You men take the horses and report back to your post. Wire Washington I'm on the way with the prisoner."

A corporal acknowledges. "All right, Sergeant. Be careful, they may come after him."

Sergeant Major Prince appreciates has loyal troops and acknowledges the warning. "Thank you, corporal."

John and Sergeant Prince walk to the waiting train and get on board. As they move through the train car people stare at John's

211

chains. They sit down opposite each other, and Sergeant Major Prince says, "Mr. Ross, when the train starts moving, I'll take your chains off."

John looks at Sergeant Prince kindly and says, "Thank you, Sergeant Major."

The train begins to pull away from the station, John looks out the window sadly and watches as the train passes people standing on the station platform. The Conductor moves through the car taking tickets from the passengers with the call, "Tickets, tickets."

He stops and looks at John and the Sergeant Major. "Excuse me, Sir, but the Injun will have to sit two cars down with the livestock."

Sergeant Prince responds as John sits quietly. "What makes you think this man is an Indian."

"I know he's got light skin and all, but I know that's, John Ross. A drawin' of his face is in all the newspapers about him bein' the leader of the Injuns and them fightin' with the South. I got rules, Injuns sit in the livestock car."

Sergeant Prince gives the conductor a disgusted look. He says, "Sir, this man is a political prisoner of the United States of America, and he is a Head of State. I order you, with full authority of the United States Army, to give the proper respect and accord to this man."

The conductor is a little startled at the outburst. "Don't get all uppity," he says, "I ain't goin against all of that. Whatever it was you said, you got tickets?"

The Sergeant Major is stern. "Go on about your business, the paymaster in Washington will issue a voucher when we arrive."

The conductor just wants the sergeant out of his hair, what little he has left. "All right, all right, don't git goin' again."

He walks on. "Tickets, tickets."

Prince and John have a smile between them about the conductor. "I am sorry, Mr. Ross. Not everyone feels the same as people like him."

John replies, "Thank you, sergeant."

# CHAPTER TWENTY

## PARK HILL OKLAHOMA

### 1861-1864

### I AM YOUR SAVIOR

Everyone feels the pressure of this mammoth war. Time grows short for the Cherokee as the brutal combat of the war moves closer to them each day. Again, a massive race for their survival is happening with the primary difference from the past being the colors they fight under and against.

Sergeant Major Prince takes John's manacles off. John looks out the train window as the images of the trees and mountains pass by in the night. He thinks he sees a very slight image of Quatie, smiling at him. John draws comfort from her image and continues to watch as it fades away.

The train roars down the tracks passing herds of buffalo resting for the night the lush Kansas and Missouri prairie grasses. The train rolls into the night coming ever closer to its destination.

John and his captor spend three days on the train with several stops and changes. They finally arrive in the political city. The train rolls to a stop near a large sign, warning everyone who sees it where they are: Washington, D.C.

There is another sign back in the Cherokee Nation, it reads Park Hill city limits in the dim moonlight, and the Park Hill population is growing as a column of one-thousand Confederate Cavalry ride toward Park Hill. They stop at the outskirts of the town, taking stock of their situation.

The troops are dirty and dusty with the dust so thick that it is not possible to see rank or emblem. The Commander at the front of the column yells out an order. "Company A, move to the north and form a skirmish line."

An officer's voice sounds off in the distance. "Company A, move out." Three hundred men speed their horses to the north end of the city and take up positions as their company commander yells orders.

The Commander yells out another order. "Company B, split your columns and take the east and west."

Another officer's voice sounds off in the background. "Split columns, east and west, yoo!" Three hundred soldiers split their columns and one column rides to the east while the other rides to the west.

The Commanding officer at the head of the column, yells again. "Sergeant Jumper, your company will stay here for a rear guard. You follow me."

Sergeant Jumper says, "Yes, Sir." He gives the command. "Company C, form a rear perimeter.

The commanding officer yells out again to his best top sergeant. "Secure this area, time is valuable, Union troops may still be in Park Hill or Tahlequah."

Other sergeants can be heard in the background yelling orders while the companies of men move into their positions.

As they wait, there is silence. At close observation, it is not possible to tell who they are.

The mounted cavalry company at the north end of the city sits waiting as their horses fidget and snort.

A single horse's hoofs are heard on the trail speeding toward them. The Commander yells out. "Hold your positions. Let him pass."

A soldier in the same dusty condition as the troops he passes, rides hard from the northeast. He moves through the lines of the company at the north end of the town.

The soldier runs his horse down Main Street of Park Hill to the Commander and stops.

He speaks in a very low tone, while catching his breath. "Sir, Tahlequah has been secured. We control the city and its perimeter, including John Ross's offices, the Treasury, and all the access roads."

The commanding officer thanks the messenger. "Good work, Major. Relay my congratulations to the other officers. In a few minutes we will control our city again. Move out, Major."

The Major answers. "Yes, Sir."

He turns his horse and speeds back to Tahlequah. The Commander is alone with Sergeant Jumper in the middle of the street. "Sergeant, rifles ready."

The sergeant repeats the order to the men. "Rifles ready."

Nine hundred troops of the one thousand, raise their rifles to firing positions. The Commanding Officer speaks to Sergeant Jumper again. "Sabers."

The sergeant yells out to his men. "Sabers ready!"

The remaining one-hundred soldiers pull their sabers to the fighting position with a clang of unity. The Commander speaks directly to Sergeant Jumper. "Follow me, Sergeant."

The sergeant yells out to a small guard detachment of ten men. "Guide on me!"

The Commander moves his horse to the center of the small suburb. Sergeant Jumper and his soldiers follow, ready for combat.

The commanding officer stops his gray horse. He wipes his face with a bandanna then dusts off his uniform. The shining stars on his shoulders show the rank of General. He yells out to the people of Park Hill. "Your city is under the protection of the Confederate States of America."

The General turns in his saddle as he looks at the hidden community and continues to speak. "Don't be afraid. I am General

Stan Watie, and these troops are Cherokee. Resume your business, your Capital City is secure. I have assumed governing the Cherokee Nation by Marshall Law. After the Union Army is defeated, we will be given complete control of the region. Any Union sympathizers may surrender to any soldier and be guaranteed good treatment."

People look out the windows and doorways as General Watie coaxes them. "Come out and greet your army, your own people!"

The people slowly begin to walk out. Stan Watie smiles and yells for his Cherokee sergeant. "Sergeant Jumper!"

Sergeant Jumper appears. "Yes, Sir!"

Stan Watie is ready to relax the atmosphere. "Steady the rifles, post the guard and let the men socialize with their kin."

Sergeant Jumper shouts the commands. The horde functions in a smooth mode. "Rifles ready, sabers ready, too."

The rifles and sabers go down with a clang as they are put away. The sergeant completes the order. "Post your guards."

Fifty soldiers from each position ride away with unintelligible commands shouted in the background. Sergeant Jumper completes his commands. "The rest of you put away your horses, then you are dismissed to visit with your friends and family, dismissed!" The soldiers dismount and go about putting away their tired horses and visiting the towns people.

Stan Watie issues another command. "Sergeant Jumper, get a detail and build a big fire in front of John Ross's house." The sergeant is hesitant. Watie completes his order. "Find some cattle and pigs to roast, it's time to celebrate our victory."

The sergeant feels relieved. "Yes, Sir, right away!"

# CHAPTER TWENTY ONE

## WASHINGTON, D.C.

### 1864-1865

### POLITICAL PRISONER

John Ross thinks about Park Hill and his home back in the Nation. He wonders what has happened in his absence. John feels time is short for his people, if he can't find new allies.

Sergeant Prince and John Ross get off the train and are whisked away in the dark of the night by a Government carriage and Federal agents.

John wonders where he is being taken. Sergeant Prince is under strict orders of secrecy, and John is not able to get a clue from this good soldier.

They arrive in the heavily guarded government coach. Two armed government guards ride on top and two more on either side. The carriage stops and John looks out. The White House is in his view. It is heavily guarded and protected by ramparts that clash with the beautiful landscape.

The beauty of the White House and the trappings of war seem contradictory to John Ross. He says to himself, "This is the place where our people's problems started. This must be the place where they are resolved."

Sergeant Prince gets out of the carriage. Guards stand ready while John Ross exits. He looks around at the many wartime guards.

Soldiers are everywhere, enough to defend in a substantial enemy. All right here on the front lawn of the White House. Sergeant Major Prince says. "This way, Sir."

He follows the sergeant major to the front door. Two White House guards stand at attention on either side. The sergeant major stops in front of them. "This man is John Ross, we are expected."

The ranking guard knows his job. "All right, sergeant major. You and the gentleman stand by." The guard turns and goes inside. The second guard stands vigilant.

The sergeant and John have a few moments to wait, and for John to realize he is actually at the home of the President of the United States of America. The office that contributed to his people's poor situation. The guard returns and opens the door. "This way gentlemen." Sergeant Prince and John turn and follow the guard.

The White House Guard takes them down a long hall, the walls covered with pecan panels. They are led down other halls with other guards, and John and Sergeant Prince follow close behind their lead guard. Eventually they reach a door with guards standing on either side. Their lead guard speaks to one of the guards at the door and, after hearing a "come in," he announces the presence of Sergeant Major Prince and Principal Chief John Ross.

A kind and strong voice is heard from inside the study. "Thank you, Sergeant Major Prince. That is all. Give my regards to your family."

The Sergeant Major smiles as he hears the familiar voice of his Commander and Chief. "Yes sir, I will, Mr. President." Prince turns to John. "It's been an honor knowing you, Sir."

John and Sergeant Prince shake hands while John responds to his new friend. "It was my honor to know you, Sergeant Prince."

The sergeant nods his head as he turns and walks away. John enters the study. He is most pleased to see the man who goes with the voice, President Lincoln. The President stands and walks from behind his desk to meet John. "Principal Chief Ross, I've finally met the man I've heard so much about. Please sit down, I've been wanting to talk with you."

Mr. Lincoln shows John a pair of leather wingback chairs near a fireplace. They walk to the refined chairs and sit down. Mr. Lincoln gets comfortable and begins to talk. "How are your people faring in this dilemma of ours?"

John looks at Lincoln sadly. "I'm afraid, our future is very uncertain under these circumstances." They both contemplate for just a moment and then continue their conversation about the Cherokee Nation.

John Ross is unaware of events at Park Hill in which Stan Watie enjoys his moment of triumph.

Bon fires burn high with four cows and six pigs cooking on spits. General Watie watches his men laugh and talk with their people. He turns and stares into the fire.

Two soldiers ride in with torches burning and dismount. They extinguish the flames and carry the torches to a nearby holder and put them away. Stan Watie watches. Sergeant Jumper walks beside him. "You know, Sir, our people have adapted well to this occupation."

"Yes, Thomas. There is only one obstacle to total harmony." The Sergeant watches Watie. He picks up a torch and lights it in the fire. The General continues. "And that obstacle is terminated now, once and forever."

Stan Watie walks to John Ross's vacant home and breaks out a front window with the burning torch. Sergeant Jumper is dumbfounded. General Watie sets the curtains on fire. He walks to the next window and repeats the deed, then throws the torch inside the house.

Stan walks back to the main street in front of the residence to watch his old enemy's stately house burn. The crowd of people and soldiers don't move. They just look on sadly. Stan Watie says, "Burn in hell, John Ross."

Flames from the burning mansion fill the darkness. Sergeant Jumper walks next to General Watie and watches the burning house. He says to General Watie, "You have burned our Cherokee brothers home. Is this something we do to people of our own tribe?"

Stan Watie looks at Sergeant Jumper understanding his brotherhood with John Ross and detesting it. "Time is running out for both of us. The time is now for me. John Ross is a prisoner, his time has passed. If I do not take this nation and its power now, our way will end and the White government will rule.

John Ross scrutinizes his situation while looking out a window in the White House study. The President relaxes with him. John has a premonition that things are not well back at his Park Hill home.

President Lincoln smiles while he listens to John speak. John says, "You know our people favored the Union, but our Council could not get Union troops to defend us while we built our own army. The Confederacy lorded over us, ready to destroy the entire Nation if we chose the Union. So, I had to sign the Alliance after the Council approved it. If not, our Nation would have been destroyed, again."

President Lincoln is kind. "You are a great statesman, John. Your people should be proud. I am sorry we could not help in your hour of need."

A White House guard opens the door and walks in with a message. He hands it to President Lincoln and leaves. The President reads the short message. He gives John the news. "John, I had hoped this would be good news. I tried to negotiate a trade for prisoners and bring our soldiers home and send their boys back to them. One of the boys on our list serving with the Union was your oldest son."

John looks hopeful as the President continues. "But I'm afraid I have bad news, your son died in the Confederate Prison Camp fighting for our freedom."

John stares at the fire. He is stunned by the news. Tears won't come to his eyes. John is numb from the pain and anguish.

The old Chief relates to Cal. "As you may imagine, at that moment I was defeated. I couldn't talk or think."

John recalls to Cal fond times with his sons as they played on their lawn giggling and wrestling. The old Chief speaks to Cal in a sincere tone hoping to convey his feeling for his dear sons. "We were fortunate the boy's grandmother could see ahead and sent the boys ahead with my wife's cousins to the New Cherokee Territory hoping to protect them from harm during the round up. I missed them so much."

John gazes at Mr. Lincoln. He stands and walks out of the study in bewilderment. President Lincoln tries to console him as he walks away. John slowly walks down the long hall past the guards. One of the guards shows him to his bedroom. He stops and turns the knob on his door. It feels as if he isn't opening the door. It feel as if his body is moving without his conscious intent.

The room is lit from a high burning fireplace. The flames cast a shadow across the elegant wall and furniture. John sits silently in a corner grieving for his son. "God, why do you allow this? My people are good. My son did not deserve to die. The White government's kill us and kill us and kill us! Why are we being destroyed?"

John thinks he feels and sees Quatie's faint ghostly image surrounding him and embracing him. He hopes it is genuine. John surrenders not knowing if it is real or imagined. John feels comforted by her spiritual image no matter which it is. He blurts out a cry from his injured soul. "Oh, Lord, help us."

John is stronger. He pulls a tin-type picture from his coat pocket. In the picture Chief Ross sees his cherished Quatie and their two sons. A picture taken when the boys were very young, just after he came home from the Creek War. He makes a promise to himself. "I will right these wrongs, if it takes the rest of my life."

Quatie's image still surrounds John. She becomes a soft blue light and fills the room. John continues to be comforted by her real or imagined image. He sits back in his chair and closes his eyes. "Has our time ended? At least let me save the lives of the few that are left."

The next afternoon, President Lincoln and John have dinner together. Mr. Lincoln tries to cheer his new friend up.

The elderly John recalls that time for Cal. "Over a period of about three years President Lincoln and I became very good friends, and he truly understood the Cherokee.

"We had dinner one night and the next day I received the news that the President had been shot in the head. I was told he struggled for life, but it was not to be. Mr. Lincoln died and with him the Cherokee Nations hopes of survival. A quiet death at a coward's hand for such a great man."

Cal feels the regret. Chief Ross continues, "President Lincoln had promised not to treat the Cherokee as a conquered Nation when the war was over. But in his death our Nation's agreement was forgotten."

In short order the war ended, and Chief John Ross, Principal Chief of the Cherokee Nation and prisoner of war, was released.

General Stan Watie and his Confederate soldiers were finally cornered and they surrendered under a flag of truce to the Union Army.

Union soldiers massed in force, just to be sure old Stan didn't get any bright ideas.

After General Watie's surrender, the Cherokee Nation was charged with Crimes of Secession against the United States of America. The Cherokee, being a Sovereign Nation and not a state nor a part of the Union, fought the charges of secession. The Nation was never politically powerful enough to win. The Tribe, therefore, was caught in the middle of a bitter political battle to punish the South.

# CHAPTER TWENTY TWO

## CHEROKEE NATION

### 1865-1866

### SURVIVAL.

John hurries home to the Cherokee Territory in Oklahoma. He wants to negotiate a new lasting peace with the Government of the United States of America.

The elderly chief rides in his carriage with his driver. This conveyance was authorized by his former friend, President Lincoln. His driver is Master Sergeant Paine the young private that went through the Ethan Springwater affair, now much older, wiser, and married to a Cherokee woman. He and John Ross are having a friendly chat along the way about old times in the Cherokee Nation. The open carriage rolls along a dirt road, just outside of Tahlequah the Cherokee Capitol City.

It is the middle of the day when John's carriage moves through the suburb of Park Hill. He sits alone inside the carriage watching the scenery and also seeing the destruction of war. He passes an open meadow with over two thousand fresh graves. The sight of such needless death grieves him.

While on the road in Tahlequah, John sees a newly freed slave wearing tattered clothes. The now free man travels with his wife and four children walking beside the open road. They carry a few meager belongings. It makes John think, "This is another, 'Trail of

Tears' for a different people." He passes a Cherokee man with no legs sitting on the edge of the road wearing parts of a Union uniform. The injured man talks with a Cherokee soldier wearing a torn and battered Confederate uniform. John sits back in his carriage as he feels overcome with the sights of war. After a few more minutes of that kind of pain and need, they arrive in the business community of Tahlequah, many White men, Union troops and Carpetbaggers now occupy the Capital City.

John's carriage rolls past Union Army Headquarters. Two soldiers take down a sign: "Confederate States Army Headquarters, Cherokee Nation, General Stan Watie, Commanding."

John's carriage stops next to a large Union Army Garrison Tent with the sides rolled up. There is a long table and chairs inside. A Well-dressed man stands at the head of a seated group of politicians both Cherokee and White. John gets out of his carriage and walks inside the tent. The man at the head of the table, U. S. Government Commissioner Albert Blake, looks at John as he enters. "Be seated, Sir."

John acknowledges and sits down. Talmidge, walks in, holding papers in his hand and sits behind John. He leans forward and talks to John while the Commissioner speaks. "John," Talmidge hands the papers to him. "These are the papers of the Washington Committee on the Civil War. They leave us blameless."

The Commissioner begins to speak. "Well gentlemen, this is your demise. We, the United States Government, have charged the Cherokee Nation with Crimes of Secession from the United States of America.

Talmidge and John continue to quietly talk as Commissioner Blake continues his speech. "Thank you, Talmidge. I will have great use for this."

The Commissioner looks at John as he speaks. "The Government will appoint Elias C. Boudinot, Principal Chief of the Cherokee Nation."

Elias C. Boudinot, son of Elias Boudinot, signer of the Dirty Papers, smiles and acknowledges as the Commissioner continues his statements. "Your Nation will be split into two districts. It will be governed by Federal Officials, White men from Washington, D.C. and your new Principal Chief."

John Ross stands and interrupts, he is frail but up to this. "Sir."

The Commissioner is put out. "Please, no interruptions."

John is firm. "Sir, I must insist. I am the Principal Chief of the Cherokee Nation, elected by the people. I would like to make a statement."

Commissioner Blake is stiff and boring with a lot of mean mixed in. "Sir, you are not Principal Chief of the Cherokee, as you heard, you and your leaders are traitors to the United States of America."

John shows anger for the first time representing his people. "Sir, I am not a traitor nor are the other leaders of the Nation." He holds up the papers. "As this Federal Commission on Civil War crimes clearly states, the Cherokee Nation is exonerated due to their imposing circumstances during the war. Exonerated, Sir."

The high commissioner doesn't want to hear anything that will change his plans. More than that, he has a one-track mind and that impairs the process. Commissioner Blake lashes out. "Enough, I am the law in this matter, the orders I gave will stand."

John tries to reason with the bureaucratic commissioner. "Elias C. Boudinot represents railroad interests trying to cross our lands. You cannot expect our nation to get fair treatment under these circumstances. Surely you know he was a Confederate legislator and not elected by anyone."

The commissioner wants to end this appeal and proceed with his own plans. "I frankly don't give a tinkers damn, Mr. Ross. The Cherokee have put themselves in this precarious situation, and I intend to carry out all United States policies in this enforcement. You want it different, take it up in Washington."

John is disgusted with the bureaucrat Commissioner's privileged behavior. However, he knows this bureaucrat is right, and the cruel political game is now in play. John turns. "Excuse me, gentlemen."

John Ross pats his old friend Talmidge on the shoulder and walks from the tent. Three White settlers sit on a hitching rail making rude and vulgar comments to John as he passes. John opens the door of his carriage. While stepping in, he is interrupted by the colorful Colonel Sevier. "John Ross!"

John looks back at the colonel before entering the coach. His driver reaches for a double barreled shotgun. John looks at the driver. "No, Mr. Paine. That's Colonel Sevier, He's many things, but he will not murder without the law with him."

Sevier hurries as fast as a very old man can to the carriage. His limp slows him further, but a large hickory stick helps him walk. He stops beside the waiting carriage. "Mr. Ross, I have been your enemy for many years, but now I understand what my country and army has done to your people. I am sorry for my part in it. If Commissioner Blake has his way your Nation will be dissolved."

John wants to be kind to his old enemy but feels he must also be truthful. "Colonel, the time is here, our Nation will live or die based on our actions in the next few days. So many times before I thought this time had come, but when it really comes, you know the real moment of truth, and it is now."

Sevier appears to sincerely want to help. "We have fought through many wars. Our eyes have seen men shot to pieces and slaughtered by the thousands. I thought the removal from Georgia, and the brutal Trail of Tears, was the cruelest work of all. Now I think they will surpass those cruelties, if the men of Washington go unchecked. Don't let them do it, John. Life's clock is running out for us, but even at this late date I remain at your service."

"I'm afraid our only hope is in Washington. I can't stop it here. But, I am curious why you fought against us for so long and seem to fight so hard for us now."

"I confess over the years I have learned much about your people through my marriage to a Cherokee woman who I love very much. I now fight for our three Cherokee children. You're the only one that can do it, Chief Ross. I am here for you, but you must do it." The jeering settlers cast remarks in the background. Sevier turns his aging body to give the settlers a cold glance.

John Ross feels the union of his and Colonel Sevier's desperation to save their people from further brutal destruction. "All right, Colonel. I will do the best I know how."

Colonel Sevier backs up and smiles. "Old enemies or not, John Ross, I am now a steadfast friend."

John nods, gets in his waiting carriage and looks at his driver. "Please take me to the train station, Mr. Paine."

Sevier watches, smiles a little and yells out to John. "I'll see you in Washington! Talmidge Watts will be there too."

Mr. Paine turns the horses around in the road, and they move away. Colonel Sevier watches them fade into the distance. He turns and walks past the rude settlers. As the first one makes a new remark the Colonel knocks him out cold with his hickory stick and watches the heckler fall from his perch on the hitching rail to the hard ground. Sevier then takes another powerful swat with his stick at the remaining two as they run from his purposeful wrath. Sevier smiles and slowly walks on.

Night falls on Washington, D.C. at the Brown's Indian Queen Hotel. John and Cal have spent the entire day together, instead of the few minutes that John Ross had planned. But what a great day they have had.

John is very old and tired, but he is happy with his newfound friend. John says, "When I arrived here from the meeting with Commissioner Blake, I got only one concession from the White Government. They promised not to split our Nation. We would be left united in exchange for blind obedience. Their victory is harsh and remains harsh. The politicians are still intent on carrying out the full penalties for Crimes of Secession. A price we must pay for our part in this intrigue"

Cal can hardly let go. "I never dreamed an ancient Indian Tribe would be able to accomplish so much and come so far."

John is exhausted from his day of storytelling. "Ancient yes, ignorant in the ways of life no. I'm sorry Cal, but I need to rest."

Cal stands. "Chief Ross, I'm sorry I kept you so long. This story though, is more than a legend. It is a lesson in history about a great people. A people badly abused by the Government of this Country."

John is pleased. "Don't be sorry. I am glad you are the one I met to tell our story. Tell it for the people. Tell it for your mother and grandmother."

Cal walks to the door. "I promise, the public of the United States will hear of this."

Chief Ross is very pleased. "Someday, Cal. I know the Cherokee people have found a good friend today." John and Cal shake hands and Cal walks out closing the door softly behind him.

Chief Ross slowly walks to his English made four poster bed. He sits on the edge just relaxing. John picks up a book titled: "Crimson Nation." He lies down on the bed and opens the old book and begins to read. In a few seconds a large tear comes to the corner of his eye as he slowly goes to sleep.

In a few hours daylight radiates through his stain glass window. John is at peace. Nothing in his genteel room is out of place, except his open book lying by his side. There is a knock on the door. "John, It's Talmidge, John."

Talmidge's key clanks in the lock. He opens the door and walks inside. Talmidge looks down at his dear friend, Chief John Ross, the legendary Principal Chief of the Cherokee Nation. Talmidge goes to him and quietly touches John's forehead with his palm. Large tears form in his aging eyes. John's childhood friend and the Cherokee Nation have lost their most prized possession, a loyal friend in a real time of need. He reflects about his old friend. "Time has run out for us all, dear friend. You're the lucky one."

Talmidge stares out the broad draped window. Tears roll down his elderly face. "You fought a good fight, old pal."

Grandma Dirteater is sad and tired as she speaks to little Samuel sitting on her front porch.

Samuel is tired but still listening to every word, "Boy they were really good friends."

Ms. Dirteater runs her fingers through Samuel's hair, "Yes they were sweet boy. In eighteen sixty-six, John Ross died in his sleep at the age of seventy-six, serving his Cherokee people faithfully for over sixty years. Without its faithful caretaker the Cherokee Nation was spread to the four winds. Today, in the modern world, a new Cherokee Nation is evolving, born again. They are rich in history and tempered in the fires of battle, still dealing in good faith with their national neighbors the United States of America and that young Samuel is the story of my people. I'll tell you about your people tomorrow."

THE END